Praise for *The Riverman*

An Indie Next Title

"Every culture has a magical river story. Some rivers promise the pleasures of eternal youth, while others promise the paradise of eternal salvation. *The Riverman* promises a more exhilarating alternative. Dive into this book and you may never resurface."
—Newbery Medal winner Jack Gantos

★ "Lines between reality and fantasy blur in this powerful, disquieting tale of lost children, twisted friendship and the power of storytelling."
—*Kirkus Reviews*, starred review

"Starmer weaves his fictional cloth out of gritty realism and sparkly fantasy, holding the whole together with lovely, careful language."
—*Newsday*

"Every page feels so carefully written that, although we can't predict what will take place, we feel certain that the author knows exactly where he is taking us." —*The Wall Street Journal*

"This blend of magical realism and mystery blurs the line between reality and fantasy, setting up a creepy unease that both disturbs and propels the reader forward." —*The Bulletin*

"In this dark, twisting tale, readers are never sure if Fiona's story is true or not, and they won't want to stop reading until they find out. . . . This magical tale is sure to please readers of urban fantasy, and with its theme of missing children and changing friendships, it will be perfect for fans of Neil Gaiman and Charles de Lint, too."
—*Booklist*

"Readers will find themselves confronted with deep, unanswered questions regarding the relationship of collective imaginary worlds to reality, the evolving nature of memories and friendships, and the unknowability of people. Those ready to explore darker realities will devour this book."
—*School Library Journal*

"Starmer explores the relationship between creation and theft, reality and fantasy in this haunting novel. . . . The novel's strength is in the pervasive aura of unknowing that Starmer creates and sustains."
—*Publishers Weekly*

"There is a lot to ponder and recommend in this unusual tale." —*VOYA*

THE RIVERMAN

AARON STARMER

SQUARE
FISH

FARRAR STRAUS GIROUX
NEW YORK

SQUARE
FISH

An Imprint of Macmillan
175 Fifth Avenue
New York, NY 10010
mackids.com

Square Fish books may be purchased for business or promotional use.
For information on bulk purchases, please contact the Macmillan Corporate
and Premium Sales Department at (800) 221-7945 x5442
or by e-mail at specialmarkets@macmillan.com.

Library of Congress Cataloging-in-Publication Data

Starmer, Aaron, 1976–
The Riverman / Aaron Starmer.
pages   cm — (The Riverman trilogy; [1])
Summary: "The first book in a trilogy about a girl who claims she is
visiting a parallel universe where a nefarious being called The Riverman
is stealing the souls of children and the boy she asks to write her biography
because she fears her soul may be next"—Provided by publisher.
ISBN 978-1-250-05685-6 (paperback)
ISBN 978-0-374-36310-9 (ebook)
[1. Friendship — Fiction. 2. Fantasy.] I. Title.
PZ7.S7972Ri 2014   [Fic] — dc23   2013027900

Originally published in the United States by Farrar Straus Giroux
First Square Fish Edition: 2015
Book designed by Elizabeth H. Clark
Square Fish logo designed by Filomena Tuosto

1 3 5 7 9 10 8 6 4 2

AR: 4.9 / LEXILE: 730L

To Hannah

Too many conflicting emotional interests are involved for life ever to be wholly acceptable, and possibly it is the work of the storyteller to rearrange things so that they conform to this end. In any case, in talking about the past we lie with every breath we draw.

—WILLIAM MAXWELL,
So Long, See You Tomorrow

BEFORE

———————✦———————

EVERY TOWN HAS LOST A CHILD. SEARCH THE ARCHIVES, ASK the clergy. You'll find stories of runaways slipping out of windows in the dark, never to be seen again. You'll be told of custody battles gone ugly and parents taking extreme measures. Occasionally you'll read about kids snatched from parking lots or on their walks home from school. Here today, gone tomorrow. The pain is passed out and shared until the only ones who remember are the only ones who ever really gave a damn.

Our town lost Luke Drake. By all accounts he was a normal twelve-year-old kid who rode his bike and got into just enough trouble. On a balmy autumn afternoon in 1979, he and his brother, Milo, were patrolling the banks of the Oriskanny with their BB rifles when a grouse fumbled out from some bushes. Milo shot the bird in the neck, and it tried to fly but crashed into a riot of brambles near the water.

"I shot, you fetch," Milo told Luke, and those words will probably always kindle insomnia for Milo. Because in the act of fetching, Luke slipped on a rock covered with wet leaves and fell into the river.

It had been a rainy autumn, and the river was swollen and unpredictable. Even in drier times, it was a rough patch of water that only fools dared navigate. Branch in hand, Milo chased the current along the banks as far as he could, but soon his brother's head bobbed out of view, and no amount of shouting "Swim!" or "Fight!" could bring him back.

Experts combed the river for at least fifteen miles downstream. No luck. Luke Drake was declared missing on November 20, and after a few weeks of extensive but fruitless searches, almost everyone assumed he was dead, his body trapped and hidden beneath a log or taken by coyotes. Perhaps his family still holds out hope that he will show up at their doorstep one day, a healthy man with broad shoulders and an astounding tale of amnesia.

I saw Luke's body on November 22, 1979. Thanksgiving morning. I was almost three years old, and we were visiting my uncle's cabin near a calm but deep bend in the Oriskanny, about seventeen miles downstream from where Luke fell. I don't remember why or how, but I snuck out of the house alone before dawn and ended up sitting on a rock near the water. All I remember is looking down and seeing a boy at the bottom of the river. He was on his back, most of his body covered in red and brown leaves. His eyes were

4

open, looking up at me. One of his arms stuck out from the murk. As the current moved, it guided his hand back and forth, back and forth. It was like he was waving at me. It almost seemed as though he was happy to see me.

My next memory is of rain and my dad picking me up and putting me over his shoulder and carrying me back through the woods as I whispered to him, "The boy is saying hello, the boy is saying hello."

It takes a while to process memories like that, to know if they're even true. I never told anyone about what I saw because for so long it meant something different. For so long it was just a boy saying hello, like an acquaintance smiling at you in the grocery store. You don't tell people about that.

I was eleven when I finally put the pieces in their right places. I read about Luke's disappearance at the library while researching our town's bicentennial for a school paper. With a sheet of film loaded into one of the microfiche readers, I was scanning through old newspapers, all splotchy and purple on the display screen. I stopped dead on the yearbook picture of Luke that had been featured on Missing posters. It all came rushing back, like a long-forgotten yet instantly recognizable scent.

My uncle had sold the cabin by then, but it was within biking distance of my house, and I went out there the following Saturday and flipped over stones and poked sticks in the water. I found nothing. I considered telling someone, but my guilt prevented it. Besides, nine years had passed. A lot of river had tumbled through those years.

The memory of Luke may very well be my first memory. Still, it's not like those soft and malleable recollections we all have from our early years. It's solid. I believe in it, as much as I believe in my memory of a few minutes ago. Luke was our town's lost child. I found him, if only for a brief moment.

Friday, October 13

———— ❖ ————

THIS STORY, MY STORY, STARTS HERE, WHERE I GREW UP, THE wind-plagued village of Thessaly in northern New York. If you're the first to stumble upon my tale, then I can assume you're also one of the few people who've been to my hometown. But if my words were passed along to you, then you've probably never even heard of the place. It's not tiny, but it's not somewhere travelers pass through. There are other routes to Canada and Boston, to New York City and Buffalo. We have a diner downtown called the Skylark where they claim to have invented salt potatoes. They may be right, but no one goes out of their way for salt potatoes.

Still, this is a pleasant enough corner of the world in which to live, at least when the wind isn't raging. There are parks in every neighborhood and a pine tree in the center of town where they string blue lights every Veterans Day. There's a bulb for every resident of Thessaly who died in a war, dating back as far as the Revolution. There are 117 bulbs in all. Unnoticed, we played our part, and there's plenty of pride in that.

My neighborhood, a converted plot of swamp and woodland that was supposed to attract urban refugees, is the town's newest, built in the 1950s, a time when, as my mom constantly reminded me, "families were families." Enough people bought in to justify its existence, but it hasn't grown. At the age of eight, I realized that all the houses in the neighborhood were built from the same four architectural plans. They were angled differently and dressed in different skins, but their skeletons were anything but unique.

The Loomis house had the same skeleton as my house, and I guess you could say that Fiona Loomis—the girl who lived inside that house, the girl who would change everything—had the same skeleton as me. It just took me a long time to realize it.

To be clear, Fiona Loomis was *not* the girl next door. It isn't because she lived seven houses away; it's because she wasn't sweet and innocent and I didn't pine for her. She had raven-black hair and a crooked nose and a voice that creaked. We'd known each other when we were younger, but by the time we'd reached seventh grade, we were basically strangers. Our class schedules sometimes overlapped, but that didn't mean much. Fiona only spoke when called upon and always sighed her way through answers as if school were the ultimate inconvenience. She was unknowable in the way that all girls are unknowable, but also in her own way.

I'd see her around the neighborhood sometimes because she rode her bike for hours on end, circling the streets with the ragged ribbons on her handgrips shuddering and her eyes fixed on the overhanging trees, even when their leaves were gone and they were shivering themselves to sleep. On the handlebars of her bike she duct-taped a small tape recorder that played heavy metal as she rode. It wasn't so loud as to be an annoyance, but it was loud enough that you'd snatch growling whispers of it in the air as she passed. I didn't care to know why she did this. If she was out of my sight, she was out of my thoughts.

Until one afternoon—Friday the 13th, of all days—she rang my doorbell.

Fiona Loomis, wearing a neon-green jacket. Fiona Loomis, her arms cradling a box wrapped in the Sunday comics. Fiona Loomis, standing on my front porch, said, "Alistair Cleary. Happy thirteenth birthday." She handed me the box.

I looked over her shoulder to see if anyone was behind her. "It's October. My birthday isn't for a few months. I'm still twelve and—"

"I know that. But you'll have a birthday eventually. Consider this an early present." And with a nod she left, scurried across the lawn, and hopped back on her bike.

I waited until she was halfway down the street to shut the door. Box on my hip, I skulked to my room. I wouldn't say I was scared when I tore the paper away, but I was woozy with the awareness that I might not understand anything about anything. Because an old wool jacket filled the

9

box, and that recorder from her handlebars, still sticky and stringy from the duct tape, sat on top of the jacket. A cassette in the deck wore a label that read *Play Me.*

"Greetings and salutations, Alistair." Fiona's voice creaked even more when played through the flimsy speaker, but it was a friendly creak. "I hope this recording finds you and finds you well. You've gotta be wondering what it's all about, so I'll get right to it. You have been chosen, Alistair, out of many fine and distinguished candidates, to pen my biography.

"I use the word *pen* instead of *write* because when you write something you might just be copying, but when you pen something it means . . . well, it means you do it like an artist. You dig up the story beneath the story. Last year, you wrote something in Mrs. Delson's class called 'Sixth Grade for the Outer-Spacers.' It takes a unique mind to come up with a tale like that. I hope you can bring that mind to the story of my life."

"Sixth Grade for the Outer-Spacers." It was a stupid thing I had whipped off in an afternoon. It was about a bunch of aliens who were old, but looked like human kids. For fun, they would visit Earth and enroll in middle school and do outrageous and exceptional things. It was my explanation for bullies and sports stars and geniuses and rebels and kids you envied because they were fearless.

Mrs. Delson had called it "promising," which I took to mean it was promising. But you eventually realize something if you're inundated with empty compliments like that—*You've got loads of potential, Alistair! You've got the makings of someone great, Alistair!* It's all part of a comforting but dishonest language that's used to encourage, but not to praise. I know now that *promising* actually means *just okay.* But just okay was good enough for Fiona, and with every word she spoke on that tape I became more entranced by the idea that I had talent.

"Choice is yours, obviously," Fiona said. "Maybe you want me to sell it to you. To sell a book, you need a description on the back. So here's mine: My name is Fiona Loomis. I was born on August 11, 1977. I am recording this message on the morning of October 13, 1989. Today I am thirteen years old. Not a day older. Not a day younger."

A faint hiss came next, followed by a rampage of guitars clawing their way out from the grave of whatever song she had taped over.

Saturday, October 14

<hr/>

TEN MISSING MONTHS. I WAS NO MATH WIZARD, BUT I KNEW that a girl born on August 11, 1977, didn't turn thirteen until August 11, 1990. October 13, 1989, was ten months before that date. Fiona had my attention.

I'm not sure how many times I listened to the tape. A dozen? Maybe more. I was listening to it in bed the next morning when the phone rang. My sister, Keri, knocked on my door, and I stuffed the tape recorder under my pillow.

"It's open."

Keri ducked in and tossed the cordless phone my way, flicking her wrist to give it a spin. When I caught it, she looked disappointed, but she recovered quickly, closing her eyes and shaking her hands in the air like some gospel singer.

"It's Cha*rrrrr*lie Dwyer!"

I glared at her, and she shot me with finger guns and slipped away.

"Hey, Charlie," I said into the phone, feigning excitement.

Charlie was Charlie, blurting out the worst possible question. "If someone asked you who your best friend is, would you say that I'm your best friend?"

I paused for far too long, then replied, "Yeah, Charlie. Most definitely."

"Got it," he said, and hung up.

The first thing you need to know about Charlie is.that in his backyard there was a clubhouse, built by his older brother, Kyle, five or six years before. In that former life, it was a fortress for neighborhood kids to collect and scheme and just be kids. When Kyle outgrew it, Charlie let it fall into disrepair. Feral cats took over, but rather than scare them away, Charlie left cans of tuna for them and gave them names. It stunk of feces and urine, and no one wanted to go in it anymore. The teenagers in the neighborhood would watch in disgust as the cats squeezed through the rotten holes in the clubhouse's shingles. They'd say things like, "It used to be so amazing."

As for Charlie, he was mostly an indoor cat, declawed so he could paw remotes and Nintendo controllers. We had been neighbors and friends since toddling, but it was a friendship of convenience more than anything. So when he asked me if he was my best friend, I should have been honest and said *No, I don't have one.* With those simple words, things could have turned out differently. Or not. Speculating is pointless.

Sunday, October 15

THE NEIGHBORHOOD WAS THICK WITH SPIES. THE MOST notorious was Mrs. Carmine. She lived up the block and nursed a smoking and a gardening habit, which kept her in the front yard, eyes hunting. Whenever she saw my parents, she updated them on my perceived mischief. Like the time when Charlie and I were nine and he showed me how to play a game he called Postal Percussion.

"Saw your boy and the little Dwyer boy bicycling with drumsticks in their hands," Mrs. Carmine told my mom. "Know what they used those sticks for? Whacking mailboxes. Good thing they got skinny arms and didn't break nothing, or else they'd be up on charges. Messing with the mail is a federal offense, you know?"

Of course my parents did know, and they educated me on the fact by grounding me for a week. All I did was ride along. I didn't *whack* anything. I actually told Charlie to quit it, but Mrs. Carmine always had her own version of events.

The Carmines lived across the street from the Loomises. I was desperate to talk to Fiona, but there was no way I was going to let Mrs. Carmine see me knocking on her door. She would build some sordid tale out of it and present her diorama of lies to my parents the next time they were out for an evening walk.

I couldn't deal with that, and I couldn't deal with calling Fiona either. Sure, I could have looked her number up in the book, but I had never called a girl before. There were far too many factors to consider. What if her father answered? What would I say to an answering machine? What if *she* answered?

No, my plan was to wait. I hadn't seen or heard from her on Saturday, so I spent Sunday hanging out in my front yard. She was bound to ride by, giving me the chance to flag her down and casually tell her that I thought her tape was "weird but cool" and that I would "entertain the notion of writing her biography." Entertaining a notion seemed like something a writer would do, and I didn't want to come off as a desperate amateur.

At the very least, I knew that she appreciated creative thinkers. Or a younger version of Fiona did. When we were in kindergarten and first grade, our parents used to spend some time together. The Loomis family would wheel a cooler over and join us for barbecues on the deck. Fiona had a brother named Derek and a sister named Maria, and they were already teenagers back then, which might as well have made them movie stars. They intimidated me, but my sister, Keri, was always angling for their approval, inviting them to her room with enticements like, "I took the arms off a Ken and put them on a Barbie. Wanna see her flex?"

And while those three were in the house, our parents would turn their attention to Fiona and me. Sitting in a line of lawn chairs, sipping from their glasses and bottles, they'd watch us play and they'd whisper to one another. Sometimes our moms would giggle.

We whispered too. "Let's trick them," Fiona said one afternoon. "Pretend a nuclear bomb fell. And we're melting 'cause of the radiation."

"What's a new clear bomb?" I asked.

"Just pretend you're melting," she said.

We flopped onto our backs and writhed in the grass, and I remember my dad started cracking up, but Fiona's dad said, "Don't encourage her. She takes things too far. She thinks the world is a joke."

That was one of the last occasions when our parents hung out together. For reasons I didn't know at the time, they drifted apart, but those words stuck with me for years. Even on that Sunday, as I waited for her to show up, I wondered if the world was still a joke to Fiona. Was that what her so-called birthday present was? A joke?

Luckily the afternoon was mild and calm and there were things to distract me from such thoughts. I raked the leaves. I kicked a soccer ball against the house's one patch of exposed foundation. I sat cross-legged on the roof of our minivan and counted the cars as they passed.

Five more cars and she'll be here.

Make that seven more.

Fifteen cars more and I go inside.

No Fiona.

Monday, October 16

IT WAS BACK TO SCHOOL THE NEXT DAY, AND CHARLIE SAT by me at lunch, which limited the social options. Charlie was tolerated more than liked. Kids had given up on teasing him back in fifth grade when it became obvious that you can call a guy *Captain Catpoop* all you want, but if he embraces the name by having it ironed onto his own T-shirt, he basically has you beat.

As Kelly Dubois walked past, her tray supporting a mountain of chicken nuggets, Charlie asked me, "You think she does it?"

"Does what?"

"It." He pounded his fists on the table like he was demanding dinner. *"Ba-dush, ba-dush, ba-dush. Wokka wokka wokka."*

I hate to admit it, but I smiled. One thing that Charlie possessed was a talent for making funny sounds, which didn't exactly redeem his obnoxiousness, but tempered it a bit. He was eager to shock *and* eager to please, a combination that tugged sympathies in every direction. My sympathies, at least. Girls weren't as conflicted.

So when a girl-shaped shadow swooped onto the Formica, I assumed Charlie was in for rolled eyes and a diagnosis of *disgusting pig*. I turned to see Fiona, brown bag in hand.

"Am I interrupting?" she asked, pulling out a chair.

"Not at all. We were talking about Kelly Dubois and her nocturnal proclivities," Charlie said through a nasty grin.

It would take a lot more than that to scare Fiona away. She sat down and said, "Okay. Not sure what that means."

"Whatever you want it to mean," Charlie told her as he stripped aluminum foil off of his can of soda.

"I don't want it to mean anything," Fiona replied. "Why don't you go over and ask Kelly what it means to her? I'm sure she'd be thrilled with your company. While you're at it, you can tell her why you wrap your soda in foil."

Charlie shook his head. "Keeps it cold, darlin'."

"Something new every day." Fiona smiled and dug deep in her sack to find a Ziploc of Oreos. She began twisting off the tops.

"Why are you here?" Charlie asked. "Don't you usually sit with the Wart Woman and Fishy Fay-Renee?"

The unfortunate soul known as the Wart Woman was Kendra Tolliver, a tomboy who fielded a bumper crop of warts on the fingers of her left hand. Some kids claimed that if she touched you, warts would sprout at the point of contact. Some kids even believed it.

As for Fishy Fay-Renee, that was Fay-Renee Donleavy. She had braces and wore turtleneck sweaters. I have no idea why she had two first names. I have no idea why she was considered *fishy*. She probably ordered a fish sandwich once in the lunch line or something stupid like that.

Fiona sighed as she peeled the cream from one Oreo and placed it on the cream of another. "I will rejoin more refined company momentarily," she said. "For now, I have business. With Alistair."

I shrugged and hinted at a nod.

"Ooo," Charlie crooned. "Risky business?"

"Hardly," Fiona assured him. She stacked on another two layers of cream and put a lid on the super-cookie. She turned to me. "So. Are you in?"

Rehearsing my response hadn't helped, because all I could say was, "I . . . Yeah . . . I think I am."

"Good. I'll come by after school."

Charlie started to raise his hand, and I slapped it back for fear he'd make an obscene gesture. It didn't seem to bother him, though. He was too busy watching Fiona lick her finger and then run it along the cookie cream until it was smoothed out and singular.

When she finished, she held the cookie up like a trophy. "Quadruple Stuf," she said. "Can't buy that in a store."

Then she took it down in one bite and chewed it as she stood and set off into the rumble of the cafeteria.

*   *   *

Every girl who invites herself to your place has the same intention—that's what Charlie's older brother, Kyle, told me once. Kyle knew his share of girls, but obviously he didn't know any like Fiona.

That afternoon she rang our bell, and I was quick to answer. "Hey," I said, opening the door and motioning with my head down the hall. "This way."

"I remember where your room is," Fiona said. "We played Legos there once."

"Oh. Hello, Fiona." My mom, fresh from her after-work shower, stood at the top of the stairs, her postal uniform expertly folded and tucked under one arm. She looked down at us as she brushed her wet hair. Water dripped over her turquoise sweat suit.

"Hi, Mrs. Cleary," Fiona chirped. "Alistair said he'd help me with some homework."

"He did, did he?" My mom moved the brush over her mouth to conceal a smile. "Well, it's . . . it's been a long time."

"It has," Fiona said.

"And if we keep this up, we'll have no time for the homework," I interjected. "We'll be done by dinner." I tugged at Fiona's sleeve and took off down the hall without saying another word to my mom.

Minutes later, Fiona was sitting on my bed, her back resting on pillows against the wall and her lap holding the tape recorder. "I'd prefer you in the tweed," she told me.

"Excuse me?"

"The jacket I gave you. It was my grandpa's. He's dead. But he was a writer, too. It still has his library card in the pocket. As my grandma told me, it probably has some inspiration left in it too."

I pulled the box out from under my bed and retrieved the natty old thing. The sleeves were about five inches too long, and my hands were buried up to the fingertips.

"Well, isn't that civilized?" Fiona said.

Not true, but I played along. "So how do you want to do this?" I slumped into a beanbag chair that I kept in the corner.

"I talk and you interpret. Simple." She pressed *Record*. "Kilgore here will keep the record straight."

"Kilgore?"

"The tape recorder. I name things. If you name things, then you treat them better." Fiona motioned with her chin to a poster tacked to the opposite wall. "Does she have a name?"

"She" was a bikini-clad model spraying a Lamborghini with a garden hose and, no, she didn't—at least, not one I knew. I lowered my eyes.

"We'll call her Prudence, then," Fiona said. "Now whenever you wake up, you can say, 'Good morning, Prudence, how's tricks? Still in the car washing game, I see.'"

"'How's tricks'?"

"'How's things,'" Fiona explained. "Slang from the good ol' days. Learned it from a kid in a newsie cap."

"A newsie cap?"

"We're getting ahead of ourselves."

Yes we were, but I didn't even know where we were supposed to be starting. Perhaps the obvious place. "You were born . . . ?"

"Ah yes, chapter one," Fiona said. "I was born on August 11, 1977. I was born *in the sack*, which means I came out with the amniotic veil still around me. Some people say that makes me a clairvoyant, but I'm no clairvoyant."

She punctuated the point with a finger in the air, and then she moved the tape recorder and wedged it in between her feet, giving it the optimum angle to catch her voice.

"I was born here in Thessaly," she went on. "Or if you want to be technical about it, at Rose Memorial in Sutton. My dad worked as an insurance adjuster then. Mom didn't work because she thought raising kids was work enough. There aren't a lot of pictures of me from those days because I'm the third-born, and apparently cameras don't work on the third. Maybe we're vampires."

She smiled, and I smiled back, because I could certainly relate. I was the second of two kids. Our bookshelves were stacked with photo albums of Keri diaper-clad in the garden, on the hammock, with her face in a bowl of ice cream. There were far fewer pictures of me, a mere year and a half younger.

"My first memory is from when I was two years old," Fiona continued. "I was playing in our sandbox. Cody, our

German shepherd, tried to steal my sand bucket, and I went to grab it back and Cody bit me on the arm and dragged me across the yard until my face hit the pole of a bird feeder and my nose broke and there was blood on my arm and my face. I remember the blood tasted dirty and hot. They put Cody down after that. I have this nose and this scar to show for it."

As she rolled her sleeve up, the purple ghost of the attack revealed itself. It was like a centipede crawling toward her bicep. My reaction must have been swift and obvious.

"I know," she said, and then launched into her best Valley girl impression. "Grody to the max."

I had never seen the scar before, but I had often wondered why Fiona always wore long sleeves, even in the summer. I stumbled through my response. "I just . . . I . . ."

"Make a note," she said. "'A gnarly scar eats at her girly arm.' Something like that. That's what a writer would do."

"Good idea." I scooted the beanbag chair over to my desk, reached up, and grabbed a pencil and the mostly empty notebook I had reserved for Social Studies. Below a doodle of Abe Lincoln riding a skateboard, I wrote: *Big scar. Purple. Somewhat gross.*

She gave the scar a kiss and rolled her sleeve back down. "I remember other things from that time. Images and stuff. My mom in the driveway shoveling snow while wearing a yellow dress and a paisley coat. Me and my dad sharing a strawberry milk shake. Derek and Maria making a house of baseball cards. I've been told anecdotes from that time too, about how we used to do stuff as a family, but I think it's best to stick with my memories."

"Probably best," I said, but what did I know? My creative endeavors amounted to a handful of stories, only a couple of which I had actually put to paper. I didn't have the first clue about what it took to "pen" someone's biography. Fiona's faith in my abilities was flattering, but as the warmth of flattery dissipated, a spiny chill was all that remained. This girl actually expected something from me. It finally struck me how strange that was.

"My second memory is from a bit later," she said. "I was four and I was in bed and I was listening to the radiators clicking. You know how they click? Well, the clicks were different this time. It was as if the radiators were talking to me, as if—"

"Fiona?" I stood up, though not as quickly as I would have liked. *Beanbag chairs.*

"Yes?"

I set the notebook on the desk. "Why are we doing this?"

Fiona pulled a pillow out from behind her back and hugged it. Tilting her head, she replied, "Because we're weirdos, Alistair. We're the aliens."

"I don't know what that . . . I am not a weirdo," I said. "And that's not what I'm asking."

"What are you asking, then?"

"I'm asking . . . I hardly know you anymore. Why not write this yourself?"

Fiona looked at me straight and serious. "To say the things I'm going to say, I need someone who hardly knows me. I need a witness with an imagination."

Sometimes I wondered if that was my problem, an abundance of cluttered rooms in my mind. She had me pegged, though, and she had me worried. "You're only twelve," I said. "Why do you need a biography?"

She shook her head and put it simply. "As I already told you, I'm *thirteen*. And tomorrow my soul could be gone."

I didn't know until later how literal that statement was. Or else I wouldn't have said what I said. "I'm not sure I want to do this."

Fiona considered those words for a moment, and then sighed and whispered her reply: "And we can't do this if you have doubts."

The recorder at her feet, the tape and its spinning reels. That's where this all started. I reached down and pressed *Stop*. "You should take this back."

She spread her feet and let the recorder fall. "No," she said, getting up and brushing past me. "It's yours. I don't take things back."

TUESDAY, OCTOBER 17

SCHOOL AGAIN. IT WAS ONLY SIX HOURS A DAY, BUT THOSE hours were whirlpools. Fight against them and I'd lose— swept up, sucked down, smothered by nausea. My best bet was to stand and endure.

Enduring usually meant daydreaming. I suppose everyone is a daydreamer, but I was better at it than most. I could appear attentive, eyes at the board instead of the window. I could even answer the occasional algebra question if called upon. But for most of the day, I was lost, exploring phantasmal worlds where I was starring in a movie or living on some tropical island with a beautiful girl.

Not this time, though. Fiona invaded every daydream, her face appearing from behind trees, her voice—metallic and pleading—crackling out from clouds and television screens.

By sixth period Social Studies, I gave in and opened

my notebook to the scribble of words from the previous evening.

Big scar. Purple. Somewhat gross.

I wrote a few more.

Ten missing months? Soul . . . gone? Talking radiators?

Images of radiators with toothy mouths, chattering like auctioneers, brought a smile to my face, but it was an uncomfortable smile. I had opened myself up to someone who was obviously a bit . . . sick. That was the best word for it, sick.

"Fiona is nutzo, you know?" my sister said as we walked home from school that afternoon.

"She's not my—"

"Girlfriend? She was in your room."

"A school project. A—"

"I don't care." Keri tightened the straps and hiked up her backpack so that she could more easily handle her load of books. "Mom was asking about her."

"Gawd . . ."

"You could have the wedding reception at the Skylark. Salt potatoes and helium balloons!"

"Shut up." I reached for Keri's ponytail. She knew what would come next.

Wriggling away, she teased, "I got a secret about your fiancée."

I pushed her backpack and she stumbled forward but didn't fall. "I *said* shut up!"

"I'm serious. One night I saw her bury something in the swamp."

I stopped. "You're kidding me."

"It was, like, a few weeks ago," Keri said with a shrug. "I couldn't sleep, and it was surprisingly hot so I had my window wide open. I heard a banging sound and I looked out and I saw Fiona with a shovel by Frog Rock."

Our backyard bordered a swamp, along the edge of which sat a giant boulder shaped like a bullfrog. If the moon was out, we could see it from our windows at night, standing guard in front of a wall of cattails.

"She wasn't just out for a walk or something?" I asked. My suspicions were well-founded. Once, Keri told me there was a mouse in our attic playing a tiny violin. It turned out to be an old sock and a creaky hinge.

"I'm serious. She dug a hole. Dropped something in. Covered it up."

"Which was?"

"Beats me." Keri threw her hands in the air. "I'm not messin' with Heavy Metal Fifi."

"Who?"

"Something me and Mandy call her."

Mandy was a fourteen-year-old with the haircut of a newscaster and a fondness for old movies. She was a frequent sleepover guest at our house, always arriving with a tin of chocolate chip cookies and something black-and-white she'd taped off of TV.

"And you never told anyone?" I asked.

"I told Mandy. I'm telling you. Thought you should know before you invited her back."

"Don't worry," I said. "I'm not inviting her back. Who knows? Maybe she'll move away sometime soon and we'll never see her again."

There is another afternoon I remember, another barbecue. Our parents were busy with the hamburgers and sangria, while Fiona and I—maybe six years old, probably seven— had ventured into the swamp, to the edge of the cattails on a mission to capture things that squirmed.

"How 'bout the big daddy?" Fiona joked, pointing to the boulder.

"You mean Frog Rock?" I asked. "Keri says he keeps us safe. Keeps coyotes away."

"Really?"

"Keri says so."

"What else does the frog keep?" Fiona asked. "Does he keep secrets?"

"What do you mean?"

Instead of answering, Fiona pushed through the cattails and grabbed the notch in the rock that doubled as the frog's right knee. Bouncing three times for confidence, counting it off, then pulling, shooting a foot skyward, trying to land a sneaker—rubber on granite—missing, slipping, trying again, and again, and then getting it right, she scrambled up the surface until she was face-to-face with the frog. She cupped her hands against the side of its head. She whispered to the stone.

"What are you whispering?" I asked.

"A secret," she said. "Between me and Mr. Hopper."

"I can keep secrets," I told her, and I reached for the notch so I could pull myself up too. I wasn't tall enough. Even jumping, I couldn't grab it. Watching me struggle, Fiona smirked. I think she liked knowing that she could do something that I couldn't.

"Prove it," she said. "Prove you can keep secrets."

"How?" I panted and wiped my palms on my shirt and leaned, defeated, against the stone.

"Tell me one," she said. "A secret of your own."

I'm sure that I had secrets, but I couldn't think of any that quickly. So I looked down at my feet and said the first thing that came to mind. "If we ever move away, to another house, I mean, then I'm gonna bury something, right here next to this rock."

It was instinct more than an answer. The soft ground was gumming my Velcro sneakers, my mind was on mud and secrets, and secrets were buried treasure.

"What would you bury?" Fiona asked.

"I don't know. Money?"

"That's stupid," she said, and she wrapped her arms around the frog's neck. "Isn't that stupid, Mr. Hopper?"

"Okay, fine." I looked to the yard for inspiration. In our weedy sandbox were action figures, strewn about like all casualties of play. On the stump of a willow tree was a deflated rubber ball that Keri and I used to throw at each other while yelling "Bombs over Tokyo!"

"How 'bout . . . something to tell some new kid that I was here first," I said.

Fiona put a finger up—*Eureka!* "I once saw spray paint on a bridge that said *Kilroy Was Here.*"

"Who's Kilroy?" I asked.

"Beats me. But he was once there. And now I know about it."

Writing *Alistair Was Here* on something and burying it in the ground seemed weird, but I had no idea what else might symbolize me, what object might communicate that I was a kid who lived in this house his whole entire life, and that it was my house before it was some other kid's house.

"How 'bout . . ."

"How about you don't tell me right now?" Fiona said. "But if you move away, then you can bury something here for *me* to find. And *I'll* dig it up!"

"Okay," I said, warming to her variation on my theme. "But what if you move away first?"

"Then I'll bury something for *you* to find. And *you'll* dig it up! One catch, though. Whatever we bury, it has to tell a secret."

I actually liked this scenario better. It felt like we were forming our own super-exclusive club. Membership: two. "It's a deal," I told her.

"More than a deal," she replied. "It's a pact. Do you know what a pact is?"

"I think so."

"Good." She slid down the rock.

"Should we prick our fingers?" I asked. "Like blood brothers . . . or sisters?"

She grimaced and shook her head. "A handshake oughta do."

I dug. How could I not?

It had been at least five years since we'd made that pact, five years in which we had hardly spoken to each other. It might seem strange, but once our parents stopped being friends, so did we. A lot of it was the *she's a girl and I'm a boy* divide that happens in elementary school. Part of it was convenience. She didn't come around anymore, and even though she lived up the street, it was like she'd moved away.

Now she had buried something for me. It could only mean that she was actually moving away. Maybe over the last few weeks her family had been packing up the house and the moving truck would be showing up at any moment. Or maybe it was only Fiona who was leaving. After all, I hadn't seen a For Sale sign anywhere. Whatever was happening, I wasn't going to wait to find out. You'd better believe I was going to dig.

That night, after my family went to sleep, I set a flashlight on the knee of Frog Rock and I went to work with a camping shovel. The ground was soft, but not soaked. Every autumn the swamp dried up and chilled to the point where it was more a frosty and muddy glade than it was a wetland. It felt like hours, but it probably wasn't even twenty minutes before I struck something that wasn't a stone or a root. I clawed the dirt away and unearthed a handle.

Moments later I was sitting at our picnic table with a long metal box in my lap. It was a relic, a green rectangular thing with a hinged top and rusty latches and a few fading, peeling baseball stickers on the outside. And on the inside? A soupy mess of dirty water and worms, but also a Ziploc, sealed and wrapped in rubber bands to keep its lumpy contents safe. I wiped the bag against damp grass to remove most of the muck and I rolled off the rubber bands.

I'm not sure what I was expecting to find in there. A diary? Maybe a key? Certainly not what I found.

It was a white handkerchief. Fiona had used Magic Markers to draw a rough grid of forty to fifty squares on it. In most squares, there was a name written. *Chua Ling, Boaz Odhiambo, Rodrigo Hermanez, Jenny Colvin*, and others. Some names were written in red ink. Some in green. Some were full names. Some only first names or initials. Next to a few, there were also the names of places. *Kenya, Argentina, Milwaukee*. In a square near the edge, *Fiona Loomis Was Here*.

A few of the squares had *X*'s on them. A few had ?'s.

At the bottom there was a note:

Dear Alistair,

You've found this because the Riverman has taken me. By now, he might have taken all of these kids. Someone must warn the green ones. Someone must stop him. I don't know what to do anymore.

So confused. So scared.

Fiona

Wednesday, October 18

———◆———

THE HALLS AFTER THE SECOND BELL WERE ALWAYS A MUDDLE of tension—kids trading halfhearted shoves and taunts as they jostled from homeroom to first period through the gantlet of mustard-yellow lockers. I spotted Fiona in the mix, shuffling alongside her friend Fay-Renee. They weren't talking to each other, but you could tell they were tuned to the same frequency simply by the way their eyes moved in tandem. I stepped in front of them, and they zeroed in on a milk stain on my shirt and followed the path of my buttons to a zit on my chin, until finally settling their pupils on mine.

"Hey," I said to Fiona. I pinched at my earlobe, shielding the zit with my wrist and the stain with my arm. "Can we talk for a sec?"

Fiona nodded *it's cool* to Fay-Renee, who shrugged and stepped back into the swell.

"What's up?" Fiona asked.

"Tell me about the Riverman," I said.

I might as well have admitted to torching her house. Her reaction isn't easy to describe. It was almost like watching a sand castle struck by a wave.

"He found me?" she asked as she braced herself against the lockers and closed her eyes.

"What?"

"Are you him, or did he send you to get information on me?" Her arms fell limp. Her head fell to the side.

"Huh?"

"I'm so sorry." She opened her eyes. There was a tiny swirl of rage in them, but mostly it was sadness. "Actually, no. I'm not sorry. But I guess it had to come to this. If he can't find me there, then he finds me here."

"I don't know what you're talking about." I pulled the handkerchief from my pocket. "This was buried behind my house."

The rage bloomed into a tornado, and she snatched the handkerchief and hissed, "What the heck are you thinking?" She didn't have pockets, so she stuffed the handkerchief down the front of her shirt and shouldered past me.

Chasing her, I said, "I should be asking you that. I don't know if this is a prank or you're just plain nuts, but—"

Before I could finish my thought, Fiona had a hand on my mouth and she was pushing me against the lockers and whispering to me, "Don't ever show that to anyone. Understand? People will suffer. Hundreds of people. Thousands."

Over her shoulder, I saw that Charlie was watching us.

He was making kissy-faces at me, puckering his lips so much that you could hear a wet squeak over the buzz of the crowd. I pushed Fiona's hand away and said, "Whatever. Forget I even brought it up."

Bulling into the throng of my classmates, I headed to first period.

When I was embarrassed, confused, or simply lonely, I would take long, hot showers. I would sit in the tub and lean forward and let the water massage my neck and scalp. I wouldn't close my eyes. I liked to watch the water cascade off my head.

That night I showered until the hot water ran out. When I was finished, I put on my pajamas and headed to the living room to watch TV. I didn't want to talk. I didn't even want to think.

On my way through the dining room, my dad handed me a coffee can overflowing with potato peels, eggshells, and the ends of carrots and celery. "A man's work is never done," he said.

"Crap."

"Hey there now. We don't pay you for your witty commentary." He took a side-sip from his beer and cocked his chin. "When I was your age—"

"You probably had to carry a hundred pounds of compost ten miles down the road every night."

"Forget that." He laughed. "No one composted back then.

Besides, my parents hired people to do everything for us. That's why I hire you."

As far as chores go, taking the compost out was fairly painless, and combined with doing the dishes and dragging the trash cans to the corner, it was worth the five dollars of allowance each week. Still, on cold nights, with wet hair, it could be downright painful.

"Hilarious," I groaned, and my dad gave me a pat on the shoulder and escaped to the living room.

I slipped into a jacket and a pair of mud shoes and took the route through the garage to the backyard. It was blustery, and I could smell burning wood in the air. Fireplace season had started, a clear indication that there was no looking back. It was only going to get colder.

The compost heap was out by the swamp, not far from Frog Rock. As I emptied the can, I looked over to the spot where I had dug up the metal box the night before. Out of the darkness a figure emerged.

Fiona.

"You called me nuts," she said.

I stepped away from her. "You made me look like an idiot today, pushing me and snapping at me. If you're playing some weird sort of game, I don't want to be involved."

"Not long ago, even twenty years ago, they'd put kids in asylums. If a kid was talking about things that adults didn't understand, they'd lock that kid away."

"I don't know if you realize how much you're freaking me out," I said. "Please leave."

She shook her head and asked, "Why'd you decide to dig? Did you know the ammo can was down there? Did you know about the map?"

"The map?"

She held up the handkerchief.

"If I explain, will you leave?" I asked.

She took a moment to think about it. She shrugged.

Honestly, any curiosity I had about that handkerchief was overpowered by my desire for life to return to how it was before Fiona showed up at my door, to when she was nobody but an odd girl who lived down the street, a former friend and nothing else. Someone to forget. "Keri saw you bury it," I explained. "Like a stupid idiot, I went and dug it up last night."

"Does anyone else know?"

"Keri told her friend Mandy, but they don't know what you buried."

"Do you trust them?"

"What's that supposed to mean?"

"Exactly what it always means." Fiona pulled a plastic lighter out of her pocket, sparked it up, and dipped the corner of the handkerchief into the flame. Nothing at first, then fire scrambled.

"What the . . . ?"

Placing the burning handkerchief on a stone, Fiona said, "You were only supposed to find that as a last resort. If I was already gone. Now I'll have to teach you. About everything. I thought writing things down, recording things, would be a good way to keep track of all the details, so that people someday know the truth. But if that stuff falls into the wrong hands, there's no telling what might happen to the others. It's better if you memorize it all."

"I'm not memorizing anything," I said. "You *are* nuts. They *should* lock you up."

Disappointment whittled ridges in her brow. "The only thing I'm asking you to do is listen."

"And you said that if I had my doubts, then it wasn't going to work."

"It's too late now. You know about the Riverman. You need to be convinced."

"Convinced of what?"

Fiona crouched down to get a closer look at the burning handkerchief. She kept her eyes on the flames as she said, "There's a boiler in our basement, in a room where my dad keeps tools and boxes of holiday decorations. The boiler feeds water to all the radiators in the house. That night, when I was four years old, the night I heard the radiators talking? Well, the radiators told me to go to the boiler. As I said, they were clicking. But I understood the clicking. They had a voice, and I did as they asked. I went to that room and I climbed up on a box and pulled the hanging string to turn on the hanging lightbulb, and I climbed down and stood next to the boiler, and the clicking told me to wait for one moment longer, and I asked out loud, 'Wait for what?' And that's when it happened, when it opened up."

The handkerchief was shriveled and black now, infested

with little red embers. Fiona didn't look at me, and I certainly couldn't look at her. Because I had abandoned something once in the thicket of images and sounds and smells that made up my early memories, and Fiona's story was now returning that uncomfortable moment to me. Simply put, what had happened to her had happened to me, and I knew what she was going to say next. And that terrified me.

"Without a noise," Fiona continued, "without a flash of light or anything like that, the outside of the boiler disappeared. Vanished. A cylinder of water hung in the air where the boiler was. A perfect, unbroken cylinder. It was gorgeous, and I reached forward to touch it. As soon as the tips of my fingers reached the water, I was pulled in. For the first time, I went to Aquavania."

Wind grabbed the remains of the handkerchief, tore it into bits of ash, and tossed it into the air, where some of it fluttered and landed on Fiona's face and painted black freckles on her cheeks.

"You're ridiculous," I whimpered, and I threw the coffee can at her feet, partly in anger, partly to keep her eyes off mine. "I'm through with you."

I trudged to the house, fighting the urge to look back.

THURSDAY, OCTOBER 19

I DIDN'T SLEEP. I LAY UNDER MY COVERS, ON MY BACK, drawing out my breaths to keep myself calm. That image of water floating in the air was too much. It was too familiar.

It took me back to when I was six years old and I won a goldfish at a school fair. I named the fish Humbert and kept him in a bowl on my dresser and fed him flakes twice a day. Humbert died after four or five months, and I took it badly. There was a coffin made of cardboard and a funeral in the backyard. Charlie attended and played taps on a recorder. Charlie's brother, Kyle, called us "a coupla wusses," but we didn't see it like that. Humbert was our friend, the sea monster in our action figure battles, the shark under our model race car bridge.

I didn't want to be alone on the night of the funeral, so I asked Charlie to stay for a sleepover. We curled up in our sleeping bags on the floor next to the TV and faded off within its glow. That night I had what I always thought of as the most vivid dream of my life.

I was called from the sleeping bag by the voice of Humbert. I'm not sure why I thought it was Humbert's voice, but I did. The voice led me back to my room, where the fishbowl still sat on my dresser. There was only water left in the bowl, but I spoke to it like Humbert was inside.

"I'm sorry for not feeding you enough, or feeding you too much, or whatever I did wrong."

Without warning, the bowl disappeared and a globe of water was floating over the dresser. I was tempted to reach out and touch it, but I didn't. I marveled at it, for it was both the loveliest and scariest thing I had ever seen. I closed my eyes.

When I opened them, I was back on the living room floor, neck-deep in my sleeping bag. A rainbow of colored bars glowed on the TV, announcing that programming had ended for the night and dead air would be broadcast until morning.

At dawn, I dumped the water out of the bowl and put it in the trash. I didn't tell anyone about the dream because I didn't want to revisit Humbert's passing. It was time to move on, a sentiment echoed by my dad that night after he dragged the trash to the curb.

"You're growing up, bud," he told me. "Becoming a little man. I'm thinking it's time you had some chores."

*　　*　　*

I feigned sickness the morning after Fiona met me on the edge of the swamp. Keri wasn't buying it, but "stomach stuff, uncontrollable and unpredictable" was more than enough detail to convince my parents. My dad treated me like I was a mugger, sidling to the door with his hands up and toast in his mouth. "Yikes," he mumbled. "I carry that plague to the hospital and I'll wipe out the entire east wing."

My mom was more sympathetic. Before leaving for her job at the post office, she handed me a box of saltines and some ginger ale and told me, "Take it easy, on your belly and on the dragons."

There were no dragons in the video games I played, but I knew what she was saying. She didn't want me ending up like Charlie, under the spell of television and computer screens every waking hour of the day.

It didn't make a difference. Video games, TV shows, books—none was a sufficient distraction. No matter how hard I tried, I couldn't shake Fiona's story and the memories of that dream from years before.

I paced.

The house seemed smaller, more sinister. Lightbulbs seemed to flicker. White walls seemed subtly filthy, streaked with faint tea-colored stains. Acid climbed the cliff of my throat. I needed fresh air.

I was leaning against a tree in my front yard, counting the shingles on my neighbor's garage, when Charlie's brother, Kyle, pulled up in a battered gray van. A guy with a reputation like Kyle's deserved a motorcycle or a muscle car, but I guess he didn't have enough cash for either. He rolled down the window and asked, "Skippin'?"

"Sick."

"Of algebra? Of women?"

I shrugged.

"Does your mom act like a mom? Call to check up on you and all that?"

"Only after lunch," I said. "She's working the window this morning."

Kyle rapped his fingers on the door, a happy little drumroll. "Then we have some time," he said. "Hop in. I could use a copilot today."

Accepting a ride from Kyle Dwyer was probably number one on my parents' Don't list. They weren't fans of the Dwyers in general, but while Charlie only annoyed them, Kyle frightened them. He was a badass of the old mold. Wore a cigarette behind his ear, carried a butterfly knife, kept his van stocked with a stack of blankets and a candle in a jar and a jug of something sweet and alcoholic to ease things in his direction.

It would have been a waste of time to ask Kyle if he was skipping too. He was still on the books as a senior, but graduation was hardly in the cards. I knew he was the worst sort of role model, but the one thing he always gave me was an honest answer.

"Where we going?" I asked as I climbed into the van.

"Do you know Gina Rizetti?"

"I don't."

"Waitress at Hungry Paul's?"

I shrugged and we were off.

"Doesn't matter," Kyle said as he struggled to find second gear. "She's a girl who can get things. Lives in one of those dumps under the bridge. I gotta see if she's got any fireworks that I can sell to these lacrosse players for their field party. Anyway, could take a few minutes, and I got a chain saw in the back of the van and some fresh cartons from the reservation, and the locks are broken and I don't want some desperate tweeker snatching it all."

"So I'm . . . ?"

"Standing guard."

My stint as a guard was an uneventful one. I sat in the van as Kyle went into a little blue house with a soggy sofa on the front porch and a rusty swing set and cracked plastic kiddie pool in the yard. Though the neighborhood was more ramshackle than I was accustomed to, it was a bright day and no one was walking around or acting the least bit menacing. I listened to voices on AM radio battle through the static and I waited.

After a few minutes, Kyle returned with a box that he tossed in the back as if it were a bag of laundry.

"You like Roman candles and bottle rockets?"

"I guess so." I had heard of them, but such things were forbidden in my house.

"These jocks better like 'em, because that's all they're

getting." He turned the key and the phlegmy engine gave its all.

"Can I ask you something?"

"Shoot, little man," Kyle responded as we pulled into traffic.

"Do you trust all of your memories?"

Kyle faked a flinch. "Whoa. Getting all philosophical on me now?"

"Forget it."

"It's cool," he said. "Truth is I'm lucky if I remember half the craziness that comes my way. And sometimes I remember things how I want to remember them, if you get what I'm saying."

"Yeah, I guess I do," I said. "But if I can't even trust myself, how am I supposed to know if I can trust a girl?"

I should have expected the laughter that followed, but it hurt anyway.

"Never mind," I said.

"No, no." Kyle coughed away his giggles. "It's a fair question. Guess it depends on the girl. You got one who's lying to you?"

"I don't know. Seems like it. Either that or she's crazy."

"What's her angle?"

"What do you mean?"

"What does she want?"

"She wants me to listen."

"Don't they all. Girl named Josie Pruitt used to tell me that she had this modeling contract with some big agency outta Paris. Couldn't shut up about it. Believe me, she was pretty, but not Paris pretty. Down the line I find out there ain't no contract, only a bunch of nudie shots taken by her cousin down in his basement. No surprise, really. So the best thing I can tell you about a chick who lies a lot is this: there's probably some messed-up stuff going on in her life."

It was as clear an explanation as one could expect. "I guess she might be having problems at home."

Saying it out loud suddenly made me feel better about things. Logic began to break the code. For instance, the similarities between Fiona's story and my dream were most likely coincidental, perhaps inspired by an image we both picked up from the same movie. And the rest of what she was saying? The missing months and the radiators and the Riverman and all of that nonsense? There was a reason for it too. Horrible things, taking place behind closed doors, can warp the mind. My dad was a social worker at the hospital in Sutton, and he was always telling us about people who came in with bruises or worse, and how they rarely admitted to how they got them. They made up stories instead, crazy, unbelievable stuff. *Coping mechanisms*. That was the term. So while he might not have used the exact same language, even my dad agreed with Kyle.

"A chick who's having problems at home will give it up quicker than most," Kyle explained. "But I warn you, little man. Might not be worth the hassle, especially if she's got a whack-job for a father, or stepfather . . . or whatever."

"Yeah."

"Is she hot?"

"I don't know."

He laughed again. "Well, get that straightened out before you go sticking your tongue in her mouth."

We didn't make any other stops. Kyle told me he needed to "nap off a long night," and he deposited me at the end of my driveway.

"Thanks," I told him as I stepped down from the van.

"Anytime," he said. "Just don't go telling li'l brother we hung out, okay? He can be a jealous kid."

"I know."

"Bet you do." Kyle chuckled to himself, shot me a salute, and pulled away.

Almost as soon as he was gone, I was on my bike, pedaling the short distance to Fiona's house. I'm not proud to admit it, but I was searching for depravity, for squalor, for anything to confirm that Fiona had more than enough reasons to be dark and disturbed.

I had passed by her house countless times over the years, but it had been a while since I'd really looked at it. It was basically the same as I remembered it from the few times I visited when we were younger. The hedges that lined its south side could have used a trim, but they weren't exactly overgrown. The paint was mostly unmarred, the mailbox relatively straight. Outward appearances can only tell you so much, though. I needed a closer look.

I was pretty sure Mrs. Carmine had a job and would be less active on a weekday morning, but I still kept an eye out for her as I hid my bike in a pile of fetid leaves. With the coast clear, I took my chance, jogging along the side of Fiona's house, where I used my peripheral vision to peek in the windows. I'm not sure what I expected to see. Men dressed in ball gowns? Iron maidens and other medieval torture devices? Corpses hanging on hooks? Of course, what I saw was entirely normal. A bedroom, a bathroom, striped drapes.

I ended up in the backyard, which was equally unremarkable. There was a small garden with a wooden archway at one end and a sundial at the other. There was a deck with a glass table in the middle of it. There was a bird feeder from which a squirrel was trying to pry seeds.

As soon as I moved closer to the house, the squirrel hopped off the feeder and darted for a nearby tree. It wasn't me that he'd heard. It was the back door opening.

"Nice as it'll be in a long while, I think. Best we appreciate it." The voice was a man's, raspy, with a touch of Southern drawl.

My first instinct was to run, but when I saw a wheelbarrow tipped onto its side next door in the Andersons' yard, I changed plans. I dropped to my belly and crawled like a soldier until I reached the wheelbarrow. Then I curled up behind it and looked back on the scene.

A man with brown shoulder-length hair and a tatty beard unfolded a lawn chair a few feet from the bird feeder. It was far too cold out for a T-shirt, but he wore one—black with a cartoon demon on the back and what looked like a list of cities. His right bicep was emblazoned with a tattoo of a skull encased in a helmet. Once the chair was in place, he returned to the house and escaped my line of sight.

"I got a blanket if you feel a chill," I heard him say. When I saw him again, he was pushing a wheelchair across the yard.

An old woman sat in the chair, hunched over so much that it was a wonder she could hold her head up. But hold it up she did, at least for a few moments, long enough to spot the tree where the squirrel had found harbor.

"Can't do much about them thieves," the man said. "Add more seed. Birds won't starve." He guided the wheelchair over to the lawn chair and engaged the wheel locks with his foot.

The squirrel stole my attention for a moment. I watched as it made a spiral ascent up the tree and hid behind a cracked bulge in the bark. When my eyes returned to the man, I noticed that he was holding a small pillow—a red embroidered throw, the type you'd find on a couch or an armchair. His arms trembled slightly as he held the pillow in the air above the canvas of the wheelchair's back.

The canvas came up as far as the bend in the old woman's spine, and that bend was now the highest point on her body. She was curled like a cooked shrimp; her head had fallen and was almost touching her knees. If her posture were better, then her head might have been in line with the pillow. The man might have been pulling the pillow over her face. He might have been smothering her. As it was, he was miming a murder, going through the motions like a golfer taking practice swings.

Strange wasn't the word for this moment. Bizarre. Because it didn't stop there. The man then drew the pillow toward his own head. He pulled both sides until the fabric and stuffing took on the contours of his face. The old woman remained in her chair, not saying a thing, hardly moving, certainly not turning around to see what was going on behind her.

Somewhere in the distance, a woodpecker went to work on a tree, and the rattle startled the man. He yanked the pillow from his face and shook his head violently, as if trying to dislodge water from his ear. Then he slipped the pillow behind the old woman's bent back, ran his hands through his mane, and let out a rumbling and exhausted breath. Finally, he sat down in the lawn chair.

And that's where he stayed. Neither he nor the woman said anything or even moved much. They looked out past the yard into the grays and browns of the swamp.

I watched them for nearly thirty minutes, first waiting for something else to happen, and then falling into a gentle hypnosis, not exactly a feeling of comfort, but a surrender to the boring and meaningless.

"Lunch?" the man eventually asked.

The woman responded with a barely noticeable nod. They went inside.

FRIDAY, OCTOBER 20

———◆———

MY TREPIDATION TRANSFORMED INTO COMPASSION. WHAT I had seen in Fiona's backyard confused me. I still had no idea who the man and the old woman were, but there was something going on there, something peculiar, something potentially violent. It wasn't illegal, so I couldn't really tell the police. And since I didn't want to admit to snooping, I wasn't going to tell my parents either. Yet the image of the pillow smothering an invisible face—of the pillow smothering the man's own face!—was not something to ignore. This was not the kind of person you wanted living in your house.

After a long, dreamless sleep, I went to school with a renewed sense of purpose. I would listen to Fiona, listen carefully to what she was *really* saying. Cries for help aren't always cries. Sometimes they're stories.

"Do you mind?" I asked, hovering over Fiona with my tray of French fries.

She looked up from her Oreos. "Sure. I mean, no. I don't mind. Kendra and Fay-Renee are waiting on chicken nuggets, but they'll be here in a jiff."

"That's fine," I said as I sat. "I got a table with Mike and Trevor today, but I wanted to stop by and let you know I'm sorry about the other night."

Fiona paused, as if searching the depths of her memory. "Oh," she said with a wave of her hand. "Forgotten. Ancient history."

"Are you busy this weekend?"

"Not that I know of."

"Why don't I go over to your house and we can talk about Aquaville?"

"You mean Aquavania?" Her eyes narrowed.

"Exactly."

"I don't think you should come over. Our house is a mess."

From the little I'd seen through her windows, I might have said their house was the opposite, but I wasn't going to challenge her. The goal was to be comforting, trustworthy. "That's fine," I said. "Anytime, though. Anytime you wanna talk about anything."

Fiona surveyed the cafeteria to see if anyone was listening. "You don't have a ton of friends, do you?"

It was true. I knew almost everyone in seventh grade, but when it came to friends, there were only a few guys I hung out with at school. Outside of school, there was only Charlie.

"I . . ."

"I don't, either," Fiona said. "I'm fine with that. Kendra and Fay-Renee are nice and all, but there are more important things, more important people."

"You called me a weirdo the other day," I said. "I'm not a weirdo, I'm a—"

"Alistair?"

"What?"

"It's not about being a weirdo. I'm gonna be telling you secrets. It's about keeping those secrets. No blabbing to Mike. Or Trevor. Certainly not to Charlie. People's lives depend on it."

"Okay. Sure."

"Tomorrow morning, at that rock. Eight o'clock. You listen. You don't run away. No matter what I say."

I stood up and ran my finger across my chest in a big *X*. The timing was unfortunate. Kendra and Fay-Renee had stopped amid the round tables, only a few yards in front of me, and Fay-Renee was whispering to Kendra, who was pretending to gag herself. It didn't bother me, though. Because I knew that Fiona would be telling me something that she may never have told anyone else.

I knew that, at least for this moment, I was important.

That evening, as I washed the dishes, I received another phone call from Charlie.

"You won't believe what I found!" he squealed. "A box of

fireworks in the back of Kyle's van! Tomorrow morning we go out and catch some toads and we launch them into space on bottle rockets."

"Sounds fun," I lied. "But I can't. I'm busy."

"Some time later then?"

"Yeah," I said. "Definitely."

Saturday, October 21

———— ◆ ————

I ARRIVED EARLY, AND FIONA WAS ALREADY SITTING BEHIND Frog Rock on a lawn chair. There was a chair set up for me as well.

I sat. "Morning."

She looked me over. "Why the change of heart?"

"I . . ."

"Felt sorry for me?"

"No," I said. "Needed to hear more."

"It doesn't matter. You're here."

"I am. I forgot to bring the tape recorder, though."

"And to wear the snazzy jacket," she joked. "That's fine. Like I said, I changed my mind. I don't want you recording this. I want you memorizing it."

"I can try to do that."

"You better. Because I'm gonna talk your ears off."

Talk she did. We were there for more than two hours,

with Fiona telling a story so fantastic, so ridiculous, that I had trouble keeping a straight face. I did my best, though, and I let her get it out. I didn't question the details. I tried to remember them. I didn't call her a liar. I listened.

In the time since, I have told the same story, but in my own words, to those who loved her and those who missed her, and the ones like me, who were trying to read between the lines.

Now I'm telling you.

THE LEGEND OF FIONA LOOMIS

The moment that Fiona Loomis touched the cylinder of water, she felt a tickle in her fingers. The tickle carbonated her body, spreading from her fingers to her arms, to her chest, to her feet, until everything was fizzing and the lightbulb above her was not a lightbulb at all. It was the sun.

She fell from the sky, her body stretched out and gently curved like a corn husk. She fell for a very long time, but she fell slowly, just like a husk or maybe a feather or a flake of snow. When she hit water, she hardly felt the impact, but she kept going, deeper and deeper into the dark, farther from the sun.

There were no fish, no colors other than blue, and it wasn't until the blue was almost black and her eardrums began to ache and her lungs began to strain that Fiona had the thought that would begin her story.

There once was a girl who could swim.

At four years old, Fiona had never swum before. She'd never seen the ocean or been in a pool, but once the thought entered her mind, a wish was granted, and she began to kick her feet like a dolphin kicks its tail and to move her arms like the fronds of a jellyfish, and she rose up through the water until she reached the surface.

Fiona bobbed in a vast ocean. There was no land in sight, no boats, no animals to speak of. It was now her instinct to tread water, because she was a girl who could swim. It was also now her instinct to tell a story.

The girl who could swim was very lonely and she wanted a friend.

This thought brought forth a cylinder of water, grabbed from the ocean by an unseen force and held in the air in front of Fiona.

One day she met a bush baby.

The cylinder of water morphed into the shape of a bush baby, with giant eyes and knobby fingers and ears that were stiff and alert. It was translucent at first, a creation born of water, but the water soon took on the red of blood, and the beige of skin, and the brown of fur, until there was a real-life bush baby in front of Fiona, exactly like the ones she had once seen in the nocturnal building at the zoo.

As soon as it was fully formed, the bush baby fell from the air into the water, and Fiona watched it sink into the dark.

The bush baby could swim, just as good as the girl.

With that thought, the bush baby shifted its path and pulled itself up through the water until it was treading next to Fiona.

The bush baby was named Toby, and he was smart and he could talk too.

Toby smiled and said, "Hello, Fiona, it is so nice to see you."

Fiona smiled and said, "Hello, Toby, I'm so glad we're friends."

"What brings you to Aquavania?" Toby asked.

"I don't know," Fiona replied. "I touched water and then I was here."

"Ahh," Toby said, raising a little finger. "You're new. So much to learn."

"What is this place?"

"It is everywhere and nowhere. It is where stories are born."

"What stories?"

"Stories we tell children. Magical worlds. They exist. They are born here in Aquavania and they seep into the minds of the people who write the books and paint the paintings and film the movies. Why, you're creating a world right now. A world where a girl named Fiona swims with her bush baby friend named Toby."

The only world Fiona wanted was the world where she came from, with Mommy and Daddy and her brother, Derek, and her sister, Maria.

The thoughts about swimming and the bush baby had been made real, and so too was this one. Fiona felt the fizz fill her body again, and in a flash she was back, standing on the box, her hand on the warm boiler, the lightbulb dangling above her in the basement of her family's home. She went upstairs and clambered into bed.

Three years would go by before the radiators spoke again.

Fiona had tried to forget about her trip to Aquavania, but it was one of the only things from her days as a four-year-old that she remembered. She told her family about it a few times, and they called it "nothing but a silly dream."

The night the radiators did speak again, Fiona was not so willing to follow. She had recently stopped sleeping with a night-light, so maybe it was the darkness of her room—punctured only by the glow-in-the-dark constellation stickers on the ceiling—but the voice didn't sound as inviting as before. It had a mischievous bite to it.

"I don't want to go there," Fiona whispered as she pulled the sheet up over her head. "It's wet and lonely and scary."

"It doesn't have to be that way." The voice crackled in the air, an irresistible enticement.

Fiona peeked out from the sheet and asked, "What can it be?"

"Almost anything."

To a girl of ample imagination, "almost anything" was far too tempting. So she snuck back down the stairs to the room with the boiler. The boiler disappeared, and the cylinder of water hung there. She touched the cylinder. She went back to Aquavania.

Toby was floating in the ocean, waiting for her.

"It's been so long," he said.

"You've been waiting ever since I last visited?"

"More or less. Time is different here. People like you arrive precisely when you need to and go home exactly when you left."

"I don't know what that means."

"You will."

There was a rumble in the ocean. It was Toby's stomach.

The bush baby named Toby liked popcorn, and he liked to eat it on the beach of a beautiful island where amazing animals lived.

A dome of water rose up from the ocean, and geysers burst out of it and froze into the shapes of palm trees. Ferns and creatures and soft earth followed, and Fiona and Toby soon found themselves sitting on the sand, inches from the surf, a giant bowl of popcorn resting between them.

"Wonderfooool!" Toby exclaimed, his mouth full of popcorn.

Fiona giggled and ate the popcorn until she

couldn't fit another kernel in her stomach, and then she and Toby explored the brand-new island. There were glorious birds with neon wings and corkscrew beaks. There were waterfalls as tall as skyscrapers and enormous swimming holes full of singing sea lions and ringed with flowers that smelled like bacon and pie, which were Fiona's favorite smells.

"Did everything come from my mind?" she asked.

"It did," Toby told her.

"But I don't remember thinking about all of it."

"Your mind is constantly wishing, even if you don't realize it. It's all in there somewhere. Aquavania is the place where it's released."

"Anything I can imagine can come true?"

"Yes and no. You are the author. But these things are now alive. They are no longer a part of you, but you are responsible for them."

"Like a pet?"

"Sort of," Toby said. "Thoughts change. Evolve. On their own. Be careful, though. Aquavania is a strange and powerful place, and you are not the only one here."

"There are others like me?"

"Yes."

"Does everyone get to come here? My brother? My sister? My parents?"

Toby shook his head and pointed to Fiona's ears. "Only the children with the imagination to hear." Then he pointed to her eyes. "Only the children with the willingness to see."

"So only young people?"

"Not every child is young," Toby said.

The explanations were too weird and exhausting for Fiona to contemplate. Instead of pressing Toby further, she imagined a bed made of marshmallows hanging from vines under the shade of palm trees, and Aquavania gave her exactly what she imagined. She climbed onto the bed and fell asleep.

When she woke the next morning, she was still on the island with Toby and all the other animals. This frightened her, for surely her parents were missing her back home.

Fiona left Aquavania to go home, but assured Toby and the animals on the island that she would be back.

Once again, Fiona was instantly transported to the box in the room in her basement, her hand on the warm boiler.

She hurried upstairs, expecting to find her family awake and worried, but it was still dark and everyone was still asleep. When she reached her bedroom, she checked her clock. She had been in Aquavania for nearly a day, but according to the clock, she hadn't even been gone three minutes.

Her family was likely to tell her it was only a dream, but she knew it was more than that. She was no longer that naïve little four-year-old who confessed every-

thing. She was the ripe old age of seven, and Aquavania was now her secret. And she was going back.

Fiona's version was more detailed, and she told it confidently, as if she'd been rehearsing it for years, patiently
waiting to get it off her chest. It wasn't without emotion,
but it was precise and focused, and I didn't know what to
make of it other than wanting to hear more.

More would have to wait.

"Alistair!" my mom hollered.

I peered around Frog Rock and saw her standing on the
back deck. Worry ruled her posture. Her neck was craned.
Her arms dangled helplessly.

"I'll be a second," I whispered to Fiona as I got up from
the chair.

Fiona responded with a curt nod, but I could tell she
wasn't thrilled about the interruption. She had only just
begun her story.

"What?" I barked as I stepped into the grass. "I'm busy."

"Thank god," my mom whimpered. "Oh, thank god."

She dashed toward me, and we met halfway through the
yard, where she wrapped her arms around me and squeezed
me as if to test my existence.

"There's been an accident," she told me. "Fireworks.
Charlie is in the hospital."

Sunday, October 22

---·◆·---

THE DETAILS WERE GORY INDEED. ACCORDING TO MY MOM, Kyle woke to a bang sometime around eight thirty on Saturday morning, but, like everyone else in the neighborhood, he had ignored it. It was the beginning of hunting season and men with muzzle-loaders were thick in the forests nearby. At nine o'clock, when Kyle ducked behind the clubhouse for a smoke, he found Charlie unconscious, his hands a mangled mess, and the box of fireworks nearby. Some of the feral cats had gathered and were licking the blood off of Charlie's body. Kyle shooed them away with a stick, carried his little brother to the van, and ferried him to the hospital. The doctors said Charlie was minutes away from dying of blood loss when he arrived and, for at least a few minutes, Kyle was a hero. When he admitted that the fireworks were his, his reputation resumed its default position. He was irresponsible, dangerous, an unforgivable variety of older brother.

People had wondered if I was involved. My alibi was solid, backed up by Fiona, though we didn't reveal the nature of our conversation. "We were making up a story together," she had told my parents and the police.

A boy and girl hanging out behind a rock? Making up a story? They certainly didn't believe that, but they also didn't believe we had anything to do with Charlie's accident.

I wasn't allowed to visit Charlie until Sunday morning. He had spent hours in surgery and needed time to sleep off the effects.

My dad drove me to the hospital, and on the way he told me, "When I was a kid, even younger than you, there was a guy down the street who I was friends with. One day we were playing ball. A few days later and he's diagnosed with polio. He died not long after that."

"You think Charlie is gonna die?"

"No, no, I don't think that," my dad assured me. "I'm trying to tell you that life will sneak up on you sometimes. Even though you're a kid, it doesn't mean you're invincible."

"I'm aware, Dad."

The truth is, I wasn't aware. Not really. But I would be.

There were cartoon puppies and pinwheels on the fading wallpaper of Charlie's room. The same motif was echoed in the sheets and blankets. This was the children's ward, and it didn't matter if you were four or fourteen; everyone got puppies and pinwheels.

Movies had taught me that hospital rooms were terrifying places, with screaming and crying and human vegetables hooked up to wheezing machines. Charlie's room, while slightly depressing, wasn't nearly so bad, and Charlie himself—tucked in and mounted on his mechanical bed so he had a perfect view of the TV—looked almost serene.

"Hey," I said as I stepped around the curtain. My dad waited in the hall, gathering the prognosis from Charlie's parents.

Charlie gave me a devilish grin as he pulled his hands out from under the blankets. He waved two gauzy lumps.

"Hey, buddy." The words crawled out from his dry throat. "Missed the grand finale."

"Jeez," I replied. I looked at the heart rate monitor. The blips were steady.

"It's okay," Charlie said. "Stupid bottle rockets. Wrap twenty together and they pack a wallop."

"I'm sorry."

"What? Why? I'm sorry you missed it. How many times do you get to see a kid blow off five of his fingers?"

"Oh man . . . that many?"

"Two on the left hand, three on the right."

My first thought was, *How will Charlie ever play video games again?* And while that may seem shallow, it had probably been Charlie's first thought as well.

"I should have been there with you," I said. "To stop it."

Charlie shook his head. "You were busy."

"I guess."

"Did you tape all of yesterday's shows?"

"I . . . no." This was a big difference between us. Had I been the one in the hospital, he would have been presenting me with a VHS of all the television I'd missed during my hours of surgery and recovery. Instead, I brought him a bag of gummy bears. I set it on his tray next to his barely touched breakfast.

"Oh well," Charlie said. "I guess there's always summer reruns." Gummy bears were his favorite, but they couldn't make up for missing a day of television.

"Want me to open them?"

He raised the wrapped remains of his hands, and with a grin he said, "What do you think?"

Shortly after that, a nurse whisked into the room to change the bandages, and I used it as my cue to escape. Down the hall, I found my dad sitting on the edge of the reception desk, cradling a cup of coffee to his chest. Standing next to him, Charlie's dad held the ribbon of a Mylar balloon that was shaped like a cat's head.

They seemed an odd pair. My dad—clean shaven, athletic, a polo shirt and khakis. Charlie's dad—bearded and balding, paunchy, tinted glasses, a red nylon jacket and dark corduroys. Yet their conversation had a natural sweep to it.

". . . and they both had about a billion wasp stings. Remember that?" Charlie's dad mused.

"How could I not?" my dad replied. "We were putting

calamine lotion on him for over a week. Man, those boys were so tiny back then."

A gentle punch to my shoulder greeted my arrival, and I tried my best to sound chipper. "How goes it, old man?" I said to my dad. For some reason, he always got a kick out of me calling him *old man*.

"Mr. Dwyer and I are sharing some old memories of you guys," he replied.

"Real nice of you to visit," Mr. Dwyer told me. "You know, Charlie asked to see you almost immediately."

"Well . . . thanks." I wasn't sure what I was thanking him for, but I didn't know what else to say.

A blast of air from an oscillating fan on the desk sent the cat balloon into orbit, and the three of us watched it until my dad stuck out a hand. "Hal," he said. "We'll have that drink soon."

Charlie's dad joined him in a firm handshake. "You bet, Rich. Long overdue."

"It'll be tough," my dad explained a few minutes later as we walked through the hospital parking lot. "He'll need you to be sympathetic. You can invite him over for dinners if you want."

"You don't like Charlie," I said. "I know that."

"Charlie's a nice kid. Sure, he can be exhausting—"

"I'll go over to his house. Every day after school. He doesn't have to come visit."

"Whatever you can do. Show him you care."

We walked past Kyle's van. It was haphazardly parked, wheels over the lines. "Did you see Kyle in there?" I asked.

"Smoking lounge."

"What are they gonna do to him?"

My dad shrugged and pulled out his keys. "What *can* you do to him? He didn't give Charlie the fireworks. Kyle shouldn't have had them, but he's eighteen years old. I'm sure he's got worse in his van."

"He's not a bad guy, deep down," I said.

My dad slipped the key into the door. "Deep down, no one is. But you make choices."

Monday, October 23

———◆———

I WAS BACK AT SCHOOL THE NEXT DAY, THE EVENTS OF THE weekend informing everything. At lunch, I sat with Mike Cooney and Trevor Weeks, as I often did. They were a couple of guys who weren't considered cool or lame or anything other than harmless. Trevor had an appetite for gossip, though, and he peppered me with questions about Charlie. I was quick to dispel rumors that Charlie had blown off his arms or that he'd been building a bomb to put under the bleachers in the gym.

Only once that day did I pass Fiona in the hall. Though I didn't say anything to her, she whispered something to me: "Hang in there."

I spent the afternoon overanalyzing those words. Were they a reference to worrying about Charlie? Or a promise that more of her story was to come? As wild as the story was, I was hoping it was the latter.

At the end of the day, Principal Braugher called an emergency assembly. We filled the auditorium, where a police officer droned through a lecture on the dangers of fireworks. When it was over, Braugher made an announcement.

"School policy for possession of fireworks is now an automatic suspension and a visit to the police station. I hope that's clear. And I hope everyone keeps Charlie in their thoughts and prayers."

Ken Wagner, never one to pass up an opportunity for attention, coughed out a "Captain Catpoop," which was met with a smattering of giggles. We were dismissed.

"Did you get to see his nasty hands?" Keri asked me on the walk home.

"They were wrapped in bandages."

"Think they'll give him steel pincers?" Keri curled her fingers and gestured at me with an exaggerated sneer.

"I don't know."

"Ooo. Think he'll dress up as a lobster for Halloween?"

Frankly, I was sick of talking about Charlie. I knew that he would be home soon and I'd probably be seeing more than enough of him. So I quickened the pace, hoping it would put an end to the banter.

"Are we taking the *long* cut now?" Keri huffed as we made a turn a few blocks from home. Yes, I had chosen the longer route, but I had also chosen the one past Fiona's house.

The man I had seen in the backyard was now in Fiona's garage. The crunch and growl of heavy metal provided a sound track as he bent over a machine that looked a lot like the motorized sander my dad kept mounted to a table in our basement. But instead of using it to smooth out a piece of wood, the man appeared to be pressing something metal against the spinning belt. As he worked the metal back and forth, it caught the glare of a shop light and I saw it clearly. He was sharpening a long, thin blade.

I stepped back and nearly tripped over my own feet. As a spy, I obviously failed.

"You're a stalker!" Keri squealed.

"Am not!"

Before I could defend myself any further, I heard the whir of bike wheels. Fiona coasted past and looked back over her shoulder.

"Busted!" Keri cheered, pointing a finger at me.

Fiona jammed the brakes and skidded out. She waited until we caught up.

"Hey, I was about to—" I started to say, but Fiona cut me off, staring Keri down with an odd intensity.

"You saw me burying something one night?"

Keri turned her head to the side. "I don't know anything about that."

"Yes you do," Fiona said. "Do you want to know what it was?"

Keri turned back. "I. Don't. Give. A. Crap."

"It was love letters to Alistair," Fiona said. "We're dating now, in case you were wondering."

The bluntness caused Keri to hold her hands up in surrender. "If you say so."

"I . . . we . . . uh . . ." I stuttered myself into silence. The logical reaction was to call Fiona a liar or to laugh it all off as a joke, but I was ditching logic in favor of emotion. I kind of liked what she'd said.

"I'll leave you two lovebirds alone," Keri told us, and she was true to her word, double-timing it to our house like she was racing curfew.

"Who's nosier, your sister or that Mandy girl she hangs out with?" Fiona asked, but I wasn't going to let her off the hook that easily.

"Really? Dating?"

"Oh, come on." Fiona rolled her eyes. "I've been to your room. Your mom found us behind that rock. It's what everyone is thinking. The more you deny it, the more they'll believe it."

"How do you know?"

"Because I'm older than you. Wiser."

"Oh right, a wise old thirteen," I said, forgetting the promise I'd made to myself to humor Fiona for the sake of uncovering the truth.

"Actually, I'm fourteen now," she said.

"What?"

"Let's go to the park. To the swing sets. No one will bother us there. You need to hear more. Things get complicated."

THE LEGEND OF FIONA LOOMIS, PART II

Fiona Loomis returned to Aquavania many times throughout her childhood. Only at night, though, and only when everyone in her family was sleeping. The radiators would call to her, and she'd creep down to the liquid portal in her basement and enter a world she was growing to love.

Toby was always waiting, and so too were all the creatures and landscapes Fiona had dreamed up. Life went on without her, on its own time line. Fiona could be away from Aquavania for a week, only to return and find that ten years had passed. Or she could be away for a month and find that only ten minutes had passed. There was no way of predicting the time gap, but whenever she was gone, the palm trees and vines and ferns would climb and twist and grow. The animals would form couples and have babies and become families. When things got old, they wilted. Things passed away.

To say it was always harmonious would be a lie. Sometimes Fiona would introduce a new creature and anarchy would ensue. Take, for example, the levitating bandicoots. The problem with levitating bandicoots was that they could eat almost anything in Fiona's world, but they preferred to eat the highest flowers of the orangeberry spruce. Those flowers were the staple of the paisley giraffes' diet. Without them, the giraffes starved.

So once when Fiona returned after some time away, she found bandicoots so chubby that they could hardly levitate and paisley giraffe carcasses strewn everywhere. It horrified her, but it also taught her that her powers weren't perfect. Sure, she could create more rules—she could make the bandicoots hate orangeberry spruce flowers or make the giraffes less finicky—but she also had to let this world figure itself out. It was as real a place as any.

"Am I God here?" Fiona once asked Toby.

"In a manner of speaking," Toby told her.

"Everything else grows old here, but I don't, do I?"

"Your body doesn't," Toby explained. "But your mind does. Your body only grows old in the Solid World."

"The Solid World?"

"The place you come from. Home."

By *home*, Toby meant Thessaly—Fiona's house, her family. But to Fiona, Aquavania was starting to feel like home as well. Every time she visited, she made the island bigger. She gave it levels. Her mind conjured up enormous trees with intertwined limbs that served as walkways through the canopies. Smaller branches wove together like tangles of fingers and formed tunnels.

Below the canopies, Fiona created an aviary so thick with birds that it looked like layers of undulating feathery quilts. Whenever she jumped from the treetops, wings cushioned her. For fun, she would summon the rain and ride the feathers like a waterslide.

When she dug into the ground, she unearthed mint chocolate chip ice cream. When she called out into the wind, a giant flying squirrel would scoop Fiona up and let her ride on his neck and survey her creations.

Sometimes while soaring, Fiona would look into the distance, over the ocean as far as the light reached, and she would see a haze. At first, she thought little of it, assumed that when she built a bigger world, the haze would move farther away, like the skin of an expanding balloon.

But that didn't happen. As her world got bigger, the haze got closer, and by the time Fiona was ten years old, she began to worry about these unknown hinterlands. One day, she called out for the squirrel, and it scooped her and Toby up. And as the squirrel dipped and barrel-rolled, Fiona pointed out past the ocean and commanded, "Fly us into that haze!"

The squirrel refused. It flew no farther than the coastline. This was beyond shocking, because it was the first time that the squirrel hadn't followed her instructions. It was the first time that *anything* in Aquavania hadn't followed her instructions.

Rightfully upset, Fiona decided to solve the problem the way she solved all her problems: by thinking the answer into existence.

The flying squirrel could speak, and it could tell Fiona why it refused to fly into the haze.

"I don't know why I can't fly there," the squirrel said. "It's simply beyond my abilities."

The squirrel continued to glide along the coastline as Fiona pondered the mystery.

"Is it the edge of Aquavania?" she asked Toby.

"It is *an* edge," Toby replied.

"I should have known better than to ask you. Why do you always speak in riddles?"

"I speak all that I know. I have never been there. I have only been here."

"If you weren't so darn cute, I'd throw you off this squirrel," Fiona said, and then she had a thought that would open her world up in a way she could never have imagined.

There was a bridge that was as long as a bridge could be, and it reached from the island into the haze and to what lay beyond the haze.

A gleaming spout of water shot out from the island as if it were a fountain, and the spout stretched all the way into the haze. It froze in place, a gentle translucent arch with a pathway wide enough for a girl and her bush baby. Fiona asked the squirrel to set them down, and the two began their hike toward the haze.

Hours later, they weren't even a fraction of the way there.

"Am I an idiot, Toby?"

"Is that a rhetorical question?"

The bridge had a conveyer belt so that Toby and Fiona didn't have to walk anymore.

A conveyer belt made of milky quartz started churning and moving them forward, but the haze was still a long way off. Fiona knew that it didn't matter how much time it took, how many days she stayed in Aquavania; she would always return home to the basement at the exact moment she left. She was ten years old and had already spent six weeks of her life in Aquavania, six weeks that didn't exist back in the Solid World.

Still, the journey to the haze was taking far too long.

And the conveyer went faster, and faster, and faster . . .

The world blurred. The only thing she could see was Toby's face, which shuddered from the g-force like a fighter jet pilot's. Any faster and she would have made herself sick. For all the things she could create, Fiona could not change herself. That was one of the restrictions of Aquavania. She couldn't make herself prettier or taller or more accustomed to Mach 2 speeds.

For three days Fiona and Toby zoomed along the conveyer belt, holding hands and surviving off of ice cream.

"You told me I can't age here," Fiona said to Toby. "But can I die here?"

"Yes," he replied.

"Can you . . . die here too, Toby?" Fiona could hardly get the question out.

"I will die only when you need me to die," Toby explained. "I am your first creation. I am not like the others."

Fiona turned away. She couldn't bear to look at him. "What happens to us here?" she asked. "I mean, when we die?"

Toby's voice was weak. It had a tremble to it. "I don't know."

When they weren't definitive, Toby's answers were usually playfully and frustratingly vague. He almost never said *I don't know.* As soon as he did, the conveyer belt stopped, and they were confronted with the edge of the haze.

There was no seeing through it, so Fiona reached out to touch it. It slapped her back like she was an insolent dog.

The haze let Fiona touch it.

She reached for it again, and again it slapped her away.

"I think this is something beyond your control," Toby said.

"But I need to know what's behind it."

"Remember how I told you that Aquavania is where stories are born?"

"Yes."

"There are many stories to tell. Yours is not the only one. Maybe this is the end of yours."

"Mine ends when I decide it ends!" Fiona barked as she tried to step into the haze. It knocked her onto her rear.

"I'm only saying what you already know," Toby said.

This was true. Fiona was not so arrogant as to think she was the only person who'd ever come to Aquavania. Toby had already told her as much. But then, she had never wished to meet anyone else here. This was a place to be alone with her creations.

Just as she thought this, there came a whisper through the haze.

The girl named Chua needed nothing more than to meet someone smart and new so that she could share her story.

This wasn't Fiona's thought. It was someone else's, and as it emerged, it brought with it a wave of water that snatched Fiona from the bridge and pulled her through the haze.

That fuzzy feeling—the bubbles in her body that accompanied trips to and from Aquavania—tricked Fiona into thinking she was returning to the Solid World, but instead of emerging next to the boiler in her basement, she emerged in the center of an ice cavern.

The cavern was as large as a football stadium. Its roof was at least one hundred feet high and covered not only in icicles but in numerous polar bears that hung upside down by their feet like bats. A few other polar bears were flying through the air, aided by fleshy and furry propellers that grew out of their backs.

Not far from Fiona, a girl wearing a parka with a woolly hood sat on a throne made of ice.

"Hot chocolate!" the girl hooted. "Success!"

"Hello?" Fiona surveyed the cavern. Toby was nowhere to be seen. She didn't recognize this place.

"Welcome welcome welcome!" The girl pushed herself off from the throne and slid with a surfer's stance across the ice to Fiona's side. She stuck out a hand. "Name is Chua."

"Mine's . . . Fiona."

As she shook Chua's hand, Fiona took in more of the surroundings. The walls of the cavern were covered in tiny lights that were constantly changing colors. The changes appeared random at first, until Fiona realized they were broadcasting messages about her.

SHE'S SCARED.

SHE'S COLD.

"You'll catch your death," Chua said. "How about a walrus skin coat?"

"That would be"—before she finished speaking, Fiona felt the warmth of animal fur on her skin and looked down to see that she was now wearing a perfectly tailored coat—"fine."

Fiona needed Toby to be there with her, to tell her what was going on.

It didn't work.

Fiona needed to go back to her world, to a safe place, a place where she was in control.

This wish didn't work either. No matter what Fiona thought, it didn't come true.

"First time crossing over?" Chua asked.

"Excuse me?"

"Don't sweat it," Chua said. "You're a guest. Relax. Enjoy your visit."

Chua stomped the icy ground, producing a ripple of cracks. From the cracks, a small beak poked up like a bud. A head followed the beak, and suddenly there was a penguin in front of them, shaking wet ice from his velvety coat.

"Greetings and salutations," the penguin said with a bow.

"This is Baxter," Chua explained.

"And who is this lovely young lady?" Baxter asked.

Fiona was too dumbfounded to respond.

"I know it's ludicrous," Baxter said. "Penguins and polar bears existing in the same geographical region. Yet it's how our Chua likes it."

"This is Fiona," Chua told Baxter. "She crossed over for the first time. I was lonely and I wished for a new friend, and she must have been near the folds."

"The folds?" Fiona asked.

"That's what we call them. The borders of our worlds."

"So I'm in your world now?"

"She learns quickly," Baxter said.

"Yes," Chua said. "But don't worry. Anytime you want to go home, go ahead and tell me and I'll wish you back."

"How many worlds are there?" Fiona asked.

"Oh, I don't know," Chua said. "Hundreds? Thousands? Millions?"

Baxter tilted his head and held out his wings like two open hands. He didn't have the vaguest idea.

"I've met six other kids here," Chua went on. "I've been to four other worlds. But they know other kids, who know other kids, and blah blah blah. So I suppose there could be countless worlds."

"Are the other worlds like this?" Fiona asked. "Icy and strange?"

"Oh, no no no," Chua said.

"Are all minds the same?" Baxter asked Fiona.

Fiona shook her head. "In my world I have a bush baby and miles of vines that you can swing on and braid into just about anything."

Nodding, Chua seemed mildly impressed. "I have this."

She put two fingers in her mouth and whistled. The ground softened and sagged like elastic. And like elastic, it held their weight for a moment and then snapped back, sending Chua, Fiona, and Baxter rocketing into the air. As they went up, the polar bears went down, fluttering past them like a snowfall of fur. When it looked like Fiona would strike the icy roof, Chua whistled again and the roof burst into a glittering cloud.

At the apex of their flight, the two girls and the penguin hung in the air for a moment, and Fiona looked down to see that the polar bears had never hit the ground. They were hovering and swarming together like bees to a hive. Gravity took hold again and pulled the three back toward the bears.

As they fell, Chua whistled twice more. With the first whistle, the ground exploded exactly as the roof had, leaving nothing but a dusty sparkle. With the second, the walls of the cavern exploded too, but not before broadcasting a final message.

PLANET POLAR BEAR IS COMPLETE!

When they touched down, Fiona, Chua, and Baxter landed on white fur. The polar bears were no longer individuals. They had merged into one enormous ball of fur that was pulsing and floating in the open air like a miniature planet. The dusty particles left over from the walls and roof and ground were now stars in the endless sky that surrounded them.

"Holy moly," was about all Fiona could say.

Chua winked and said, "Baxter, be a good li'l bird and fetch us some potato chips."

Baxter nodded and jumped in the air, his pointy wings poised like a diver's hands. There was no water anywhere, so Baxter dove straight into the furry ground. It swallowed him completely, and he was gone before Fiona could make sense of what had happened.

It didn't faze Chua one bit. "Stay the night if you like. Sleepover?" she asked.

"I . . . I . . ." Fiona was rarely one to stutter, but she was also rarely one to attend sleepovers, let alone ones in magical lands. There were occasional birthday party invitations back home in Thessaly, and her friend Kendra had her over on a few Saturday nights to hang out and watch videos, but that was it.

Chua clearly sensed Fiona's apprehension. "If you'd rather return to your world, I can wish you back," she said. "But I think we can have some fun here, don't you?"

"I think . . . I might like that," Fiona finally replied. Why not, right? Chua was obviously a girl of great talents and knowledge. There was no telling what she could teach Fiona about Aquavania.

Chua stepped forward and put an arm around Fiona. It felt nice to have a new friend.

"You know there's only one thing left to do, then?"

"What's that?" Fiona asked.

Chua's dark hair brushed against Fiona's face as she leaned in and whispered, "Riverman, Riverman, blood to ice."

The words reeked of menace, and Fiona's body felt like it was split in half. She looked down to see a bright blue icicle embedded in her chest and Chua's hand pulling away. Falling backward, Fiona clawed at the icicle to try to get a grip, but it was burning cold and far too slippery.

"What did you do?" Fiona cried.

"Riverman, Riverman, blood to ice. Riverman, Riverman, blood to ice."

Fiona arched her back and planted her shoulders in the fuzzy ground and tried to dislodge the icicle. It was no use. The icicle was melting, and the liquid was seeping into her as if her body were a sponge.

Chua loomed, arms out and eyes wide, as if in a trance. "Riverman, Riverman, blood to ice. Riverman, Riverman, blood to ice."

"Why are you saying that? What have you done to me?"

Fiona closed her eyes and began whimpering, and she didn't stop whimpering until she realized that she wasn't in pain. She had been stabbed in the chest—she had felt the icicle tear into her!—and yet it didn't hurt anymore. Not one bit.

Opening her eyes, she saw that the icicle was no longer there and there was no injury. She wasn't even wet. Chua was standing above her, smiling.

"I'm sorry," Chua said. "I didn't think you were him, but I had to know for sure."

"You didn't think I was who?"

"The Riverman," Chua said.

This is where I stopped Fiona. It had taken her almost three hours, but she had finally mentioned the name that had haunted me for nearly a week. I blurted out the inevitable question. "Who the heck is the Riverman?"

Fiona sighed. "He's the one who's coming for us. All the kids in Aquavania."

Headlights swept over the backstop behind the swings and splashed our shadows onto it. In the empty lot, a truck engine rumbled.

"Fi!" someone yelled. The voice had teeth.

"Crap," I said. "It's late, isn't it? Is that your dad?"

"Uncle."

A cigarette torpedoed out of the truck window and hit the lot with a flurry of sparks.

"Well past dinner," her uncle called out from the cab. "Been sent to find ya."

Fiona stood from her swing as I turned myself in a circle, twisting and tightening the chains like the rubber band on a balsa plane.

"We're just talking," Fiona called back.

"Don't matter one bit. Need you home, Fi."

The look Fiona gave me could have been two things: panic or longing. Maybe it was both. Whatever it was, it struck me hard. She wanted nothing more than to stay there with me.

"I have to tell you the rest, as soon as possible," she said.

"Call me."

"Can't risk it. He could be listening in on my phone."

"Your uncle?"

"The Riverman."

"He's here?" I asked.

The moon was strangled by clouds. It was as dark out as it gets. "He could be anywhere," she said.

There were pebbles at my feet, and as Fiona lifted her bike and walked away, I worked my feet through those pebbles and kept tightening those swing chains. There are countless stories where a boy tosses pebbles at a girl's window and she opens it and climbs down and he saves her. He always saves her.

Fiona hefted her bike into the truck bed. Opening the passenger side door activated the interior light and illuminated the face of her uncle. It was the same man from the backyard and the garage.

Lifting my feet, I launched into a spin. I closed my eyes and tucked my legs to spin faster as the truck pulled away.

Tuesday, October 24

On the walk to school the following morning, Kyle's van pulled up alongside me and Keri. "Got a second?" he asked.

Sniffing toads might have induced a similar expression on Keri's face. Her lip curled, and her head sank into the valley between her shoulders.

"Don't worry about it," I told her, placing a hand on her backpack. "He's cool. Go on without me."

Your funeral, her eyes said, but she wasn't going to mourn. She kept moving, leaving me next to the van.

"Get in."

"I can't be late," I said.

"Get in."

We drove around the block, circling a couple of times while listening to the radio. When I tried to speak, Kyle turned up the volume to quiet me. At first I thought it was because he wanted to enjoy the music, some oldie with a lot of *ooo wa ooo*s. By the third loop, I discovered the real reason. Kyle was crying.

He wasn't bawling, but there were tears, plump and real, and he was wiping them away. I'm not exaggerating when I say that this shocked me more than any story Fiona had told.

"Hey, are you—"

"Shut your face," he said.

He eased the pedal down, the van sped up, and he cranked the wheel to make the next turn. The tires yelped.

"I don't know if you should drive like—"

"I almost killed the little prick," Kyle sniffled. "Can you believe that? Chriiiist! Five fingers. If it wasn't bad enough for him already."

"It wasn't your fault."

He shook his head. "Does that make a difference?"

I wasn't sure if I knew the answer. I tried to roll down the window to get some air, but the handle didn't budge.

"I never told anyone you came with me for the fireworks that day," he said.

"Okay."

"Not that it matters. But I want you to know I can keep secrets."

"Okay. Thanks."

Kyle cranked the wheel again to make a left turn, and it felt for a second like the van might tip. I braced myself against the door until we were on an even keel.

"You've never once ratted me out," Kyle said. "You knew I stole the stop sign from Seven Pines and Cheshire. You saw me doing donuts in the field by the playground. I ain't ever been busted for those things."

"Uh-huh," I said, because this was basically true. The sign I had found in his clubhouse years ago, and I was too intimidated by Kyle to report it to my parents. The donuts happened more recently. It was an early Sunday morning, and I was out on my bike when I spied Kyle's van tearing away from the playground, muddy curlicues in its wake. Again, I didn't bother telling anyone. Kyle was in trouble all the time, and it didn't seem necessary to pile onto his problems.

"You're a kid who keeps secrets," he said. This wasn't a question.

"I am," I assured him. My cheek brushing the window, I looked at my reflection in the side-view mirror. *I am*, I assured myself.

"Good," he replied. "Because everyone around here thinks I'm as dumb as monkey nuts. While you can't half blame them, that ain't the whole story."

"I know."

"I've saved money. Near a thousand dollars at this point."

"That's a lot."

"It's enough."

Kyle eased off the pedal, finally, and my heart stepped down a couple of rungs.

"What will you do with it?" I asked.

Kyle wiped his face again, and his fingers left red splotches on his cheek. "There will be a hiking trip. Out to the Adirondacks. March, probably, when there's still tons of potential for snow but people act like it's spring already. I'll pack light. Won't be prepared. That won't surprise a single joker. Storm will roll in. My tracks will be covered. They'll find my pack in some half-baked lean-to. Maybe my boots somewhere. Maybe a bloody bandage. God, I don't know. Something to make them think I was busted up."

It was now our fourth loop around the block, and the glare in my window made everything outside look like a Polaroid.

"What are you saying?" I whispered.

"I'm saying that sometimes when it seems like a guy is dead . . . it's really a guy is starting over."

No wink, no smile, nothing. He wasn't kidding. "Can't a guy start over without . . . faking?" I asked. "You know, use his money to move away?"

Snapping and peeling with his teeth, Kyle removed a crescent of thumbnail and spat it on the dashboard. "I don't need this place trying to track me down," he said. "People can cry a little, remember the good, and forget the rest. Clean slate. It's better that way."

"Why are you telling me this?"

"At least one person needs to know. You're a kid who can keep secrets." When he said it this time, it felt almost like a threat. He stopped the van right in the spot where he'd picked me up.

"I am," I assured him.

His hand lunged toward me and I flinched, but he was only opening my door. This wasn't his first time kicking someone out of his van. "They're bringing him home this afternoon," he said.

"Good."

He rolled his eyes. "Life goes on."

Why me, why me, why me, why me, why me . . .

Sitting on the toilet, lid down, in a bathroom stall on the second floor of school, I let the lullaby of fate lull me into a stupor. I didn't volunteer to carry such secrets, and now that they were put upon me, by two different people no less, I was starting to feel the weight. Where was my loyalty? Did I have a responsibility to tell anyone else about these things?

I looked over at the wall.

What are you looking here for? The joke is in your hand!

It was a classic bit of bathroom graffiti, crafted in blue marker above the flimsy aluminum box that dispensed waxy toilet paper. In my backpack, I kept a black Sharpie, always on reserve for doodling on the covers of my binders. I used it to add my own message to the stall.

Screw you Fiona Loomis!

The moment I dotted the exclamation point, I regretted it, and I ransacked the dispenser for paper to wipe the wet ink away. I got most of it, but there was still a faint specter, so I redeployed the Sharpie until the only evidence was a solid black bar.

I'd like to say I don't know what compelled me to write such a thing, but I had a pretty good idea. I was angry. A little bit at Kyle, for being so honest. More so at Fiona, for being so obtuse. Mostly at myself.

Stories taunted me. Even ones I didn't believe dared me to see them through to the end. The idea of Aquavania was absurd, but Fiona's fear seemed so real. I suspected that the end of her tale would reveal the true source of that fear, and I hated her for roping me in, but I hated myself even more for letting her drag me along. Because the tension—the not knowing—was unbearable.

Why can't someone spoil the ending for me? I thought. But from my frustrated question came a strange realization. Perhaps . . . someone . . . could.

I scribbled a new message.

In the story of Aquavania there is a Riverman and a girl. Who is the Riverman? Is the girl in danger?

My logic went like this: Every boy in the school frequented that stall. It was the farthest from the door and a veritable gallery of graffiti, so if they weren't there for bathroom emergencies, then they were there for casual reading or, like me, for alone time, to soothe the ant farm of *why me*'s in their veins. On Fiona's tape, she said that I had "been chosen . . . out of many fine and distinguished candidates." So maybe I wasn't the first boy she had approached.

Maybe some of these other "candidates" were my classmates, and they had heard more of the tale.

It was a long shot, but what other shot did I have? My vaguely worded plea was a way to keep Fiona's secret while possibly discovering if it was a secret worth keeping. I was hoping I could return to the stall tomorrow and see a reply along the lines of, *You've been talking to Fiona Loomis, haven't you? There's no Riverman. She's not in danger. She's messing with you. You're being tricked.*

Being tricked was a happy ending in my book. It meant I could walk away.

I was called to Principal Braugher's office at the end of the day. Under other circumstances, I might have thought I was being indicted for graffiti, but when I saw the stack of books on her desk, I knew exactly what this was about.

"Mrs. Dwyer regrets not being here to ask you herself," Braugher said, "but it would be of monumental service if you could bring Charlie his assignments every day until he's well enough to return."

"Yes, ma'am. I'd be happy to."

Next to the books sat a hunk of ceramics that lured me into picking it up. I didn't ask. I snatched. It was twisted and lumpy, and I wasn't sure if it was a paperweight or an ashtray or what, but the swirl of the glaze drew me to it. It reminded me of a vortex.

"A gift from my daughter," Braugher said.

I nodded and stared at the glaze. I had used this stuff in art class before. When applied, it went on white, but when fired in the kiln, it blossomed. I must have been staring at it for too long, because Braugher eventually asked, "Is everything all right, Alistair?"

"Fine. Perfect." I set the object back on the desk.

"It's scary, I know. He'll be okay, though."

"Yes, ma'am." I was struck by an urge to cry, to let loose right there in the principal's office, to confess that I feared for Fiona, for Kyle, for everyone and everything in life, but I swallowed the feeling back down. I was a kid who kept secrets.

"Alistair?"

"I'm sorry," I said. "I . . . You worry, right? About the kids in this school? About them being okay?"

"More than anything. That's why I do this job."

Most people liked Principal Braugher. She could be strict, but she could never be accused of not caring. After years on the job, she still showed up in the cafeteria every few days, ordered from the lunch line, and sat among the strays at the long tables. Whenever there was a students-versus-teachers basketball game, she played point guard and dished out assists and words of encouragement. There was even a rumor that she took a salary cut to keep the chess club going after it was removed from the budget. Of course, she never admitted to it, but that only made people suspect it was true.

"I just want everyone to make it through the rest of the

year safely," I told her, grabbing the stack of books. "And next year too."

Braugher bit her lip and fixed her eyes on mine. "That's very sweet of you. You do know that you can come talk to me, or one of the counselors, anytime you need to?"

I did know, but I also knew I had made promises. I nodded and I left.

That evening, when I brought the books to Charlie's house, his mom said the same thing: "That's very sweet of you." Only she complemented the words with a hug.

Mrs. Dwyer was a heavy woman, and as she embraced me, I felt the soft terrain of her body. It was comforting, but the longer she held me, the more I thought about something my mom often said: *She doesn't have control of anything over there.*

"How's he doing?" I asked when Mrs. Dwyer released me from her arms.

"He's sleeping," she replied. "But he misses you. Come see him tomorrow?"

"I will," I said as I climbed onto my bike.

It wasn't too chilly out, so I pedaled around the block rather than going straight home. The lights were on at Fiona's house. I hadn't seen her all day, and I contemplated popping in, but thought better of it. I needed to hear the end of the story. But as maddening as it was, I couldn't demand answers. Not from Fiona, at least. If she was going to trust me, she needed to reveal things when she was ready.

Sleep that night, when it came, was fitful.

Wednesday, October 25

———◆———

THE MORNING ARRIVED WITH SNOW ON THE GROUND, ALMOST a foot. A late-October snowfall in Thessaly wasn't unheard of, but forecasters had only warned of a dusting. The plows certainly weren't prepared for such an early onslaught.

In the kitchen I found Keri parked by the radio, monitoring the scroll of school delays and closings. It was a tortuous ritual, because Thessaly was always near the end of the list and, God forbid, if its name wasn't announced . . .

. . . *all Sutton area schools are closed, all Thessaly schools are closed, Willomac is operating on a two-hour delay* . . .

Keri slapped the counter in triumph. "I'm calling Mandy."

Before she could reach the phone, it rang. I was the closest, so I answered.

"Get over here. Now." It was Charlie.

*   *   *

There was an addition on the Dwyer house, a sun-drenched room in the back, where I found Charlie on the couch buried under a silk comforter. A menu screen for a video game lit up the TV on the other side of the room. A controller was resting on the cushion of a La-Z-Boy.

"How about that?" Charlie said. "Snow day on a day I don't even have to go to school. Them's the breaks."

I forced a smile. "You've been playing video games?"

Charlie looked at me sideways and held up his bandaged hands. "Can a dolphin play video games?"

"Uh . . ."

"I got flippers now. So you have to play for me."

A dragon swooped across the TV screen. "I don't know this game," I said.

"Brand-new. Kyle bought it for me. Penance."

"Penance?" My vocabulary was pretty good for a kid, but Charlie's was usually a few steps ahead of mine.

"Payment for guilt," he informed me. "Avoid the same debt, Sir Alistair, by grabbing your sword and fighting for me." He pointed to the video game controller.

I did as asked, and for the next three hours I continued to follow orders, guiding a swordsman through a world of fire-breathing salamanders and phosphorescent blobs. Charlie's ability to predict what might come next in the game was uncanny, but my coordination left something to be desired. I couldn't perform at the level expected, and even though Charlie didn't insult me, I could hear the annoyance in his voice.

Luckily, when it came time for a bathroom break, Charlie didn't insist that my hands continue on as surrogates. He called upon his mom for assistance, which gave me a chance to pause the game and stretch my legs by doing lunges near the window. Through the glass I watched a bluebird light-footing it across the sugary snow, and beyond the bird, I saw a flash of neon. I stepped closer and I recognized her.

Fiona, decked out in her bright green jacket, was hunched over in a patch of trees past the clubhouse and the border of Charlie's yard. She had a stick in her hand and was writing something in the snow. We locked eyes, then she tossed the stick aside and tromped away.

"I remembered I gotta go," I told Charlie when he returned.

"Why? It's a snow day. You have until dinner, right?"

"I gotta . . ." *Shovel the driveway . . . do some homework . . . clean my room.* There were any number of things I could have told Charlie, but he looked so pathetic with his wrapped hands, his homemade *Captain Catpoop* T-shirt, and his faded striped pajama bottoms. I didn't have it in me to lie to him, so I simply said, "I gotta go."

Before he could milk my conscience, I had my jacket in hand and I was heading through the dining room to the door.

"You promised to help me win," he called after me.

"I will. I'll help you win. Another time," I called back as I stepped out into the snow.

When I reached the patch of trees, Fiona was long gone, but a message remained.

LIBRARY. NOW.

It was a two-mile trudge through the snow and slush to the library, but it was a trudge I knew well. The library wasn't exactly a second home for me, but it was a warm place on a cold day, a haven for my abundant curiosity.

"Hello, Alistair," the librarian, Ms. Linqvist, said as I kicked my snowy boots on the entrance mat.

"I'm always impressed when you're open," I replied.

In her hand she held a plastic toy duck. Turning a knob on its wing, she wound it up and then set it on her desk. It waddled, gears squealing, until it fell off the edge into a tiny trash can. "No school today," she said. "The party is obviously in the library."

The library, obviously, was empty, but it actually wasn't a surprise that it was open. Ms. Linqvist lived next door, and as long as she could shovel the walkway, she made sure the community had comfy seats, good books, and a windup plastic duck for amusement.

"I've got something for you," she said, handing me a sheet of microfiche film. "A young lady thought you might find this fascinating."

"What's on it?"

Ms. Linqvist shifted her attention to a stack of returns

that she was placing on a shelf cart. "Your guess is as good as mine. Newspapers, I would think."

"Is the girl still here?"

Ms. Linqvist shrugged and kept on with her work.

I could have searched the stacks for Fiona, but she clearly wanted me to see something on the sheet first. The microfiche readers were in a dark corner of the library. Hardly anyone ever used them, and today was no exception. I settled in at the machine closest to the wall and fed the sheet into the viewfinder.

I had no idea what I was looking for. The first stories I scanned through were about local politics and sports. I didn't recognize the name of the newspaper, but references to Washington, Oregon, and Idaho implied that it was from somewhere in the Pacific Northwest.

The film had a week's worth of newspapers on it, and I scrolled over dozens of stories, two or three times each, until I finally zeroed in on the one Fiona wanted me to find. It was a capsule piece, tucked in next to the police blotter.

THE SEARCH FOR CHUA LING ENDS

Police have suspended the search for twelve-year-old Chua Ling, who disappeared two months ago from her bedroom in her North Carson home. "It has been a very trying time for everyone," Police Chief Falcone says. "But unfortunately we cannot contribute any more resources without further leads." Hundreds helped in the three-county search for Ling, who was described by friends as "sweet, friendly, and incredibly imaginative."

December 12, 1988

As soon as I finished reading, there was a whisper in my ear.

"It was the Riverman. You need to hear more," Fiona said.

THE LEGEND OF FIONA LOOMIS, PART III

Chua Ling didn't believe in the Riverman, at least not in the beginning. She had heard that he was a horrible beast, a phantom, a ghoul, but she couldn't imagine that he was actually real.

On the night of their first sleepover, Chua told Fiona how she first learned of the Riverman.

"There was this darling boy named Werner. He was from Germany and spoke German in the Solid World, but here in Aquavania we all understand one another, no matter what languages we speak. He would visit me and I would visit him. We would stand at the folds and whisper sweet nothings to each other. Yes, it was sweet, but it was nothing too. We only kissed a few times. I think I might have loved him.

"Werner told me stories. He said that there are

empty worlds in Aquavania. Rumor has it they are cold and gray places, like ruins made of stacked ashes, but they are also home to rainbow-colored rivers that glitter and snake through all the muck. Ancient tablets and glyphs found in these worlds carry the same creepy warning: *The Riverman is coming. Freeze his heart and say the words 'Riverman, Riverman, blood to ice,' or else he will steal your soul.*

"Werner didn't know anyone who'd actually seen these Dead Worlds. It was something whispered about, a ghost story to remind us that, oh yes, we were gods in Aquavania, but we weren't gods of everything.

"To be honest, we didn't actually discuss the Riverman too much. Why focus on all that spooky stuff when you can talk about hopes and dreams? And that's what we usually did.

"'Sometimes I wish I had as much confidence in the Solid World as I do here,' I told Werner one afternoon. 'That's something Aquavania can't give me.'

"'You can give that to yourself,' Werner said. 'You can't create the same things in the Solid World, but that doesn't mean that you aren't amazing and special there too.'

"'Maybe,' I told him. 'It's hard to see that, though. What about you? Is there anything that Aquavania hasn't given you?'

"'Sometimes I wish I knew what my father really thought of me,' Werner said.

" 'And Aquavania can't tell you that?' I asked.

" 'It cannot,' Werner said.

" 'Maybe if we combine our wishing powers and both of us wish as hard as we can wish, Aquavania will grant us the answer,' I proposed.

"So that night, the two of us slept on these lovely beds made of tiny stars, high in the sky above Werner's world. When we closed our eyes, it was as black as black can be, but when we opened them, the stars were so bright that we couldn't see each other. Only a wonderful glow. So we held hands to assure ourselves we were side by side.

"As I dozed off, I wished for that thing that Werner needed so badly, and I knew that he wished for it too, because I could hear him whisper, 'Please tell me. Please tell me.'

"I woke up later. Coulda been minutes, coulda been hours. I heard the sound of another voice. It said, 'I will slip the answer into your ear.'

"Werner's hand was still in mine, but it was limp. I opened my eyes, and our star beds were now dim. A dark figure was hunched over my sweet Werner. I couldn't see a face, but I could see a glass fountain pen in the figure's hand. The tip of the pen was dipped in Werner's ear, like it was an inkpot. The end of the pen was in the creature's mouth. There was this horrible sucking sound, and the pen was filling up with a sparkling liquid.

"Werner's eyes were open and he was staring at me, but he wasn't moving. I let out a howler of a scream. As soon as I did, the stars let go of me and I fell. Werner must have had the power to wish at least one more wish, because a parachute puffed up behind me and slowed my descent. Below me I could see Werner's world, with its castles, forests, and grassy plateaus. Everything was losing its color, like fresh paint in the rain. It was draining out into a glorious new river that wound through the center of everything.

"A few feet before I hit the ground, my parachute disintegrated around me and I crashed into a world that was exactly as the stories described. Stacks of ashes instead of the castles, instead of the forests. It was a shadow of Werner's creation. Gray. Dead. Everywhere . . . except for the river. The river was alive and swirling with color. I wasn't sure what to do, so I touched the water. And like that, I was gone, back home to the Solid World.

"The next time I went to Aquavania, I waited for Werner. I waited for weeks, calling out for him constantly, oh so desperate for a reply. It never came.

"So I decided that if I couldn't find him in Aquavania, I'd find him in the Solid World. I knew what town Werner was from. I knew his last name. There was a German bakery down the street from me, and I told the baker that I was hoping to talk to my German pen pal. I asked him if he knew anyone from Werner's town. He did. I asked him to call that person and to see if they could find Werner's phone number. He did. And when I got Werner's number, I dialed up his house and asked for him. Thankfully there was a woman who could speak English there, and someone handed her the phone.

" 'Werner is missing,' she said. 'If you know where he is, please tell us. We are sick with worry. This is a horrible time for our family.'

"It was a horrible time for me too. I cried for days. I never thought what happened in Aquavania could affect us in the Solid World. Now I knew that it could. And the Riverman, he was real. He was after us."

"Why?" Fiona asked Chua.

"I don't know for sure," Chua said. "But remember the warning? *Or else he will steal your soul.* When I saw that sparkly stuff filling up that pen, it was like I was seeing Werner's soul. And when all the color drained out of Werner's world into the river, it was like everything he created, all of his stories, were being stolen, carried away. The Riverman must want these things. Our souls. Our stories."

"Do you think that Werner is . . . dead?" Fiona asked.

Chua shook her head. "No. That river leads some-where. That pen is somewhere. Werner is somewhere. And the Riverman is going to give him back to me."

"How do you think he got into Werner's world?"

"He must have promised to give Werner what he needed—to let him know what his father really thought of him—so Werner invited him across the folds. Like I invited you. Only Werner couldn't have expected it was the Riverman."

Fiona recalled what she had heard when she was pulled into Chua's world: *The girl named Chua needed nothing more than to meet someone smart and new so that she could share her story.*

"But you expected him? That's why you stabbed me with the icicle? You thought I might be the Riverman?" Fiona asked. She wasn't injured, but the memory of the attack still coursed through her body.

"He tricks his way into your world, feeds off your desires, pretends to be something he isn't. I've got friends in Aquavania. There's Boaz, Rodrigo, Jenny, and a whole bunch of other kids they know. They've all helped fill in the story of the Riverman. They've heard old legends too. The legends tell of the icicle and the chant. Stabbing him with the icicle won't destroy the Riverman, but it will freeze him, make him submit. And if I can get him to submit, maybe I can get him to tell me where Werner is."

"How can you be sure of that?" Fiona asked.

Chua placed her hands on Fiona's shoulders. Her grip was firm, as were her eyes. "I can't be sure. But no one can convince me not to try."

112

"What if you're wrong?"

"Well, I really hope I'm not wrong," Chua said. "Because then there will be only one chance left. The Swimmer."

"Who's the Swimmer?" Fiona asked.

"Another of those legends. The Swimmer is the person who can swim the river without getting sent back to the Solid World. If the river leads to the Riverman, then maybe it leads to Werner too, and maybe the Swimmer can find my love. You're not the Riverman. We've established that. But maybe, and this is a big old maybe . . ."

"You're the Swimmer?" I asked Fiona in the dark corner of the library.

She nodded. "I've spent a long time in Aquavania wondering if I was."

"And . . . ?"

"And I still don't know. I've never been to one of the Dead Worlds, as we call them. I've never seen the river. Chua is the only kid I know who has, and that was only because she was in Werner's world when it happened. Now she's gone too."

I looked back at the screen and the newspaper story. If this was a cry for help, it was an astoundingly complex one.

"I made a map of Aquavania," Fiona went on. "The

handkerchief. It lists all the kids I know about there. But it's a good thing I burned it, because I think the Riverman might be in the Solid World too. And he's after those kids. Your mind is my map now, Alistair. You've got to help me stop the Riverman. Before he has every soul in Aquavania."

When the library closed, we walked home together through the mist and slush. Words were thin. I was even more confused than before. I wasn't sure what sort of help Fiona expected. We split off at her house, where she left me with an apology. "I'm sorry, but there's no one else I can confide in."

Again, it was a *why me?* moment. This had all started because Fiona had admired something that I wrote. Before I knew it, she was asking me to memorize a long and complicated fairy tale, and she was begging me to help her stop some monster that I was quite sure didn't exist. It didn't add up. If something bad was happening in Fiona's life, then who were these other characters? Who were Chua Ling and these other kids?

When you pen something it means . . . well, it means you do it like an artist. You dig up the story beneath the story.

That's what Fiona had said to me. I was beginning to realize that the story beneath the story wasn't simply about some girl who was having trouble at home. It was much bigger and much more disturbing than I had ever suspected. As I watched Fiona walk past the pickup truck parked in her driveway, I started to dig deep into my imagination.

A dangerous man. Missing children. A girl too scared to tell the truth.

Thursday, October 26

———◆—◆———

THE STREETS WERE CLEAR BY THE NEXT MORNING AND
school was back on. I hauled my backpack to the kitchen
where my mom was at the counter, spreading peanut butter
and marmalade onto bread.

"Do you know anything about Fiona Loomis's uncle?" I
asked her.

My mom had grown up in Thessaly, and for years she
had worked at the post office, the only one in town. While it
wasn't a gossip mill, it was a place that everyone visited, a
place where everyone revealed themselves through their
bills and their catalogs and their boxes big and small and
long.

"You're spending a lot of time with Fiona, aren't you?"
She smiled, but it was a cautious smile.

"I guess so. She has this uncle, and he's like a heavy
metal guy and—"

"His name is Dorian. Dorian Loomis."

"You know him?"

My mom bagged a sandwich, plucked a couple of apples from the wooden fruit bowl, and washed them in the sink. "We went to high school together."

"Fiona's parents too?"

"They were older, gone by the time I got there. Dad and I got to know them later, when you kids were all little. But Dorian and I graduated together."

I wasn't sure how to put this without causing her alarm. Still, I needed to know. "Was Dorian a . . . good guy?"

My mom thought about it for a second, and she handed me my lunch. "He was a guy. Like any guy. War will change people. Some for better. Some for worse."

"He was in a war?"

"A lot of the guys went to war back then. Around here, the draft wasn't something you got out of."

They would be stringing the memorial lights up on the tree in the center of town for Veterans Day in a few weeks. My mom might have known some of the people those lights honored. This was the first time that thought had occurred to me.

"Do you think he came back for the worse?" I asked.

Maybe I didn't want my mom to understand what I was getting at, but I wanted her to look more concerned than she did. She smiled again. "As I heard it, Dorian drifted around for a while after the war. He's had his troubles, but he came home this summer and he's home for the right reason. He's looking after his mother. Fiona's grandma. She's a nice girl, Fiona. But the more time you spend with someone, the more you realize they're not perfect. Everyone comes from a different place with different problems."

"But . . . do you think her uncle is a good man?"

My mom dried her hands on a dish towel. "A girl is not her family, sweetie."

Smiling there in the kitchen, she must have thought she was giving me advice on exploring the foreign lands of a first girlfriend. She didn't ask *Is something wrong?* or *Are you worried about Fiona?*

It was baffling, but it was typical. We all see what we want to see.

"Thanks," I said, and I left for school.

I didn't know war. Skirmishes sometimes lit up our TV during the nightly news, but war was something that happened in other places at different times to faceless people.

I knew stories. My dad would sometimes tell the tale of an old friend named Herb who tried to dodge the draft by deliberately failing the psychological exam. He studied psychology texts so that he could answer the questions in a way that would make him seem woefully unstable. When the draft board called him in, an officer clasped Herb's hand and said, "Figured it out, huh? No one's ever scored so off-the-charts insane. You must be some special kind of brilliant."

They assigned Herb to intelligence, and he spent years in the jungle trying to extract information from locals about underground tunnels and weapons caches. When he returned home, he refused a government job, choosing instead to move to Reno, Nevada, where he lived off of blackjack winnings. The dealers weren't nearly as disciplined in Reno as they were in Las Vegas, and Herb claimed that when these novices drew a face card or an ace and had to check their hand for blackjack, he could read subtle clues in their eyes that would tell him whether to hit or hold. Odds tipped ever so slightly in Herb's favor, but ever so slightly was always enough in the long run.

When his winnings were large, Herb carried a lot of cash, but also a holster that bulged in his jacket and made people think twice about pulling fast ones. He didn't pack a gun, though. After what he'd seen in the war, he hated guns. Instead, he kept his winnings—his wad of twenties and fifties—in the holster.

One night Herb was grabbing a bag of cheese curls at a gas station when a fidgety cashier—also a veteran—saw the bulge and the flash of leather. The station had been robbed a few weeks before, so the cashier now kept a shotgun hidden in a box of candy bars beneath the register. As Herb stepped to the counter, the cashier buried his hand deep in the box and curled a finger around the trigger.

Just a few minutes before, Herb had slipped some bills to a man who had approached him in the parking lot. The man wore a camo jacket and carried a piece of cardboard with a message inked on it: *We gave our souls for your freedom. All we ask you to give in return is your spare change.*

The cash Herb gave this other veteran was the cash he kept in his pocket so that he didn't have to dip into the holster stash and startle the civilians. Luck goes as luck goes, and giving away all his pocket money was one of those things that made Herb's luck go the wrong way. Because when Herb placed his cheese curls next to the register, he placed his other hand in his pocket. No cash there, so he went for the holster.

The shotgun blast didn't knock him on his back or into the display of snack cakes, but it tore his shoulder open. The cashier didn't keep firing. He ducked down behind the counter and prayed for things to end.

Herb stumbled outside into the parking lot and collapsed on the ground between the gas pumps. The panhandler was still there and he raced over to help, but when he saw the holster and the wad of bills sticking out from the bloody and shredded jacket, baser instincts took over. Soon the beggar was fleeing through scrubby and vacant lots with nearly five thousand dollars tucked into his pants.

Herb survived, but lost an arm, and now lives in a cabin in some state forest where he reads a lot and talks to truckers on his CB radio.

So, no, I didn't know war. I knew stories about men who went to war, men defined by their decisions, decisions made out of desire or fear, or for survival, or simply because their spirits had been bent one way or another. And I couldn't help but apply such stories to Fiona's uncle Dorian. Was he a guy like Herb? Did he once have great potential, only to see it squandered by luck and consequence? Was he like the cashier? Perpetually scared? Paranoid? Quick to employ violence? Or was he like the panhandler? Broken? Desperate? Willing to do anything to satisfy his needs?

Maybe he was a little bit like all of them. It didn't matter, really. What my mom said was the most important thing. *War will change people.* It must have changed Dorian into the type of man who carries a sharp blade, a man who stands in the backyard pretending to smother someone with a pillow. Maybe it turned him into something far worse.

This all led me to think about Chua Ling. Why Chua Ling? Did Fiona dig up some article about a girl who had disappeared all the way across the country just to make me believe she was having trouble at home? Not necessarily. She wanted me to see the story beneath the story. The Riverman was out there stealing children. He was someone she knew. In fact, she lived with him.

I really needed to talk to Fiona alone, so I avoided her until the end of the day. After the last bell, I waited at the bike rack. Wedged in the maroon teeth of it was a solitary bike— Fiona's. Snow or no snow, she was the only kid who rode to school this late in the year. To some that made her seem tough. To others, a little crazy. Like so many things about her, it was open to interpretation.

She exited the school through the rarely used east doors and followed the brick path past the dumpsters to the bike rack. As I had hoped, she came alone. I didn't bother saying hello. I jumped right into it.

"There are others like Chua?" I asked.

She pursed her lips and nodded. I hadn't abandoned her yet, and this seemed to please her. "He's gotten others I know of," she said. "Werner, obviously. Then there's Boaz and Rodrigo. Can't find the articles in the library yet, but if you make some calls, it checks out. Missing. No evidence."

"I see." I turned my eyes to the base of the rack, where the paint was chipped and exposing the rust.

"Do you not believe me?" she asked. "I can give you full names, hometowns. I can give you phone numbers. Newspapers, police stations. Long distance, unfortunately, but—"

I looked back up at her. "No, I believe you," I said, and I did. I had no doubt that if I called those numbers I would hear stories of other missing children. What I didn't believe was that there was anything supernatural about their disappearances. That's not to say the disappearances weren't connected. I figured if I humored Fiona, maybe she'd let more truth slip out.

"I'm trying to understand how he does it," I went on. "How does he sneak into other kids' worlds, again?"

Fiona's feet shuffled in the gravel. "When you're at the

folds, it's not easy to cross over to someone else's world the first time. You have to be invited. You have to have something they need. One of the things that Chua needed was a friend like me. And I was there. So that's how I ended up in her world. It's not always so simple."

"So if I needed, say, hamburgers, and I called out that I needed hamburgers, then I'd be inviting the Hamburglar to my world?"

Fiona reached over and patted me gently on the stomach. "If you needed hamburgers, you could have hamburgers, Alistair. This is Aquavania. Not a drive-through."

Her touch made my muscles clench. "I was just—"

"It's not about objects," she said, pulling her hand away. "It's more emotional. Things you can't wish up yourself. Things that only others can provide. Encouragement. Debate. Love. Hate even, I guess. Werner needed to know what his father really thought of him. And I guess the Riverman was able to give him that, or at least the Riverman was able to *pretend* he could give him that. In Aquavania, you can create anything your mind can think up. You'd be surprised what your mind can't create. It's often the things you really need."

"So the Riverman knew what they needed. But how? You said that he might be here, in the . . . Solid World?" I still wasn't comfortable with Fiona's terminology, but I was trying.

"Everyone else who visits Aquavania also lives in the Solid World," she said. "So why wouldn't he?"

"Do you think he met Werner and Chua in the Solid World? Do you think that's how he knew what they needed?"

She ran her foot across the gravel a few times, as if she were using it to cross off theories that didn't fit the facts. "At the very least, he knew about them."

I'd never been to a police station, but I imagined maps with thumbtacks and threads connecting them to identify patterns. "What if he's a drifter? A guy who goes from place to place and meets kids and tricks them into trusting him?"

I was laying it on thick and I was looking for the recognition in her eyes. Her eyes narrowed, but she didn't give anything up.

"But how? How does he know where to find them? How does he know which kids in the Solid World have been to Aquavania?"

"Maybe he doesn't," I said. "Maybe he takes advantage of wherever he is at the time. Seeks out the easiest prey."

"That doesn't make any sense. He can't randomly have found both Werner and Chua. He sought them out specifically. They were friends."

There was no one else around. At the west entrance of the school, kids were lined up and piling onto buses or they were following the sidewalks into the surrounding neighborhoods. On the east end, it was us and us alone. I really wanted Fiona to finally confess, to admit that she was making this all up, that she was painting over the truth because the truth was too ugly to bear, or too dangerous to admit.

But she didn't do that. Instead, she grabbed the handgrips of her bike and pulled it from the rack.

"Oh my god," she said, her voice breathy and incredulous. "I get it. I finally get it. Each kid he takes gives the next kid away. The next victim. That stuff in the pen? It's their souls, but maybe their thoughts are part of their souls. And the Riverman knew what Chua needed because Werner knew what Chua needed. And now he has Chua's thoughts too. Which means he knows about me. He knows that I know. But he doesn't know what I need. No one does."

She was off before I could say anything else. But as she pedaled through the gravel and past the tennis courts, I focused on that statement: *He knows that I know.*

Friday, October *27*

———◆———

I ROLLED OVER AND CHECKED MY CLOCK. *1:37. HOLY CRAP.*
Is it possible that I overslept by more than six hours?

Consciousness pulled back from my head like the tide.
Next thing I knew I was lying in the shower, curled up as if
taking a nap. Naked, exhausted, I let the water massage
my ribs while I worried about the classes I was missing.

Next I was in the hall, half-dressed, backpack slung over
one shoulder. The tide pulled away again, and when it returned I was at the kitchen table, eating cereal. Outside it
was dark, but that didn't register.

"What on earth are you doing?" My mom, ensconced in a
duvet, leaned against the kitchen's entryway.

Milk dribbled down my chin as I looked up. I hated seeing
her face like this. It wasn't a mother's face. It was the face of
a person who was frightened and had no answers.

"I'm late," I told her. "I'm so late for school."

"It's two in the morning."

My shirt was soaked. I hadn't toweled off after my shower. I didn't even have jeans on. I was sitting there in my underpants and sneakers. *Is this sleepwalking?*

"Everything okay, sweetie?" she asked.

"Yeah . . . I looked at the clock and . . . I was confused." Embarrassed was more like it. I pushed the bowl away.

"You don't have to be up for hours. Go back to sleep. You've had a tough week. What with Charlie."

Charlie. I had forgotten about Charlie. He'd only been out of school since Monday, and I'd already screwed him over.

I burrowed into bed, but I couldn't fall back to sleep. It proved Fiona's point. I obviously needed something that my mind couldn't give me.

"I forgot to bring your homework yesterday. I'm so sorry," I told Charlie on the phone when the real morning arrived five hours later.

"You've got more important things goin' on," he told me, his voice difficult to parse. He didn't sound angry or sad or annoyed. He was almost teasing me.

"It's not that. It's—"

"Don't sweat it. You think I really care about my homework? I was expecting you to come over and we'd try to solve the necromancer's lair."

"I will. This afternoon. Right after school."

"Sleepover?"

I knew how this would go. He was going to spend my guilt before it was banked away and forgotten. "You bet," I said.

It was the end of the first marking period, and the teachers rewarded themselves by taking a breather. School was filled with filmstrips and games of Seven Up. Normally this would make for a carefree day, but my exhaustion and my anxiety were immune to such diversions.

It also didn't help that I didn't see Fiona. I was beginning to figure out her schedule, so I knew where in the hall to loiter after each bell. At lunch, I knew which tables to plot a course around. She was nowhere, and this was not a good sign.

I went to the bathroom stall where I'd posted my plea: *In the story of Aquavania there is a Riverman and a girl. Who is the Riverman? Is the girl in danger?*

There were two responses.

Hey river man, I heard you got a river of diarea, uh uh, diarea.

The only danger is you're greasy farts!

Poorly spelled comebacks weren't a surprise, but they certainly weren't a consolation.

At the end of the day, I collected Charlie's homework and, since Keri had plans with Mandy, I walked home alone. Temperatures had climbed and the only remnants from the snowstorm were scattered chunks of gray ice that lined the road and burst like rotten fruit when you stepped on them. Passing Fiona's house, I noticed that Dorian's truck was the only vehicle in the driveway and every window in the house was dark. If her family had planned a vacation, she hadn't told me, but it certainly seemed like no one was home.

All day I had been contemplating going to the police. It meant breaking Fiona's trust, but if it kept her out of danger, then I figured it was worth it. The only problem was, how would they ever believe my wild, unsupported theories?

Dorian Loomis is responsible for a bunch of missing children. Fiona knows about it, and I'm afraid of what Dorian will do to keep her quiet, I'd say.

And your evidence? they'd ask.

Microfiche, a pillow, a belt sander, and some stories about a magical land made of water, I'd have to admit.

In books, even the very best boy detectives are dismissed with a laugh. In real life, they're sent to psychologists. If I was going to be taken seriously, I needed more proof.

So I waited until after dinner, until the sun was down. I was supposed to be at Charlie's for the sleepover by seven thirty, but I set out at seven and took a detour to Fiona's, where the windows were still dark. Dorian's truck was still in the driveway, and that seemed as good a place as any to start my investigation.

As I moved toward it, the first thing I noticed was the mud splattered on the red paint. It had probably been driven off-road somewhere. That didn't tell me much, so I peered into the truck's bed. Empty, except for a few leaves and sticks trapped in the waffled grooves.

On the back window of the cab I could see there was a sticker, but I couldn't decipher what it was. Rather than walk around to the side and strain my neck to see it, I stepped onto the tow hitch, climbed into the bed, and crawled toward the cab. As soon as I reached the window, my curiosity about the sticker was replaced by a desire to know what was inside the cab.

Using my hands as a visor to block out the glare of the streetlights, I leaned into the window. It was hard to see much, but the first thing I noticed was some sort of stuffed animal on the floor. *A squirrel? Maybe a cat?*

Also, on the passenger seat, there was a lump underneath a ratty and stained towel. A small wing poked out from the terry cloth. *A toy airplane?*

"See anything interesting?" someone said.

The voice was loud and spiny and almost sent me to my back. *Oh please no,* I thought. I knew exactly who it was.

"Good evening . . . Mrs. Carmine," I said as I turned around.

Mrs. Carmine stood in the middle of the street, smiling like she'd found a quarter in a jar of buttons. "Not sure Dorian would appreciate you poking around his truck."

"Ah . . . no, ma'am, I don't know if . . ." In my eagerness to uncover evidence, I had completely forgotten about the most obvious obstacle. I didn't even have an excuse lined up.

"You don't trust him, do ya?" she said as she took a few steps closer and stopped at the edge of the driveway.

"Excuse me?" I asked. I had heard her clearly, but I was having trouble believing she would ask such a perceptive question.

"I wasn't thrilled about him moving back here neither," she explained.

I crawled my way to the back of the bed and climbed out. "I was looking for a . . . water rocket," I told her. "Shot it off and it landed somewhere around here. That's all I'm doing."

"Water rockets?" She chuckled, her throat rattly and dry. "At night? That's rich."

I couldn't keep this up. I was a terrible liar. Looking down, I said, "I'm sorry if I bothered you."

"It's no bother," she replied. "I realize that boys are curious beasts. But I'd be careful around men like that. You don't need to confirm the rumors."

I looked up. "What rumors?"

Her voice got softer, a ghost story voice. "That the man is a deviant."

"A deviant?" I asked. "What . . . what has he done?"

"If you don't know, then I'm certainly not going to tell someone so young," she said with a huff. "All I can say is keep your distance. No matter what folks claim, men like that don't change their stripes so easy."

Thoughts percolated, questions that I was sure she wouldn't answer. *Has he hurt kids? Has he done violent things?* She couldn't possibly be talking about Chua Ling and the others, because if she knew about them, Dorian would be in jail. And yet she knew something. I opted for a less salacious query. "What do the police think of him?"

She waved me off. "I've voiced my concerns, but they don't make out search warrants because of concerns. Lazy lazy, these cops. Don't worry too much about this guy, though. I'm keeping an eye on him."

"Thank you, ma'am," I said, because I believed her. But her eye only saw so far. It didn't see what Dorian had done in the past, or might do in the future outside of the neighborhood.

"Don't mention it," she said as she turned and headed back toward her front steps. "And I won't be mentioning our talk to your parents. They wouldn't be happy to know what you've been up to, even if your intentions were good. So let's not get them worried this time, okay?"

It was rare for Mrs. Carmine to practice such compassion, but seeing that she was the neighborhood snoop, perhaps she sympathized with my behavior. "Thank you, ma'am," I said again.

"You're welcome," she replied, and she made a motion with her hand that told me to *run along now.*

As I set off toward Charlie's house, exhausted and concerned, I still had no concrete evidence, but I was more convinced than ever that I was on the right track.

* * *

"Exterminate. Exterminate. Exterminate!" Charlie's voice stacked on more glee each time I sliced a creature in half with my sword.

It was a tick or two from midnight, and I had been playing the video game for more than four hours. Charlie had granted me a single break, and that was only so I would open some cans of tuna that he served to the clubhouse cats. My hands were starting to cramp, but my gaming had improved. I had defeated eight of ten big bosses, thanks in no small part to Charlie's amazing ability to spot their weaknesses.

"Back of the knee!"

"Block twice with your shield and wait for him to blink!"

"Shoot an arrow at the stalactite as soon as she's on the marble tile!"

When we finally paused again to fetch some microwave popcorn, Charlie asked what would seem to be an unusual question for an avid gamer. "Do you think it bothers the swordsman? Killing all those monsters?"

"He's an eight-bit cartoon," I said as I opened the ballooned bag and let the corny steam assault my cheeks.

"Seriously," Charlie said. "If he were a real person, would it scar him? Would he go all crybaby in his bed?"

An image scorched my mind. Red night-light. Blade on a nightstand. Homemade quilt. Fiona's uncle Dorian bathed in the red, under the quilt, on his back, looking up at the ceiling. "I guess someone who does that much killing has to think it's the right thing," I said. "Or else they don't care. Don't have any feelings about it either way."

"Who's doin' 'that much killing'?"

A figure stood on the other side of the kitchen, away from the island of light created by the open microwave.

"Didn't think you were coming home tonight," Charlie said.

Stepping forward, Kyle caught his hip on the seat of a counter stool. The stool performed a clumsy pirouette on one leg, which amused Kyle, and he waved his arms like someone coaxing a bowling ball. When the stool found its feet, Kyle turned back to us and mocked us through his grin. "Am I distawbing da widdle gawls' slumba pawty?"

"Mom and Dad are gonna wake up and get a whiff of you, and you're gonna be so toast," Charlie said.

Kyle leaned in and wiggled his fingers like a warlock casting a hex. Now that he was face-to-face with us, I could see his forehead was splotchy and red and I could smell a heavy sweetness on his breath.

"How can this be a sleepover without a game of jack-in-the-box?" Kyle asked, snatching the popcorn bag and helping himself.

"Like the stupid toy with the crank and the clown?" Charlie said. "You don't make any sense."

Kyle chewed and shook his head. Mouth full, he mumbled, "Who wanna play a *man's* jack-in-the-box?"

I didn't know what he was talking about, but I said it anyway.

"I do."

Saturday, October 28

It was technically the next day, slightly past midnight.

All the Halloween decorations were now up in our neighborhood. Poster board skeletons in the windows, cotton cobwebs on the shrubs, plastic pumpkins at the doors. They were the same ones every year, and most were dirty or fading. They definitely weren't scary. In the night fog they looked more desperate than anything.

There were three of us standing in knee-high weeds along the side of the road. Me and the Dwyer brothers. Kyle had driven us to the far corner of the neighborhood and had parked his van in a patch of dirt almost out of view. In the center of the road, under the weak glow of streetlights, he had placed a cardboard box, flipped over so its top was down and its flaps were spread like four rectangular wings. All eyes were on that box.

Kyle stood between us and pulled us in with his spindly arms. "And men and boys and mice and men and all that junk. Tonight we settle the question of who is brave and who wears maxi pads."

"You're bluffing," Charlie said.

Kyle cocked his head. "Yeah?"

"Yeah," Charlie replied. "You wanna convince us to get under that box and then you'll get in the van and rev the engine and pretend like you're gonna run us over so you can see us jump out all scared."

Kyle turned to me. "Does that sound like something I'd do?"

I shrugged. It did sound like something he would do, but I was wary of any direction this could be headed. I wasn't about to choose sides.

Kyle laughed, a cackle he reserved for his wildest moments. Or his drunkest moments. I was beginning to suspect they were one and the same. He squeezed our shoulders, then pushed us away. He stumbled toward the box.

"Pioneers. Pioneers. Grab the ladies and pour the beers!" he shouted.

"Should we stop him?" I asked.

Seething, Charlie shook his head.

When Kyle reached the box, he lifted it and wore it like a mascot's costume. It covered his body down to the elbows, which he bent so he could stick out his forearms and hands. Tottering in place, he spoke like a robot. "I am Charlie.

Beep beep. I play video games. Boop boop. I have no fingers. Blop blop."

"He's a child," Charlie whispered to me. "I'm a man. And he's a child."

I couldn't argue with that. There were times when I liked Kyle, but this wasn't one of them. Especially as he pulled his arms all the way into the box and then crouched down until he was completely hidden. As far as any driver was concerned, it was now just a box. To swerve around. Or to squash.

I looked up the road and said, "This can't be good."

"It's his stupid game," Charlie shot back. "Let's see if he wins."

Betrayal. I wasn't sure what qualified. *He hates this life! He hates this place! Who knows what he might do to himself. We have to get him out of there!* I could have said any of these things, but was it a betrayal to protect someone by revealing his secrets? I thought it might be. So I kept quiet. And we waited.

First there was a glow up the road at the crest of the hill. For a moment, that crest might have been the edge of the Earth, the bright and shapeless void where everything falls away. Then there were headlights and only headlights. Yellow and ripe and growing wider as a car moved closer. It was really happening. I had to say something.

"We've gotta—"

Gauze brushed my shoulder and two fingers jabbed my neck. "Down," Charlie commanded.

When I didn't heed, he made me heed by kicking me in the back of the knee and toppling me. Mud splattered the underside of my chin. The weeds revealed their husky browns as the first blush of headlights drenched them and us. I pulled my head up to see the car—a Jeep, actually, with a ripped fabric top—bearing down on the box.

Twenty yards. No brakes yet.

Ten. Blinding light now.

It wasn't going to . . .

There wasn't time.

Kyle was . . .

It hopped. That's my best description for what the Jeep did. It didn't swerve. It seemed to launch itself to the side at the last moment, wheels leaving the ground and landing inches from the box.

Blame it on adrenaline, but that's how I remember it. I also remember the Jeep didn't slow down. It whinnied away into the night, its taillights streaking the sky with wisps of red.

Finally, I remember the box flying in the air and Kyle, triumphant in the center of the road, raising a fist and shouting, "Pop goes the weasel!"

It should have been over at that point, but it wasn't. Kyle did a victory lap around the box and then centered it in the road again. Grinning, he rejoined us. From the weedy mess he plucked a long blade. I could tell he wanted to put it in his mouth and chew it like a toothpick, but it came out with earth still on it. He chucked it to the side.

"That was so scary," I said. Wonderful too, but I left that part out.

"It was stupid, is what it was," Charlie said.

"Who's next?" Kyle asked.

I turned to Charlie. "No chance," he told me.

"So it's established," Kyle said. "Charlie is a woman. How 'bout you, Alistair? Pink undies under those jammies?"

Yes, I was wearing pajamas. There had been no opportunity to change into more suitable clothing, so I was standing there in checkered fleece and a down vest. Not exactly the attire of a daredevil, but perhaps I had the makings of one yet. My exhaustion had morphed into a numbness that enveloped my body. Aroused by the spectacle of Kyle cheating death, my heart fed the numbness and I felt damn near immortal.

"You've played this before?" I asked Kyle.

"About a billion times."

"Gimme a break," Charlie said. "Let's go home."

"And no one's ever gotten hit?" I asked.

Kyle thumbed his chin, a thinker pose. "That's a mystery now, ain't it?"

"I guess it would have been all over the papers and TV if someone had ever been hit while playing this," I said. The logic seemed flawless.

"Maybe," Kyle replied. "Or maybe they don't run those stories because adults don't wanna fill your baby bwains with gore, gore, gore." He reached over and scuffed Charlie's hair, and Charlie ducked away.

"We can deal with stuff like that," Charlie said. "We've seen R-rated movies."

"And I've seen X-rated ones," Kyle replied. He pointed to the box. "So who's next?"

I stepped into the road.

"Don't be an idiot," Charlie said. I couldn't tell if he was genuinely concerned for my safety or if he was only competing for my loyalty.

I kept moving. I knew if I thought about it too much, I would change my mind. So I simply crouched down in the center of the road and pulled the box over me like I was a tortoise and this was my shell.

I had no idea what might happen next. My only clear feeling was that I didn't want to be alone. It wasn't my parents, or my sister, or Charlie, or Kyle that I needed. It was Fiona. I imagined her there with me, holding on to me, telling me that we would see things through together. It was a fresh and strange and terrifying and glorious feeling, and it spread through my entire body until I realized that Fiona was more than someone I wanted to help. She was someone I wanted to be with . . . all of the time.

As I cradled these thoughts, I pressed my nose against the pavement. It was just north of freezing and smelled earthier than I expected. I clawed it, like an animal starting a burrow. It was pavement, all right. I brought my fingers to my ears. I didn't want to hear any car until it was right upon me. I didn't want to think about what might happen if I was hit.

Would I be crushed? Would I fly? Pain doesn't always arrive immediately, so would it maybe even feel transcendent, if only for a second or two?

No. It would feel horrible.

My numbness was fluttering away, and I had only a vague idea about what it meant to be drunk, but I decided I wanted to be drunk like Kyle. Anything other than what I was. *How nice,* I thought, *how very nice to be obliterated. Or to be asleep. To turn the dial of my mind down to its lowest setting.*

And that's when—in the moment of my thickest loneliness and doubt—the box moved. It brushed against my knee and rose up around me like I was a roast pig being presented to a king. For Fiona to be holding the box would have been miraculous, but this wasn't that type of moment.

It was the type where Charlie was holding it.

"Get out of there," he pleaded. "I hate this game. I hate it so much."

I looked up at his gauzy hands, sandwiching the cardboard. He couldn't reach down to help me up, so I stood under my own power. I took the box from him and placed it back in the road. And then I hugged him. I can't remember ever hugging Charlie before, but I did it then, and I peered over his shoulder to Kyle, who was still standing in the grass with his chin up and his hands engaged in the politest of applause.

"Precious. So in love."

"Scumbag," Charlie growled.

"It's okay," I whispered.

"Let's go," Charlie said.

And we did. The two of us walked up the road together, away from Kyle's cackles and his muddy jeers. It comforted me to know I wasn't alone, yet I wasn't entirely sure this was how I wanted the night to end. Because when headlights appeared at the crest of the hill again, I began to regret my retreat. Surely this car was going to swerve. Minutes from now, in some alternate universe, Kyle and I would be the ones walking up that road together.

When the car screamed past us, I looked back over my shoulder. The car struck the empty box full-force, flattening it and sucking it under and kicking it out with a back tire. A gust of wind then opened the box and puffed it into a cylinder and spun it in place for a moment before depositing it next to a storm drain.

Kyle, arms to the heavens, voiced his approval. A rapturous howl marauded through our sleepy neighborhood.

Sunday, October 29

—————◆—————

The rest of Saturday was a lost day, spent bed- and couch-bound. I tried not to spend it thinking about the fact that Charlie had saved my life. Reminders would come early and often.

By Sunday morning, I was back to normal, at least physically. My eyes were open as soon as the dawn came in through the window, but I stayed under the covers and watched the rising sunlight sweep across my posters, including that one of Prudence and her Lamborghini.

The doorbell rang. I answered.

"Hey," I said. "I was worr . . . wondering what happened to you."

There was a different version of Fiona at my front door. This was one with stockings and pulled-back hair, with makeup and a skirt and a small leather handbag. Not the Fiona I was accustomed to, but I was so relieved to see her.

"Do you have nice shoes?" she asked.

"Like wedding ones?"

Her mouth was smiling. Her eyes were not. "Like funeral ones."

"Oh no, it's not—"

"My grandma. It was time. The wake is today. I'd like you to come."

The funeral home did seem almost like a home, but the tiny details weren't there. No framed photos on the bookshelves, no slippers poking out from under the chairs. The casket was set in a room with plaid couches and enormous windows. Our blacks and navy blues looked deep and rich in there. Vegetables and dip and pastries sat on a table as far from the casket as possible, and that's where many lingered, whispering and nodding and hugging and shaking hands. Even cracking jokes. Not many, but a few, perhaps inspired by good memories of Fiona's grandmother. I'd come to learn her name was Phyllis. Phyllis Loomis. Not the most unfortunate name, but certainly a mouthful.

Except for Fiona's family, I didn't recognize most of the people there. To be honest, I hardly even recognized Fiona's brother and sister anymore. Derek and Maria were at least nine or ten years older than me. College students, maybe even out in the world working real jobs. Occasionally, during the holidays mostly, I'd see them driving down the street in their beat-up sedans. Otherwise, they weren't part of the neighborhood anymore. Keri used to rave about how cool they were. She'd fawn over Derek's frayed jeans and his weightless bangs or Maria's frilly dresses and her steel-toed army boots. But that was when they were teenagers. Hair trimmed and thoroughly buttoned, Derek and Maria looked like regular people now. Regular adults mingling with other regular adults.

Standing next to Fiona's dad at the snack table, I noticed that he had lost some of his hair in the last few years and had resorted to a comb-over. He was an angular man, with a large chin and sunken eyes, and when he spoke to people it was with a deep yet soft voice. It was because of that voice that I always thought of him as a sad person, but maybe that wasn't fair because I was comparing him to my dad, who was so quick with boisterous jokes and tales.

When a ruddy-faced minister turned away from Mr. Loomis to carve a slice of cheese, I took the opportunity to offer my condolences. Since I was the only one Fiona invited to the wake, I had to speak for our family. "My parents and sister want you to know that you're in their thoughts," I told him. "All of you."

"Very well, then," Mr. Loomis said, offering no indication as to whether he recognized me or not, and he stepped away from the table to talk to an elderly woman who placed a hand on his cheek.

On the opposite end of the room, Fiona's mom received a line of well-wishers. She was fair-skinned and dark-haired like Fiona, with sharp blue eyes and a mole on her forehead.

I wasn't sure if she was pretty or not. She could have been. Some of my early memories featured her walking through our yard barefoot, pointing out different birds and plants to Fiona and me. Out of everyone in Fiona's family, she seemed the most at ease at the wake, clinking her wine glass with the glass of every passerby and saying, "To Phyllis, a hell of a gal."

You could chart the similarities in their noses, their cheekbones, the curls in their ears. The Loomis family members were clearly related, but as they wandered around the room, I could also see how clearly divided they were. They didn't talk to one another. They hardly looked at one another. I would have thought that this was a time for kids and parents to band together, but instead they were all on their own.

I remembered a comment that Fiona made when she first started telling me her story. She talked about a time when "we used to do stuff as a family." *Used to.* I had thought nothing of that phrasing at first, but watching the Loomises now, it made me wonder if they even knew how to do stuff as a family anymore.

As for Dorian, he was sitting in a rocking chair. His hair was tied in a ponytail, and his beard was trimmed. He wore a blue blazer and khaki pants like someone who christens boats. I tried not to watch him, but the movement of the chair kept drawing my eyes back in his direction. When people came by to pay their respects, he didn't stand. He would plant his feet for a moment and shake their hands and mumble a few words, then resume his rocking. His face was placid.

"Would you like to have a moment with Phyllis?" the funeral director asked when he saw my eyes turn to the casket.

"Yessir."

It was the only answer that seemed appropriate. The director must have thought so too, because he guided me forward with an experienced hand. As soon as we were standing next to the casket, he backed away. Alone, I looked at Phyllis.

Ridged and pocked, her face wore all of its years. Her eyes were closed, and I wondered if they wore their years as well. They had seen depressions and world wars and silent movies and all these things I thought of as black-and-white things. What did that face and those eyes look like seventy years ago? In black-and-white, were they a version of Fiona?

And what about in their last moments? Did Phyllis die peacefully in her sleep, as everyone at the wake was saying? Or did something more sinister happen? Did that face feel a pillow smothering out the world? Did those eyes see Dorian?

Surely a doctor had examined the body. Foul play was something doctors could detect. Or so I hoped. I didn't really know for sure, and again, I wasn't about to make accusations without more solid evidence.

"I'm so sorry . . . for whatever happened," I whispered to

Phyllis, and I gave the casket a little pat, like it was a good pet, and I turned away.

Fiona intercepted me on my way back to the snacks. "Will you go for a walk with me?" she asked.

"Always."

She chose the cemetery. It was only a couple of blocks away, and she said she wanted to see the hole before they filled it. All four of my grandparents were alive. Aside from my goldfish Humbert's funeral, I didn't have any experience with this sort of situation. It seemed a reasonable thing to want to see.

An open grave is almost as you would imagine. Rectangular. Deep. But there are roots and stones and clay and remnants that make the walls seem marbled and pulsing with life. I thought about how strange it would be to put a shiny new coffin in there. It seemed more natural to bury a body as is and let it dissolve into the earth.

"You go into a movie and it's a dark place," Fiona said softly, looking at the hole. "The point is to be distracted. I have this fear, and I've had it since I can remember . . ."

She looked around, but it wasn't like she was searching for witnesses. Maybe she was searching for a reason to stop talking, to shut the heck up and return to the wake, but I told her, "Go on."

"I'm . . . I'm afraid that I'll be sitting in the front of the theater, and I'll get so wrapped up in the movie that I won't notice until it's too late that everyone around me is dead. The whole theater, murdered, still sitting in their seats. And me in front of them, oblivious, completely entranced by the movie."

It was a puzzling thing to say, so my response leaned toward logic. "Then sit in the back row."

"That's the thing: the risk is too tempting. I can't ever sit in the back row." Fiona sighed and turned. She walked toward the mausoleum that was the centerpiece of the cemetery. As I kept pace, she told me, "It's a metaphor. For my life, I guess."

"I don't know if I get it."

"Death is all around me, Alistair. And I choose to be oblivious to it. I guess because I can't do anything about it."

"Your grandma?" I asked. "Was she . . . ?"

"It was Nana's time," Fiona said. "I'm talking about the kids. In Aquavania. I think it's so many more than I could know of. It probably goes back forever too. Kids have been disappearing since the beginning. Ancient Egyptians, Greeks, Native Americans—they all have stories about kids stolen by the gods or whatever. What if those kids had also gone to Aquavania? What if the Riverman got them all?"

"You're saying he's thousands of years old?"

"I don't know what I'm saying." Fiona sat on the top step of the mausoleum and rubbed an eye as she brushed her hair away from her face.

The mausoleum seemed more like the grandest of sheds

than it did a tomb. Boxy, mud-stained stone, two pillars flanking its entrance, a name etched near the top: *Barnes*.

I sat next to Fiona. "Is there more you need to tell me?" I asked.

THE LEGEND OF FIONA LOOMIS, PART IV

Once you visited someone's world in Aquavania, it was easy to go back. Fiona only needed to think about Chua and a signal would travel through the folds. The signal would arrive in Chua's world as a giant bubble shaped like Fiona. Chua could pop the bubble, which meant she was inviting Fiona into her world. Or she could step inside the bubble, which meant she was coming to visit Fiona's world. Once you were connected to someone—once you had their trust—you could call them up whenever you wanted. Unless that person was no longer there.

Chua was always game for a visit, so Fiona knew it from the moment one of her calls to Chua went unanswered. The Riverman had taken her.

Chua had introduced Fiona to other kids, to Jenny, Rodrigo, and Boaz. So Fiona called them all to her world. They gathered in the treetops, where Toby served nachos and they discussed the terrifying developments.

"First Werner and now Chua." Rodrigo sighed. Rodrigo was a tall boy with bony shoulders and a willowy voice. His world could best be described as a Wild West town in a tropical rain forest.

"So their souls get sucked into the pen. Where do you reckon their bodies go?" Boaz asked. As for Boaz, he dressed like an old-fashioned newsboy and he lived in the clouds. Literally.

"Ash. Like everything else in their worlds. Dead," Jenny stated. A brilliant but dire kid, Jenny populated her world with enough robotics to fill thousands of factories.

"I don't believe that," Fiona replied. "Because why aren't they dead in the Solid World too? They disappear. I think their bodies are being held somewhere, until we get their souls back."

"Perhaps we should admit we don't know a lot about this Riverman and how he operates," Rodrigo said. Always the cool head of the bunch, he was a listener, a person who considered things.

"I think that we can make him submit," Fiona stated. "Then he can tell us what happens to them. Chua was sure that you have to stab him with an icicle."

"Lotta good that did her," Jenny huffed.

"That's not fair," Fiona said. "No one else was there, so we don't know exactly what happened to Chua."

"Sure we do," Jenny said. "She tried to bait him. And she paid for it."

"Bait him?" Boaz asked. "Not sure I gather your

meaning." This was a common problem for Boaz, gathering meanings.

"Somehow the Riverman knows what people need," Rodrigo patiently explained. "And that's how he crosses over into their worlds. Chua was trying to bait him over to hers by begging for what she needed."

"And what did she need?" Boaz asked.

Rodrigo shrugged. "We all need lots of things. And we usually keep those things secret."

"I need our pals back," Boaz said.

Even a heart like Jenny's could warm to such a sentiment. They all nodded in unison and sat there silently. *But how?* Fiona thought.

"Maybe Chua wasn't strong enough," Rodrigo said after a moment.

"Chua was as tough as a grizzly bear," Fiona shot back.

"I'm aware, but hear me out," Rodrigo said, and he stood and starting pacing around them like it was a game of Duck Duck Goose. "What if you can't stop him alone? Maybe only if there are two of us? One to play the victim and one to drive the icicle?"

He placed a hand on Jenny's head.

"It didn't work when it was Werner and Chua together," Jenny said, pushing Rodrigo's hand away.

"Only because they were caught off guard." Rodrigo resumed his pacing. "Werner couldn't have known who he was inviting over. And Chua was asleep. As for us, our guest list will be unmistakable, and though we'll pretend to be asleep, you best believe we'll be wide-wide-awake when one of us hides with the icicle and the other one gives an ear to the pen."

Boaz took off his newsie cap and fanned himself with it. It wasn't hot out, but his face had gone flush. "That sounds dangerous."

"It's only dangerous if you don't know what you're doing," Rodrigo said, and now he placed a hand on Boaz's head. "That's why I will be the one facing the pen."

Boaz looked up at Rodrigo and whimpered, "And you're choosing me to . . . drive the icicle?"

Rodrigo patted Boaz's frizzy mop. "I'm only asking for a volunteer."

Fiona knew that she should volunteer, but she couldn't will herself to raise her voice. She was more terrified than she'd ever been in her life.

"So what do we say?" Rodrigo asked, his voice fortified with confidence.

Boaz looked up at Rodrigo like a sprout to the sun. Then he reached up and grabbed Rodrigo's hand. "We say . . . that we will . . . give it a shot."

Rodrigo pulled Boaz to his feet and replied, "And we will succeed, my friend. Not right now, though. First, we go back to the Solid World. We train. We bulk up. Only then will we be ready."

And in a few months, they *were* ready. Boaz took to

his training like there was nothing else that mattered. He added muscle to his doughy body. He became skilled with a cold and slippery icicle. Gathered again in the treetops of Fiona's world, the other three watched as Boaz demonstrated his newfound strength and quickness by battling a troop of demented scarecrows that Fiona summoned. The air was chaos in straw as he took down every last one of them. It was thoroughly impressive, especially to Rodrigo, who shook his head in amazement and said, "Tomorrow we do this for real. Tomorrow we meet the Riverman in my world."

And when tomorrow came, the two went to Rodrigo's world.

And that was the last time Fiona and Jenny heard from those boys.

A few weeks passed before a Jenny-shaped bubble appeared in the treetops of Fiona's world. Fiona stepped inside the bubble and journeyed across the folds to see her last remaining friend in Aquavania.

Jenny's world was all steel and circuits, a maze of electronic walls and doors that rotated and shifted at the girl's whim. Everything was dead, but everything was alive. It buzzed and growled and sniggered with beeps. To be inside of it was to be inside the intricate bowels of an android.

Luckily for Fiona, Jenny provided a guide, a crystalline silverfish that scurried and climbed and always chose the correct path, even when it meant passing through trap doors in the ceiling and inching past a whirring fan. Fiona was quite slim, but even she had to suck in her tummy as she sidled her way by the spinning blades.

The silverfish brought Fiona to the hub. The hub was a room no bigger than a walk-in closet, and every surface appeared to be a mirror. But if you looked into these mirrors, you would not see yourself. You would see fantastic images, creations of Jenny's mind. When Fiona entered the hub, an inky smudge was expanding over the mirrors and darkening the room.

Jenny floated in the middle of the hub, weightless like an astronaut aboard a space station. She greeted Fiona with a salute.

"Zero gravity?" Jenny asked.

"Yes, please," Fiona said. Like that, Fiona was floating in the air next to Jenny.

"This is goodbye," Jenny said. Conversations for her were about efficiency, about finding the quickest route to the point.

"I'm sorry?"

"The answer isn't to bait the Riverman. It's to hide from him," Jenny explained. "I like you, Fiona. You're noble and sweet and the perfect amount of kooky. But your outlook is too rosy."

Rosy was not something anyone in the Solid World would have ever called Fiona, but yes, compared to Jenny, Fiona was a parade of flowers. The mirror exploded into a kaleidoscope of color, then melted into a landscape made of candy. Teddy bears danced across the candy. They wore impossibly wide and toothy smiles.

"All I want is us to be safe," Fiona said.

"And I want the same. And the safest thing to do is to close our worlds off. To not let anyone else in. Ever."

This wasn't an unreasonable idea, but since meeting Chua, Fiona had grown accustomed to having friends in Aquavania, to exploring wonderfully exotic places like Jenny's world.

"You're right, but you're wrong," Fiona said.

"I can't be both."

"There's a reason why we've been lucky enough to come to Aquavania," Fiona said. "It isn't to hide. Maybe we're supposed to stop him. Maybe one of us is the Swimmer."

The seams on the teddy bears started to break, and the stuffing oozed out like pus. The candy turned brown. Swarms of flies now filled the mirrors. They had come to feed on the rot.

"There's a reason for everything," Jenny said. "But it doesn't have to be a reason you like. There is disease and disaster. Surely you don't like any reason for those things, yet the reasons exist. The reason we're here has nothing to do with luck or silly legends about the icicle and the Swimmer. It's because we're better than everyone else. We're creators, Fiona. Everyone else? They're nothing but consumers. If we stopped creating, then inspiration wouldn't find its way into the Solid World. So if hiding means we can keep on creating, then I'm hiding. Because I'm essential."

"You're wrong. It's not selfish like that." Fiona spoke the words but she wasn't sure if she believed the words.

"Yes, it is," Jenny said. "I love coming to Aquavania. Sometimes I don't want to go back to the Solid World. I'm not about to risk my life here because I want more friends."

The mirrors went blank. Jenny also had no intention of revealing all of her thoughts.

"I don't want you to risk your life," Fiona said.

"You wanted Boaz and Rodrigo to risk theirs."

Fiona winced. "That's not true."

"If you say so. How old are you, Fiona?"

This would take some arithmetic. Fiona took her age in the Solid World—where she was still eleven—and she added the days she'd spent in Aquavania. "I'm twelve," she finally said. "I'll be thirteen in a few months."

"And I'm so much older than that," Jenny replied. "Maybe someday you'll realize that goodbye can often be the best thing. Even when you're crazy about the person."

"I'm old enough to know that's not true," Fiona said.

Jenny simply shook her head. The mirrors showed images of Fiona's island. "Goodbye, Fiona. And good luck."

That was it. In a blink, Fiona was back in her world, sitting on the beach with Toby. She told Toby what Jenny had said, and the only thing Toby could say was, "You'll always have me."

It was sweet, but she needed more than sweet. She needed to warn people.

So as soon as Fiona returned to the Solid World, she pulled an old handkerchief out of a painty bucket in the basement. She took it to her bedroom and drew a grid on it. She filled the squares with the names of her friends in Aquavania and every kid she knew of there, even the ones she'd never met but had heard about from Chua and Boaz and Rodrigo and Jenny. If she didn't know a name, she wrote a question mark. If the kid had been taken by the Riverman, she wrote the name in red ink. If not—or if she wasn't sure of the kid's fate—green ink. She put X's for the Dead Worlds that they had all learned about from legends.

She brought the handkerchief to the library and scrolled through sheet after sheet of microfiche. She tried to locate information on any and all of the kids. The only article she found was the one about Chua. But she also found phone numbers in some of the mastheads of international newspapers. She went home and made calls. She asked questions to any journalist who spoke English. She tried to locate more phone numbers—for police stations, schools, any place that might be able to provide her with leads. But as much as she knew about these kids' stories in Aquavania, she knew so little about their lives in the Solid World. For some, she only knew what country they lived in. For most, she only had first names.

Throughout the summer she investigated, and after all was said and done, she didn't make contact with a single kid whose name was written in green. She didn't warn anyone.

"Four hundred and eighty dollars!" her dad had howled when he opened the family's next phone bill.

"It must be a mistake," Fiona's mom said.

"Argentina. Kenya. Singapore. Who in their right mind would be calling these places?"

Fiona was ready to confess, but her uncle Dorian spoke up. "I think it might be Mom," he said. Dorian had recently moved into the house and was looking after Fiona's grandmother. He spent morning, afternoon, and night with the ailing woman.

"Well, who in the heck is Mom calling?" Fiona's dad asked.

"No one," Dorian explained. "She's confused. I find her sometimes with a phone in her lap. Must be dialing random numbers. Doesn't do it on purpose."

Begrudgingly, Fiona's dad accepted the explanation and canceled their long-distance service. Whether Dorian was covering for Fiona, or whether this was a lucky coincidence, Fiona couldn't be sure, because she didn't ask and Dorian didn't say. But she was out of options now. She had no choice but to reveal her secret. Someone else had to know about Aquavania, if only because Fiona feared that the Riverman might find her too, and then nobody would ever learn what had happened.

Kendra and Fay-Renee seemed like obvious candidates. Though as much as they were Fiona's friends, they were hardly her confidants. Once, when she told them that she had the tiniest of crushes on Sanjay Raza, the news was all but printed in the yearbook. So there was no way she was going to open up to them about Aquavania.

Informing her family was also out of the question. There was already enough stress pushing against the walls of their home. Besides, who would have believed such outrageous tales?

"Ignore her. The girl is mired in whimsy," her dad had said to Dorian when he moved in, and all because Fiona had dared to ask if Dorian had come across any sasquatches in his travels.

No, Fiona needed a fresh mind, someone who wasn't attached to Aquavania, but someone who had the capacity to believe. A storyteller.

Her thoughts turned to Alistair Cleary. He was her neighbor in the Solid World. He was a quiet kid who once wrote a tale about aliens who came to Earth and pretended to be sixth graders.

She could relate to that story. Every time she returned from Aquavania, Fiona felt a little more like one of Alistair's aliens. And since the author of those aliens seemed to understand that part of her, she wondered if he might understand Aquavania too.

She also wondered if he would remember their pact. When they were younger, she and Alistair had been friends, and one day, standing out on the border of Alistair's backyard, next to a rock that was shaped like a frog, they had made a promise to each other. Whoever moved away from the neighborhood first was obliged to bury an object in the swampy ground next to the rock. That object could be anything, so long as it told a secret.

Fiona had the perfect thing: the handkerchief. So at the bottom of it, she wrote:

Dear Alistair,

You've found this because the Riverman has taken me. By now, he might have taken all of these kids.

Someone must warn the green ones. Someone must
stop him. I don't know what to do anymore.
So confused. So scared.
Fiona

Dorian had given Fiona an ammo can from his time
in the Army. Fiona put the handkerchief inside the
ammo can and buried it next to the rock. She had no
plan. She only hoped that she could trust Alistair
enough to tell him everything. She only hoped that if
she didn't have time to tell him everything—if the Riverman got to her first—then at least she had left him a
clue, a secret, a map to Aquavania. She only hoped
that Alistair remembered the pact.

I looked out over the cemetery at the patchwork of graves
and stones. I thought of that strange handkerchief. "Of
course I remembered the pact," I said.

"If I had disappeared, would you have dug it up?" she
asked.

"Definitely," I said. "But I don't understand. You keep
calling it a map. It's a grid with a bunch of names on it."

"Yes," she said. "And each square of the grid represents
a kid's world in Aquavania."

"But everyone's world is connected?"

"That's right," Fiona said. "You have to think of it in
three dimensions. What happens when you fold something

like a handkerchief? You can connect any two points, right? Because there are infinite ways you can fold it."

This sort of abstract thinking was a bit beyond me, but I sort of understood what she was saying. It didn't matter, I guess. The important part of this story was me. Where I came in.

"Last time we talked, you said that the Riverman knew about you. What if I told you I know who the Riverman is? And that you're right—he's here, in the Solid World."

She folded her arms, cradled herself. "I'd . . . ask you how you knew."

"Don't worry about that. All you have to know is that I'm figuring out a way to handle it. And all you have to do is stay safe." I placed a hand on her shoulder. She looked at it, but didn't push it away.

"Have you ever built anything from scratch?" she asked.

This was not the response I was hoping for. No *Thank you, Alistair*, no *Of course, Alistair, I'll stay safe for you*. Just an incongruous question. "I don't know," I replied. "What do you mean?"

"I've told you my story," she said. "That's a good thing. At least one person should know it. But I'm starting to think that no matter who the Riverman is, we won't be able to stop this. The best we can do is start over from scratch."

And that was all she said. She didn't elaborate, didn't explain. As far as she was concerned, the conversation was over. So she stood up and started walking back to the wake.

163

Even though I was tempted to, I didn't follow her immediately. I was trying to dig up more of that story beneath the story. Rodrigo's world was described as a rain forest. Maybe the stuffed animal on the floor of Dorian's pickup was connected to Rodrigo. Maybe it was a monkey or something. And the toy airplane? Fiona said that Boaz lived in the clouds. Was that a reference to the boy's love of airplanes? Were those things in Dorian's truck souvenirs he kept from the kidnappings?

I imagined that the part of Fiona's story about the telephone was close to the truth, that she suspected Dorian was responsible for the missing kids and so she made phone calls to learn more, but when the phone bill came back, Dorian caught on to what she was doing. That would explain why she said *He knows that I know.*

But what about the green names on the handkerchief? Were they other victims that Dorian had chosen? And how would Fiona know about them? Not all the pieces were fitting together, but they didn't need to. I was more concerned about her hopelessness. Why couldn't we stop this? Why couldn't *I* stop this? Because someone had to.

I sat there on the steps for a few more moments, watching a man raking the damp brown leaves. He pulled them away from the graves into mucky piles along the gravel access road. The grass he uncovered was thin and pale, and I wondered what it would be like to have the power to wish all the color back into it.

Monday, October 30

———◆———

It was a rainy morning. Misty, spitting, and cold, but not exactly a downpour. Inside the house, sitting on the stairs near the front door, my dad pulled rubber galoshes over his brown leather shoes. He spotted me grabbing an umbrella from the coat closet.

"Come here," he said.

My dad was over six feet tall, but with him sitting three steps up, it put us at eye level. "What's up, old man?" I asked.

"I'm proud of what you did yesterday," he said. "Mom is too."

I shrugged. "Okay."

"That's what a man does," he went on. "He's there when you need him to be there. Fiona is lucky to have someone like you."

"She invited me, so I went."

My dad shook his head. "It's more than that. Growing up in that house can't have been easy. And dealing with death . . . it's always hard, even when it's expected."

"What do you mean by 'growing up in that house'?" I asked.

The galoshes snapped against the heels of his shoes as he put them on. "I didn't mean anything by it. They're different from us. That's all. Believe me, they're . . . fine people." He stood up and looked down at me.

"It's hard to know what to believe sometimes," I said.

"Believe in the girl," he replied.

That's when Keri tapped me on the shoulder. "We're gonna be late."

Jacketed and loaded down with our backpacks, Keri and I slogged up the driveway. The wind blew our umbrellas inside out before we even reached the sidewalk, so we folded them up and faced the weather.

"Do you love her?" Keri asked as soon as we were out of earshot of the house.

"You are so annoying," I said.

"What's it feel like?" Behind the words there was honest curiosity. It was strange to be asked such a question from my older sister, but then again, she was barely fourteen, still an eighth grader.

"It doesn't feel like anything," I said. This was a lie. When it came to Fiona, it felt like everything.

"I'm sorry," Keri said. "About her grandma. And for saying she was nutzo."

"I don't care."

"She *is* nutzo, but she's your girlfriend, and it's cool that you have a girlfriend." She was right. It *was* cool, even if it wasn't entirely true, and yet the more time I spent with Fiona, the more I wanted it to be true, the more I wanted people to believe that it was true.

Keri scooped an acorn from the road and proceeded to fling it at a mailbox. It hit the target with a satisfying *dong*. A less skilled markswoman might have roared in victory, but this was nothing for Keri. She had always been astoundingly coordinated.

"It's a federal offense to tamper with other people's mailboxes," I told her.

She shrugged and said, "Do you guys make out?"

"Will you quit it?"

"A girl can ask questions."

Indeed. And a girl can be asked questions. I hadn't thought of it before then, but Keri wasn't all that different from Fiona. Same neighborhood, close in age. Clever, confident. Girls. Maybe their minds had a similar geometry.

"Do you want to be saved?" I asked.

Keri cocked an eyebrow. "Like Jesus?"

"Like Lancelot."

"I hang my hair out the window every night, waiting for some dude to climb up." This was a typical Keri comment, designed to provoke, but I wasn't going to be tricked into trading barbs.

"I'm serious," I said. "Is that what every girl wants? A guy to step in and save the day?"

Keri shrugged. "I guess if a monster is involved. Mostly I think a girl wants a guy who, like, tells her nice stuff. Reminds her that she matters, you know?"

A monster *was* involved, but what Keri said was equally important. Part of helping Fiona was reminding her that she mattered. And to do that, I would have to do something significant.

I decided to avoid Fiona at school until I knew for sure what I was going to do. I suspected her emotions were still all over the place after dealing with the wake. *My* emotions were still all over the place, and I didn't want to burden her with my ideas until my ideas could be put into action.

At lunch, I sat next to Mike and Trevor again. They didn't ask me about Charlie this time. Halloween was all they wanted to talk about, and how even though they were a bit old for trick-or-treating, they would still be dressing as ninjas and snatching up every peanut butter cup they could.

"Your neighborhood is Battleground this year, you know?" Mike told me.

I didn't know. Information of this sort was so low on my priorities.

"Cops were all over last year's Battleground," Trevor remarked. "Could get nice 'n' nasty tomorrow."

In other places, mischief reigned on the night before Halloween, but in Thessaly it always dominated Halloween night itself, when identities could be concealed and vandals could easily fade into the costumed crowd. An Olympic committee composed of the more popular kids decided which corner of town everyone should descend upon. It made the shaving cream assaults more intense and exponentially increased the probability of coed socializing. The chosen neighborhood was always called Battleground.

"I don't know if I'm going out," I told them.

"What!" Trevor yelped. "You live in Battleground! You have to go! It's gonna be wicked awesome. I heard Chad Burk is bringing a rocket launcher!"

"Come on," Mike said. "A rocket launcher?"

"Okay," Trevor admitted. "Maybe it's only a crossbow. But he jiggered it so he can shoot smoke bombs with it. He's got, like, a hundred smoke bombs."

"How about it, Alistair?" Mike asked. "Crossbows? Smoke bombs?"

"Maybe," I said.

They continued to press me, to insist that Halloween might be the greatest night of my life. It was a possibility, but it wouldn't really matter unless I could think of a way to help Fiona.

At the end of the day, I collected Charlie's homework and brought it to his house. I hadn't seen him since the sleepover and I was worried that he might expect me to stay for dinner. I considered leaving the books and papers on his front porch with a note saying I didn't have time to stick around, but that was bound to backfire. He'd end up calling me and booking me on yet another guilt trip.

Charlie's parents had an open-door policy for me. In many ways, they trusted me more than they trusted their own sons. Of course, they never stated this, but you could hear it in their voices. They were always saying things like, "It's good to have you around, Alistair. We wish you were here more often."

So I let myself in the front door and made my way to the back room, where I was sure I'd find Charlie. The house hadn't changed much in the last ten years. A two-year-old me could have walked through and recognized almost every chair and table and picture. The Dwyers didn't move things or add fresh embellishments. It was comforting in some ways. In other ways, unsettling. It was like they were curators at a gallery of their previous lives.

That said, when I reached the back room, I spotted something unmistakably new. A swooping, elegant, embroidered red hat—perhaps the biggest hat I'd ever seen—sat atop Charlie's head. On his body, he wore a long red coat and a billowy white scarf. A fencing foil was attached with Velcro straps to one of his bandaged hands. To the other? A hook.

"Whaddya think?" Charlie asked.

"Impressive."

"Glad I let you live to see it," he said as he used the hook to push the hat back from his brow.

"Didn't take you long to get there."

Charlie thrust the foil at me. The tip stopped inches from my chest. "Question my honor and I'll take your heart, you filthy cur."

I pushed the foil away. "You're a day early."

"Gotta see if it fits. There's big news, you know? They're happy with the healing. Sending me to school. So I'm going out tomorrow night. Then on Wednesday, it's back to class. *Bwa bwa bwa.*"

Bwa bwa bwa was Charlie's sad trombone sound, but it didn't make me sad at all. This was a relief. I could handle lunch with Charlie if it meant I didn't have to stop by his house every evening. "It was bound to happen sometime," I said.

"What do I need school for?" Charlie replied. "I could read for a couple of hours a day and learn more than what they teach in that hole."

"Don't you want to see people? Socialize?"

"With a bunch of infant morons? No, thanks."

"But you're still going?" I needed a yes. More than anything, I needed a yes.

"Yes. For Mom."

And there it was, and thank god for it. I smiled. "It will be good to have you back. I always thought you kinda liked school."

Charlie waved his hook dismissively. "Only thing I like

about it now is that my mom finally bought me a laptop computer. No more writing with my hand like a chump."

"A laptop?" I said. "Those things cost like a million bucks!"

Charlie smiled. "Four thousand . . . nine hundred . . . ninety-five . . . buckaroos. To be precise. Five times the Blue Book value of Kyle's van. Mom said I'm worth it. Besides, what choice does she have? She wants me to keep up with my schoolwork, so I'm pinkie-typing all my notes and assignments from this day forward. You kids have fun with your cursive *z*'s. This guy is getting sophisticated."

I couldn't let the obvious contradiction go unnoted. "You're not too sophisticated for Halloween, though, are you?"

This time Charlie twirled the hook. "Pretending, dear boy, is the definition of sophistication."

I left Charlie's house two hours later, after a plate of microwave eggrolls and an intense gaming session. While playing, I kept a tally in my head of the creatures I had killed. One hundred forty-seven total. Most were serpents, rabid wolves, and whatnot, but there were also a handful of people, namely sorcerers and black knights.

Only a game, I told myself as I biked home into a stiff wind. A few nights before, I had basically told Charlie the same thing. But it suddenly made me consider the cemetery and Fiona's grandma. Ashes to ashes, dust to dust, all that stuff. Death takes everyone. Most of us too early, a few of us not early enough.

As I reached my driveway, Kyle's van pulled up alongside of me.

"Hey, pal," he called out.

"Hey." After our harrowing night, maybe I should have been angry with Kyle. I wasn't. If anything, I was more impressed than ever by his recklessness. Reputations rarely held up to inspection, so now that one did, it inspired a strange sort of trust. Kyle was dangerous, exactly as advertised.

"The . . . fun we had," Kyle said with a sigh. "Sorry if I put you in a bad spot."

"It *was* kinda fun, wasn't it?"

"Well, it was something. And you got some balls on you. I'll give you that."

"I only did it because you did it."

Kyle wagged a finger and twisted his voice into a haggy cackle. "Just say no!"

I smiled and nodded. We both knew how stupid that notion was.

"Seriously, though," Kyle went on, "I was only messin' with you. If you hadn't done it, I wouldn't have thought any less of you."

Whether this was true or not didn't matter. I *had* done it. If he didn't owe me respect for that, then he at least owed me a favor.

"That girl who lives under the bridge," I said.

Kyle squinted. Elaboration was necessary. Several girls worthy of his memory must have lived under that bridge.

"The one who gave you the . . . stuff," I continued.

Nodding solemnly, he made the connection. "Crazy Gina Rizetti. What about her?"

"She can get things? Anything?"

"Most things. Plutonium? Maybe not. You building a time machine?"

"Would you take me to see her?"

"Right now?"

"No. I'm already late for dinner. Soon."

"How about tomorrow? She's shipping her kid off to Grammy's for trick-or-treatin'. So her house is free to throw a rager. Costume and clothes optional."

"Seriously?"

"Oh, it's a big-boy party, all right, but I think you can handle it. I can't be contributing to the delinquency of a minor, though. So you'll have to find your own way there. But Gina's cool. I'm sure she'd help you out. This about that girl of yours?"

"Maybe."

"You dog!" Kyle whooped. "I can only imagine."

An understatement. I shrugged my response, and Kyle took it as being complicit in some conspiracy. He grinned and said, "Rock and roll."

Then he turned up his radio and proceeded to peel out, for my benefit, I suppose. As soon as his van disappeared around the corner, I wheeled my bike to our garage.

I lingered there in the dark. I needed a few moments before going inside and facing my parents. I was thinking about something that would shock them even more than if they learned about our game of jack-in-the-box. Would they see the trepidation in my body and ask me what was going on?

Probably not, but doubt and darkness are good friends, and the longer I stayed in the garage, the more unsure of myself I became.

I'll go to Gina's, but I won't ask for it.

I'll ask for advice.

Someone else needs to know.

And that someone else wasn't going to be either of my parents. I took a deep breath and went inside.

HALLOWEEN

I DIDN'T HAVE A COSTUME PICKED OUT YET. I WASN'T opposed to them, but I wasn't like Charlie. My nerves weren't attuned to such things. As harmless as it was, pretending to be someone else infected my body like any other lie. It made me blush and stammer and apologize. Even when I was five or six, standing at my neighbors' doors with my jack-o'-lantern bucket, I tried to explain my superhero getups. "I can't really fly," I'd tell them. "Mom made this cape using curtains and the sewing machine. It isn't real."

No one dressed up during the day anyhow. That was more of an elementary school thing. Any seventh grader who dared to show up in character was definitely not celebrated for bravery. Quite the opposite. Sure, there were always teachers who wore witch hats or vampire fangs, but otherwise Halloween was a normal day of classes.

That's not to say kids weren't excited about the evening's activities, though. They dominated any and all conversations.

I still wasn't sure what to say to Fiona, but I certainly wasn't going to tell her what I was considering. In my mind I tried to justify my plans, but every few seconds my mind turned its coat.

You're crazy, Alistair!

No, you're doing what a man would do.

Tell the police, Alistair!

No, don't tell a soul. Because they won't believe you. And they will try to fix her. And you will lose her. You will never see her again.

Luckily, I didn't have a chance to even see Fiona at lunch and have what was sure to be an awkward conversation. As soon as I entered the cafeteria, Principal Braugher's secretary intercepted me. She brought me to the head office, where Braugher was sitting at her desk, plastic spiders dangling from her ears. A bowl of candy sat in front of her.

"Help yourself," she said.

I pocketed a caramel. "Thank you."

"No," Braugher said. "Thank *you.* Mrs. Dwyer says you've been a good friend to Charlie. And I appreciate your bringing him his assignments."

"It was only a few times." It was hardly that.

"Doesn't matter," she replied. "It was enough." She slid a piece of paper across her desk and motioned for me to take it.

It was a gift certificate to the Skylark. Twenty-five bucks.

"For me?"

She smiled. "Treat your family to lunch."

"Thank you. I didn't do it for—"

She waved me off. "You've got a good heart, Alistair. Good hearts deserve rewards. Last time we talked, you asked me if I worry about kids. The thing I worry about most is friendships. At your age they go in either direction. Charlie thinks the world of you, you know?"

"Maybe."

She shook her head. "That wonderful short story Charlie wrote for the *Sutton Bulletin* a few weeks ago? There's a reason he named the hero after you."

The *Sutton Bulletin* was a weekly paper that covered sports and politics and human interest stories. Occasionally they'd print poems and short fiction by locals. My parents had canceled our subscription at least a year before, when they realized they were shelling out a dollar a month for what amounted to unused papier-mâché supplies. So I had no idea what Braugher was talking about. My response was thus a neutral one. "Charlie does what Charlie does."

"And, it appears, he does it quite well."

I didn't know Charlie wrote stories, let alone submitted them to local papers. Since he didn't brag about them, I assumed it meant they weren't very good. Braugher seemed to believe he had talent, and my curiosity about this outweighed any fear I had of embarrassing him by reading something he clearly didn't want me to see. After school, I headed straight to the library.

Ms. Linqvist showed me where they kept copies of the *Sutton Bulletin*. They were in the study room, hung on a rack of wooden rods like they were towels left out to dry. I took the five most recent issues to a nearby table and flipped through them. I found what I was looking for in the October 14 issue.

ALIENS OF THE SEVENTH GRADE
A story by Charlie Dwyer

There once was a boy named Alistair, and he was in the seventh grade. He was a regular boy with regular problems. There were kids in his class who weren't regular. The day that he found out that these kids were aliens was the day that everything made sense . . .

Character names had been changed, the title tweaked, but this was "Sixth Grade for the Outer-Spacers." Word for word.

Sickness stood in for anger. Last spring, I had given Charlie a copy of my story fresh from the computer printer. He took it home and read it that night. The next morning he delivered his review over the phone: "Don't quit your day job. You'll end up starving."

Looking down at the newspaper, at Charlie's baffling act of plagiarism, I felt like I *was* starving. Sourness filled my stomach. My throat lurched. For a moment I was tempted to rip the paper up, stuff it in my mouth, and swallow it. It was a weird temptation, but an honest one. I wanted to drown the existence of such a thing. Drown it in acid.

Better senses won out, and I pushed the paper away and stood up from the table. Without saying a word, I sprinted out of the library.

The two miles I ran from the library were probably the most I'd ever run. It was still early, but little kids were already out, walking hand in hand with their parents. There were princesses and firemen and gypsies and hobos and every sort of cute animal. Probably half the kids donned cheap store-bought costumes with plastic masks that were held on by rubber bands and pressed cockeyed against their faces. When I was younger and my mom was making all of my costumes, I envied kids like this. They got to be the latest movie icon or popular toy. They were quietly and instantly recognizable, while I always had to explain.

I was still in my school clothes—jeans, a jacket, a sweater, a turtleneck—not exactly the attire of a runner. Parents exercised caution, guiding their children out of my path as I dashed by. They must have taken me for both types of mad, and I guess they were right. By the time I reached Charlie's house, I was also exhausted. On his front porch, I doubled over and tried to cough myself back to normal. The sourness in my stomach had gotten worse. I was having trouble remembering my stomach without it.

When I finally brought my head up, I saw that the front door was open and Charlie was standing there in his pirate attire.

"So what's your costume?" he asked. "Tuberculosis?"

I gulped back my nausea and said the title. "'Aliens . . . of the Seventh . . . Grade.'"

That was all it took. Charlie stared at me for a moment and scraped his hook against the doorjamb. I was a bit surprised he didn't have a canned response. Surely he knew this day was coming.

"Let's face it, Alistair," he finally said. "You were doing nothing with that story. If it wasn't for me, no one else would have seen it. A thank-you might be nice. For getting people to actually read your writing. And for saving your life."

I could have punched him right in his smug face. I could have kicked him square in the crotch. I could have watched him writhe in pain, and I could have told him that he was no friend of mine, that I owed him nothing, that he owed *me* everything, for all of the years I'd indulged him, for all of his crap I'd endured, from the morning with the wasps to the night with the sleds and any number of incidents I don't have the time or energy to delve into now. I could have done a lot of things.

I chose to walk away.

Halloween

Part II

My doorbell rang at a quarter till seven. Mike and Trevor, darkly clad and wearing backpacks, waited on my front steps. Ski masks clung to their brows, but they hadn't pulled them over their faces yet. On the street behind them, things were under way. A trio of girls dressed as M&M's sprinted by, the orbs that encased their bodies exploding into red and blue and yellow as they passed beneath a streetlight.

"We're giving you five minutes," Trevor said. "Ninja now or ninja never."

"Whatcha got there?" I asked.

Mike took his backpack off and opened it up. He pulled out rolls of toilet paper, a carton of eggs, and a can of shaving cream with the nozzle melted down so the opening was nothing more than a pinprick. "Good times," he said.

Weaponry like this was suddenly irresistible. My

encounter with Charlie had left me ravenous for revenge. I imagined the eggs flying at his face, breaking on his cheekbone, and oozing down his neck.

"I'm in," I told them.

I didn't have a lot of dark clothing, so I had to make do with a navy blue long-underwear top and black dress shoes and dress pants—the same ones I wore to the wake. Instead of a ski mask I found an old wool hat and I used the tip of an umbrella to spread the stitching and create two eyeholes. When I pulled it over my face, it only reached down as far as my chin. Ridiculous, but it concealed my identity. It would have to suffice.

"Ninja, huh?" my mom said when she saw me tiptoeing to the door. "Please tell me my son is more creative than that."

"I'm twelve," I reminded her. "I'm sorry if I can't go as a bunny rabbit anymore."

"Keri is dressed as a cat," she countered as she poured a bag of miniature candy bars into a glass bowl. "Wasn't so hard to put together."

"Really, Mom? Are you really saying this?"

She grabbed a bar, tore it open, and took a bite. She winked. "Have fun. Keri gets until ten, so you get until ten, but only tonight."

I met the guys in the yard, where Mike loaded up my backpack with my share of the supplies. "First things first," he said. "Heard that 167 Maple has a basket of full-size Snickers sitting on the front porch with a note that says *Please take one*."

"We'll be taking more than one," Trevor informed me. I had assumed as much.

A divorced college professor owned the house. I didn't know his name, but my parents referred to him as Dr. Leadfoot because he tore around the neighborhood in a little blue sports car, rarely even slowing down for stop signs. He was never out for a stroll, never participated in the block parties or the neighborhood garage sales. The windows of his house were almost always dark.

They were dark when we got there, and as we darted across the lawn toward the door, Trevor pulled his mask over his face and a pillowcase out of his backpack. "I'll take 'em all and we'll divvy 'em up later."

Mike and I nodded our approval, and Trevor assumed the lead. He leapt over the front steps and onto the porch. As promised, the basket was there, and he snatched it immediately, but when he got a look inside, his head dropped. He tilted the wicker to show us the contents: broken eggs.

"We're too late," Mike said.

"You're right on time, actually," someone responded.

An egg pelted Trevor on the side of the head. As he recoiled, a water balloon struck him on the arm. Liquid smacked his chest. Attackers were somewhere on the porch, but we couldn't see them.

"Freakin' gross!" Trevor howled, and he sprang back over the steps and hit the ground running. Mike and I fumbled through our bags, desperate for retaliation. I grabbed the first thing I found—a rotten banana—and threw it toward the porch. It struck a support beam and splattered.

"It was pee! Oh god, I think it was pee!" Trevor yelled as he sprinted toward the road.

Meanwhile, Mike was dispatching long thin ribbons of shaving cream, waving his arm in a haphazard figure eight. The cream flew at least fifteen feet, but the porch was more than twenty feet away. The grass and bushes took the brunt.

A water balloon exploded at my feet and unleashed an acidic stench. I couldn't be sure what the liquid was, but I wasn't taking any chances. "They've got pee balloons!" I screamed to Mike, and that's all he needed to hear.

Seconds later we were both following in Trevor's wake, packs over our shoulders and eggs and water balloons raining down around us like mortar shells.

"Keep goin'! Keep goin'!" Mike squealed to Trevor. There was a certain amount of glee in his voice. This was exactly the type of night he had been hoping for.

We made it across the street and kept going until we were out of range of the streetlights. Shielded behind a tree, we assessed the situation.

"Who was that?" Mike asked.

"I'm guessing Ken Wagner and Sanjay," Trevor said.

"Sanjay is such a tool," Mike added. Then he sniffed Trevor's shoulder. "Oh god, it really was pee, wasn't it?"

"Probably vinegar," I said. It made more sense. It would take a lot of pee to fill up multiple balloons.

"It's gross, whatever it is," Trevor said, peeling off his top layer. "I knew I should have brought another sweatshirt."

"Get that pee-smock outta here," Mike commanded.

Trevor did the contrary. He thrust it at us. "Lap it up, doggies."

Mike grabbed for a sleeve and yanked it away. "Buh-bye," he said as he swung it like a lasso and tossed it into the bough of a tree.

"I'm gonna get frostbite!" Trevor protested, folding his arms. He was down to only a T-shirt. It was close to freezing out.

"Really?" Mike asked. "You'd rather stink?"

"I'd rather keep moving," Trevor said. "Come on. Let's take down one of our targets." Trevor bolted again, and our only choice was to tag along.

The little kids had gone home by this point, and our classmates had completely taken over the neighborhood. Bands of three to six roamed up and down the streets and huddled in yards to plot. Many of the costumes were uninspired—girls in football jerseys and eye black, guys in rubber monster masks—but everyone had at least one can of shaving cream at the ready. Trees and cars and signs were all caked with the gunk. I could taste it in the air.

We snaked and dodged, wielding our cans with fingers on the nozzles so that any potential foes would know we had the drop on them. It was exciting, and for the first time in weeks I was smiling, genuinely. I hadn't forgotten about Charlie, but I knew he was out there alone, while I had two guys with me who didn't care how good I was at video games, who didn't steal my ideas, who wanted me as a friend because they thought I was fun.

"Better run, ya pansies!" someone yelled, and Mike pointed his nozzle back over his shoulder and let loose with a stream of shaving cream as he ran. It looked like the exhaust from a jet.

A burst of red and blue lights tipped me off to a police car down the street, and I shouted to Trevor, "Cops! Hang a ricky!"

Trevor got the message, making a sharp right turn into the O'Haras' yard. We hustled past their aboveground pool, over a chain-link fence on the other side, and kept going for a while, running from yard to yard, trying to stay buried in the shadows.

We were a couple of houses away when I realized we were heading straight for Fiona's. Trevor was leading again, and I considered asking him to shoot back across the street, but any excuse to pass by Fiona's—if only to see if the light was on in her window—was a good enough excuse for me.

As soon as we reached the border between the Andersons' and the Loomises' yards, Trevor stopped and said, "This is it, I think."

"This is what?" I asked.

"Fiona Loomis's house," Mike said.

"Yeah, so?"

"It's one of our targets," Trevor told me.

"Target for what?" There was only one second-floor room

with the light on. I was pretty sure Fiona's room was on the second floor, but from our angle I couldn't tell if the lit one was it.

"TP. Eggs. The whole shebang," Mike said. "We're messing this place up good tonight."

"Uh . . . why?"

"Because," Mike said.

"Because of what?"

"She's a pig," Trevor said.

A pig? He called her a pig? I couldn't believe it. He might as well have karate-chopped me in the Adam's apple. I started to talk, but my windpipe sealed up and I could only whisper a short reply. "She's . . ."

They weren't listening anyway. By that point they were already digging into their backpacks and removing the ammo.

I took a deep breath and tried again. "She's . . . What did you call her?"

Trevor put his thumb to his nose and started snorting and oinking.

"Naw," Mike said as he hurled a roll of toilet paper at the nearest tree. "Her nose is all twisted. It's more like one of those monkeys with the nasty old honkers."

"Shut up," I said. "What are you . . . ? Just shut up."

Trevor looked at me sideways. "Don't you know Fiona Loomis? She's weirdness squared."

"Of course I know her," I said. "She's my . . ."

I stopped short, but not because of embarrassment. It was Trevor's cheeks. I could see them rising beneath his ski mask. He was smiling.

That was all it took.

I reared back and jumped forward, drove my shoulder into Trevor's stomach, and wrapped my arms around his body. It didn't knock him over, but it knocked the breath out of him. He wheezed and coughed, and I could feel his hands pawing, trying to grab at my belt loops. His fingernails found the exposed skin of my lower back. He scraped and I clenched my teeth.

"What in the . . . ?" Mike said.

Pushing Trevor forward, I tried to get a good foothold, but the grass was wet and my shoes didn't have enough traction. I slipped backward, and as I fell, he fell, and soon we were on the ground wrestling.

"Knock it off!" Mike yelled.

While we squirmed, my hat twisted over my face, blinding me. I kicked and clawed but couldn't tell if I was winning or not. I tried to grab Trevor's arms, but now that he was in short sleeves there was nothing to get a grip on. My rib cage felt the pressure of his knee and I struggled to breathe, but it only made me fight harder. Blood rushed everywhere. My face was piping hot.

"What's . . . wrong . . . with you?" Trevor grunted.

I yanked my hat off so I could finally see my opponent. I swung my arms, trying to land a punch, but ended up elbowing the ground and his thighs. I twisted my body to get a better angle, and that's when I came nose-to-nozzle with it: Mike's can of shaving cream.

He sprayed it right in my face.

I howled and I spat the cream off my lips. Letting go of Trevor, I rolled away.

"You're crazy!" Trevor yelled.

I ran an arm across my face to wipe it clean and looked up to that window with the light on, hoping to see Fiona. Instead, looking down on me was Dorian Loomis. He raised a hand and gave a single sharp wave. If our fight was anything more than a curiosity to him, he didn't let on.

I closed my eyes and screamed, "You don't ever say anything about her! You don't ever do anything to her! You don't even think about her! Or I'll kill you! I swear, I will kill you!"

When I opened my eyes, Dorian was no longer in the window. Trevor and Mike, grass-stained and dumbfounded, were standing a few feet away, staring at me.

I scrambled to my feet and ran into the street. Mrs. Carmine, holding a bowl of Smarties, watched me from her front steps and shook her head.

HALLOWEEN

PART III

I WASHED MY FACE WITH FRIGID WATER FROM OUR GARDEN hose, ditched my hat in the bushes that lined our yard, and fetched my bike from the garage. It was barely past eight o'clock. Riding my normal speed, I could get to Gina Rizetti's by eight forty-five. As far as my parents were concerned, I was still out trick-or-treating with Mike and Trevor. I had until ten. It was possible.

On the streets the battles were still raging, so I pedaled as far from large groups as I could and rode on grass when necessary until I reached the bike path on the south end of the neighborhood. This was a risk. The bike path went for miles—under train trestles and near the banks of the Oriskanny, past nature trails and county parks—but there were no lights along it and I had never ridden it at night.

The stars cast only ten feet of visibility in front of me, and to my sides the brambles and shrubs were impenetrable.

If someone was hidden in them, I would never have known. So I didn't even bother looking around. Eyes ahead, I hummed to myself and rode as fast as I could.

My legs were aching, but I couldn't stop them moving. I couldn't think about anything other than my anger. The humming was supposed to calm me, yet it only provided a sound track to the feelings. The song I was humming was one that Fiona used to play from the tape recorder on her handlebars. It was the same one she had taped over when she recorded her message for me. I didn't realize that right away, but when I did, I hummed louder and I pedaled faster.

I arrived at Gina's a few minutes earlier than predicted. At night, her neighborhood earned its seedy reputation. Men sat in upholstered chairs on their porches, smoking and watching the street. Their drags were long and menacing and made the cigarette tips glow a sickly orange. Cars moved slowly, as if they weren't really going anywhere. They were nothing but steel wolves, out roaming.

Dogs were chained up next to rusted rebar and sheets of plywood and corrugated aluminum. They were mutts, but they all looked to be at least part German shepherd. The pathetic poster board Halloween decorations were here too, in even greater numbers than in my neighborhood. Some had been used to partially cover broken windows or missing shingles. I wondered if the homeowners would swap them out for Thanksgiving decorations as soon as the sun came up.

Cars were parked along the street and in the grass at Gina's house. I didn't have a lock, so I laid my bike down in the yard, flipped the plastic kiddie pool over it, and headed to the front door. Instead of a doorbell there were a few frayed wires sticking out of a ragged hole. The door was open a crack, so I pushed it all the way and stepped inside.

The party was nowhere near as wild as I'd expected. A group of five teenagers was lounging on a sectional, eating from bags of candy and watching a machete-wielding maniac on TV. Only a couple of them turned their glassy eyes to me. One cocked her chin, while the other shouted, "Someone's li'l bro is here!"

Down a hall in the kitchen, another group was gathered around a card table. Stalks of smoke rose and flowered as music played from a small boombox on top of the fridge.

"You gotta be kiddin' me!" Kyle stood up from the table and opened his arms. "Alistair Cleary, come for his vision quest."

I took one step into the hall and stopped. I leaned against the wall and motioned for Kyle to meet me. After a day of running and riding and fighting, my body was ready to implode.

Kyle dropped his cigarette into a plastic cup and pushed past his friends. He strutted down the hall toward me, but when he saw my face, his fell. "What gives, buddy?"

"Hide me somewhere."

"Come again?"

"I think I'm about to cry."

There were no tears, but I sat hunched over on a race car bed fighting off the tremors in my chest. We were in Gina's son's room. From the toys on the floor—windups, simple puzzles, stuffed animals—I guessed the kid was three or four years old. He wasn't there, though. It was only Kyle, and Kyle didn't say a word. He sat on a wooden trunk and watched me.

The door opened and a young woman poked her head inside. "Everything cool?"

"Yeah," Kyle said. "Give us a minute."

The woman's face was painted white like a skull, with dark rings around her eyes, black swaths across her nose, and crooked teeth drawn in over her lips. She had frizzy red hair with tall bangs and she was swirling a half-full beer bottle that she wore on the tip of her index finger. When she saw me sitting on the bed, she smiled widely. Her real teeth had a retainer bar over them.

"Are you Gina?" I asked.

"The one and only."

"Thank you . . . for letting me . . . visit." Each word came out more pathetic than the one before it, and I was sure that she would laugh at me.

But she didn't. She stepped into the room and joined me on the bed. She wrapped an arm around me and replied, "Doors are always open here."

"I think the kid needs some alone time," Kyle explained. "Seems like he's had a crap day."

"She can stay," I said. "Actually . . . I want her to stay."

Gina rubbed my shoulder. Each of her fingers had a ring or two on it. "See that, Dwyer?" she said. "Little charmer likes me. Can I get you anything . . . ?"

Kyle filled in the blank. "Alistair."

"Alistair," Gina echoed. "There's a famous witch with that name. You spell it like he does?"

I had no idea who she was talking about. "The regular way," I said.

She smiled again and sipped her beer and then set it on a plastic crate that did the duty of a nightstand. "We got juice, milk, soda, and *adult* beverages. Anything in the fridge is fair game. Whatever you want."

"Thank you, ma'am."

Her bone-white face lit up like she was at a surprise party. "Hear that, Dwyer? He called me ma'am! Stay forever if you want, big guy. Teach my son a thing or two about manners."

"He's good people," Kyle said. "Always has been."

It was the last thing I wanted to hear at that moment. "I'm not always good," I shot back.

"Ooooo, polite and a bad boy," Gina cooed. "Watch out, ladies."

I pulled myself away from her grasp, puffed my shoulders up, and said, "I fought a kid today. Because he bad-mouthed my girlfriend."

"That's what I like to hear," Kyle said, and he leaned in to get a closer look at me. He must have seen a scratch or something else that met his approval, because he nodded and leaned back.

Gina grabbed her beer and raised it in a toast. "To gentlemen."

She was drinking alone, but that didn't seem to bother her. She took the remains down in a few gulps and set the empty back on the crate.

"This kid was saying terrible things," I went on. "But that's nothing compared to what her uncle has done. He's a sick man."

Gina paused. "What's that?"

"My girlfriend's uncle. He does . . . awful things."

She didn't open her mouth right away. Underneath her lips she was running her tongue back and forth, sending a wave across the skeletal teeth. When she did finally speak, it was with a soft anger. "What are you saying, Al?"

The day had poked a hole in me. As soon as I started talking, I couldn't stop. "Her uncle. He's a war veteran and he probably saw lots of stuff that messed up his brain. He's from here, but he's been gone for a long time, only just came home after traveling all around. Germany, I think. Pacific Northwest. Maybe Argentina. All over. I don't know if he's on drugs or into Satan or anything, but he's got tattoos and black shirts and listens to heavy metal."

"I got black shirts and sometimes I listen to metal," Kyle said. "If I had the cash, I'd get a tattoo. Doesn't say much about the man."

"And he does things!" I snapped. "To kids! He goes from place to place and he . . . I don't know what he does with them after, but . . . there might be a river. Rivers are important, I think. My girlfriend, his niece, she knows about it all. She knows the kids' names, where they're from. They're regular kids who didn't do anything, and he comes for them when they're sleeping, and no one ever sees them again. And then there's Fiona's grandmother. She died, and I don't know if it was a natural death or if . . . What I'm trying to say is that Fiona lives with this man and she knows what he does, and he knows that she knows, and I can't do anything about it." The tears finally arrived and, like the words, I couldn't hold them back. "I can't do anything about it. I can't do anything."

"You're serious," Kyle said softly.

Gina was quick to fish a tiny T-shirt from a mesh hamper next to the crate. As she handed it to me, she said, "It'll be okay, big guy."

The T-shirt was covered in dinosaur decals. Wiping my face with it felt a bit like running sandpaper over my skin, but for soaking up tears, it performed admirably. "Thank you," I told her.

Gina waited until I set the T-shirt down to ask, "What I really need to know is where you heard all this stuff."

"My girlfriend told me," I said through my sniffles. "She makes up these crazy stories about some magical land and some monster called the Riverman. I don't know if it's the way she deals with it or what, but she's basically told me about all the kids. There's a newspaper article about one of the girls. She's been gone for almost a year."

"Holy crap." Kyle ran his hands up and down his thighs like he was trying to warm them up.

"And this guy lives with the family?" Gina asked. "So her parents don't suspect anything?"

"I wouldn't think so."

"Anyone told the cops?"

"The neighbor, Mrs. Carmine, she told the cops that she doesn't trust him, but I don't think she knows how bad he really is. I'm not sure there's solid evidence."

"So this is a bunch of speculating?"

I shook my head. "No. I'm sure. I'm sure. Any other option is crazy. Anything else doesn't make sense."

Kyle exhaled a long breath and stared at the hamper. Gina stood, and as she did, she picked up one of her son's stuffed animals, a koala with a Matchbox car in its pouch. She tossed it to herself as she walked around the room.

"Laura Niles had this boyfriend, Clint, who hit her sometimes," she said. "In front of her kids. Whenever he was angry and blind-drunk. She called the cops at first, but there was only so much they could do. Even if they arrested the sleaze, it's not like he'd ever get convicted. No evidence, really. Her word against his. Laura threatened to leave him, and he threatened back, saying he'd do things to her kids. Disgusting things.

"One night when Laura couldn't take it anymore, she

put bleach in Clint's glass instead of Absolut. Guy was so blasted that when she dared him to take it down in one gulp, he didn't realize what he was drinking. Stomach got all tore up, and he was in the hospital for a month. He couldn't remember what happened. And this time it was his word against hers. Like always, cops didn't do a thing. So Laura took her kids and she left him there.

"These days Clint's got a bag on his hip for a toilet, and you better believe he doesn't go hitting and threatening any women, because no woman will have a thing to do with this leaky slime."

"Karma," Kyle said.

Gina stopped tossing the koala and held it under her arm. "It isn't karma, Dwyer. It's a woman looking out for herself and for her kids because no one else is looking out for them."

"I'm looking out for my girlfriend," I said.

"Arc you?" she asked.

"I'm here asking for help."

"While she's at home with the perv?"

"Lay off," Kyle said. "He's being a stand-up guy. He cares about this chick."

"I'm sure he does," Gina said. "But this 'chick' has gotta care about herself, because Al ain't always gonna be there."

I wished I could always be there, but she was right, and my response came without hesitation, without the fear that I was overstepping the line. "I should probably get something for protection, then. Right?" I asked.

Gina raised her eyebrows and a shoulder and twisted her mouth into an expression that said *There are worse ideas.*

"Jeeeesus," Kyle said. "You can't be serious. You're not talking about what I think you're talking about?"

"What?" Gina said. "We're talking about protection. Defending the innocent."

"We're talking about kids!"

"How old are you?" Gina asked me.

"Twelve."

"And your girl?"

I paused. "Four . . . thir . . . around thirteen."

"I was pregnant with Brody when I was fourteen. Had him when I was fifteen. These aren't kids, Kyle."

Kyle put his head in his hands and ran his fingers through his oily hair. When his hands reached the back of his neck, he massaged it and asked me, "Are you really serious about this?"

I nodded.

"And going to the cops ain't gonna work?"

I shook my head.

"And does my brother know about this?"

"No."

"And does anyone except your girl, and me, and Gina, and her koala bear know about this?"

"No one."

Kyle kept massaging his neck as he bent it back and

closed his eyes. "What about money?" he asked. "Do you have money?"

I had maybe fifteen dollars and a gift certificate to the Skylark. "Not really."

"Well, I have money. So I tell you what we're gonna do. Gina, is this something you can get?"

"I know a person," she said.

Kyle lifted his head and looked at me. "Okay. Then *I* will buy this thing. *I* will hold on to it. And you and your girl will only see it if *I* decide you need to see—"

"If the girl is in danger, Kyle, then—"

"Gina! This is gonna be my money and my decision! If the chick's in danger, then I'll handle it!"

Kyle stood up. Gina took a step back. I stayed where I was.

"Chill out, man," Gina said, her pupils widening, making her eyes even darker. "We're all on the same side."

"You don't have a kid brother," Kyle said.

"And you don't have a kid," Gina shot back.

I didn't know enough about their relationship to guess what might happen next. All I knew was I didn't have enough money and I really wanted this conversation to end.

"Let's do it Kyle's way," I told them as I stood up and got ready to leave. "I want to do it Kyle's way. And let's do it soon."

Wednesday, November 1

SCHOOL THE NEXT DAY WAS AWASH WITH DISPATCHES FROM the Battleground. There were skateboard chases, lip-locks behind toolsheds, close calls with the police. My tussle with Trevor didn't make the front page, and I was determined to keep it that way. I knew it was best to avoid Trevor and Mike, at least for the foreseeable future.

And then there was Charlie.

Charlie returned to school like an astronaut from space. His shoulder supporting a bag that held his new laptop computer and his hands still wrapped in gauze, he walked into the cafeteria at lunch and Ken Wagner shouted, "Captain Catpoop!" But it was a triumphant shout—a hero's shout—and Charlie seized upon it. He spun his hands, threw his arms out like wings, and bowed low. The laptop bag scraped against the ground.

"Sorry, everyone," he announced. "No more high fives. High twos. Maybe threes."

There were laughs, some awkward, some genuine. Far too many in my mind, but my mind was in another place.

As Charlie found a seat with some kids who would have never spoken to him during his ten-fingered days, I roamed around the circular tables. Fay-Renee and Kendra, huddled together and playing a game of cat's cradle, shot me daggers as I passed them, so I headed to the periphery, hoping for a place where I could fade into the walls. That's where I found Fiona.

She sat alone at a long table eating yogurt and an apple. Our eyes met, and it was like I was looking at a new person, or maybe she was looking at a new person. In any case, things felt different. She pulled out a chair for me.

"Long time no see," she said.

"How you been?" I asked.

"Not bad. Skipped out on Halloween. Not really into that scene anymore."

"Your family?"

"They're fine. Taking it day by day." She brushed hair away from her face and looked out into the cafeteria. "Your ol' pal Charlie makes quite an entrance."

"Yeah, well . . . he's a celebrity now. Speaking of friends, why aren't you sitting with yours?"

Fiona shrugged. "On a break from them for a while. Running out of things to talk about."

It seemed a bit harsh, but I knew that girls could be fickle, so I nodded like I understood. Then I took my lunch out of the bag and lined it up in front of me. Oatmeal cookies. Orange. PB&J. None of it was particularly appealing, and one by one I placed them all back in the bag. "You wanna go to dinner?" I finally blurted out.

Fiona pointed to her yogurt. "Looks like we're already going to lunch."

"No," I said. "Like *out* to dinner. At a restaurant. The Skylark."

She considered it for a moment. "I wouldn't be opposed to such a thing."

"Tonight. Let's do it tonight. Six thirty. The Skylark."

"Why tonight?"

"Because we can't wait any longer." Before she had a chance to back out, I pulled one of her tricks. I scooped up my lunch and walked away.

Out on the floor and at the counter in the Skylark, the waitresses and customers kept things at a squawky din, but in the back booths where it was deep and comfortable, conversations could be private. I arrived early and opted for a back booth.

"We'll be needing two menus," I told the hostess, and she winked her approval.

Hands folded in my lap, I waited. I read the menu about three or four times even though I knew what I was going to order—my Skylark standard: a turkey club. I gazed across the restaurant through the wall of windows to the parking lot. There were half a dozen cars there, and I decided to occupy myself by memorizing as many license plates as possible.

CAZ1303 . . . CAZ1303 . . . CAZ1303 . . . CAZ1303 . . . MAN—

My concentration shattered as soon as Fiona coasted by. She slowed near the windows, moved her legs to the side, and hopped off while her bike was still moving, landing midstride and keeping her hands on the grips. After she guided the bike into the rack, she took a moment to straighten her clothes, then her hair, running her fingers through it while using a window as a mirror. She stood there for a few seconds, talking to herself. I couldn't read her lips, but the words seemed hurried. She took a deep breath and turned to the door.

The hostess showed Fiona to our booth, and I greeted her by standing and shaking her hand. I regretted it immediately, but Fiona smiled, and I realized that this was the first time since we were kids that I'd held her hand. Her fingers felt so slight.

"Nice to see you, Alistair."

"And you."

Fiona was wearing a denim skirt and white leggings. Her sweater was purple with little white diamond designs and it puffed at the shoulders. It wasn't as dressy as what she wore to the wake, but it was certainly dressier than what I had on. Jeans. Sweatshirt. Sneakers. I sat down so she wouldn't notice.

"I haven't been here in years," she said as she followed my lead.

"We come every few weeks. Keri likes the chili. She likes that it's beany."

Beany? Incalculably stupid thing to say, but then again, it was a struggle to say anything.

Fiona gave the menu a look. "A burger is always a good bet."

I responded with the first thing that came to mind. "Keri, my sister, she can be stupid and mean one second and then smart and nice the next, and I never know when she's gonna be what."

Fiona lowered the menu, but didn't set it down. "Okay. That must be . . . annoying for you. I'm sorry to hear that."

Water hadn't arrived yet, so I couldn't gulp away my embarrassment. I was forced to explain. "I'm not saying . . . I was just trying to tell you about something that bothers me. Because . . . you should know that we all have things that bother us."

Again, incalculably stupid, but Fiona was kind. "Thank you, Alistair," she said. "You make me feel less alone."

"Forget it."

"What? Why?"

"I'm talking about stupid little things, and you've got, well, the Riverman and—"

She swatted my hand playfully with the menu. "I don't want to talk about that."

"But that's what we talk about."

"And that's the problem. We should be talking about you. I hate to admit it, but I know so little about you."

The waitress saved me from responding. She arrived with glasses of water, but without a smile. "Can I get you kids any drinks to start?"

"Iced tea," Fiona said. "Plain. No sugar. Slice of lemon."

"The same," I said, even though I rarely drank iced tea, and never without sugar. The waitress took a mental note and was gone as quickly as she'd arrived.

"This is nice," Fiona said. "Nice and normal."

"It's just the Skylark."

"I know that, sweetie. Believe me. That's what makes it so nice."

Sweetie? Fiona had never called me that before. Was she feeling what I was feeling? Did she want what I wanted? I tested the waters. "I've been thinking about you a lot."

"Oh, Alistair, that's so . . . nice. But let's not talk about me. Let's talk about you. What did you dress up as on Halloween?"

Again, I was caught off guard. "I . . . I . . . It wasn't a costume, really . . . Trevor Weeks and Mike—"

"You went as a ninja," Fiona said confidently. "How could you go as anything else?"

There was a bruise on my thigh, a cloud of purple and

black that had risen a few hours after my fight with Trevor. It was tender, and I pressed on it to remind myself of everything that had happened the night before. "I didn't go as anything. I was only out there defending you."

"Alistair, Alistair, Alistair . . ." Fiona's voice trailed off with a sigh. Why did she keep saying my name?

The iced tea appeared in front of us, green straws sticking out like bamboo in a muddy pond, lemon slices sipping from the rim. "You kids know what you'd like yet?" the waitress asked.

"You bet," Fiona said. "I'll have a cheeseburger. Medium. And instead of salt potatoes, can I get onion rings?"

"Sure can. And you, hon?"

"Turkey club. A regular turkey club," I said as I squeezed my lemon slice over my drink and took a sip. It was unbearably bitter. I started to reach for the sugar dispenser, but resisted the temptation. If this was what Fiona was drinking, then I was drinking it too.

"Medium cheeseburger and a regular old club. Coming right up." Mental note taken, the waitress abandoned us again.

I took another sip to see if the second time was better. It was worse, and I must have winced. Fiona pushed the sugar toward me. She nodded her consent.

"How's Charlie doing?" she asked.

I sent a stream of sugar into my tea. "I don't care about Charlie."

"Really? I thought you guys were best buds."

"Not anymore."

"What happened?"

I sipped again—much better—and I shrugged. "He's Charlie. He'll always be Charlie."

She swirled her drink with her straw and said, "People can change."

I wasn't sure if this was small talk or if she was hinting at something. "Ain't that the truth," I replied.

"Soooo . . . any big tests coming up?"

It was the kind of thing that my mom asked at stoplights, the sort of question that deserved no better an answer than *I have no idea, lay off.* For Fiona to ask it was, at best, an insult. I couldn't take this anymore.

"Who gives a crap about tests?" I said. "Why are we talking like this? Why aren't we talking about the Riverman? A few days ago you said we can't stop him, but I know for sure that if I—"

Fiona put up a hand. "Not here. While we're here, let's be a couple of friends. Having a meal. Talking about things friends talk about. I want you to tell me about what's going on in your life. I want you to tell me stories about Thessaly. Things I might not know about it."

"I . . . I . . . don't wanna tell you—"

"Then I *need* you to tell me. Don't ask me why. *Please* . . . just talk."

And there it was, and it was back, the Fiona I knew so

well, the Fiona that flipped my switch and turned me into a sucker. It was in her eyes, of course, and in her voice. It was an aura around us that made me feel like I was the only person in her life who mattered.

"That's what you need?" I sighed.

"Right now, that's all I need," she said.

So I talked.

I told her about Charlie. I told her about his plagiarism. I told her about Keri and how she could be the worst sister and the best sister wrapped into one. I told her about what classes I was taking, what homework was giving me fits. I told her about memories my mom had of Thessaly from her days as a kid, about when the Oriskanny flooded and she and her cousin rowed to town on an inflatable raft. I even told her that sometimes I ate carrots dipped in ketchup and watched soap operas because I liked it when characters got amnesia. It was meaningful stuff and mundane stuff and any stuff that came to my mind. Fiona listened to it all like it was some brilliant and epic novel. She kept her responses to "Really?" and "Go on" and "Tell that one again." She laughed at the right moments and never stopped looking at me, even when she was eating her burger, the juices running down her wrist.

Dinner led to dessert, sundaes with all the toppings. The more I rambled on, the more I forgot what had led us to that restaurant in the first place. I had never talked to anyone about myself for so long, and I had never known anyone to listen so intently. As our spoons scraped the last bits from our ice cream dishes, it felt like we were coming to the end of something huge. Maybe we were.

The bike ride home was only a couple of miles, but we took it slow, detouring on less trafficked roads and utilizing the wind to minimize our pedaling. We rode side by side and didn't say much. The crickets had packed it in for the year. The only sound was the whir of our wheels.

On a dark stretch of road a few hundred yards from home, Fiona's chain fell off. We pulled over next to a pile of leaves to fix it. Kneeling by the bike, I found myself as close to Fiona as I had ever been. I handed her the chain, and she hooked it to a tooth of the sprocket. When she turned her head back, I closed my eyes and leaned in.

Images of us rolling in the leaves splashed across my eyelids, and I led with my lips.

"Hey now," she said, pushing me away.

"I thought . . ."

"Oh, buddy." She sighed. "I know what you thought. And maybe when I was your age."

"Why do you say things like that? You *are* my age. We've been the same age forever, and we'll be the same age forever. You don't have to hide things anymore. I'm here for you and I can protect you. And whatever you've experienced, however old that makes you feel, well, I can make sure you feel young again."

Fiona stood up and brushed off her knees. She grabbed

the banana seat and lifted her back tire off the ground. She stepped on the pedal and eased the crank around to remount the chain.

"I'm twenty-six years old," she said plainly. "I'm more than twice as old as you."

"What?"

"We're not the same anymore, sweetie," she said. "We never will be. And I haven't told you my entire story. You should really hear the rest."

THE LEGEND OF FIONA LOOMIS, PART V

Fiona wanted to tell Alistair Cleary about Aquavania immediately, but she also wanted to be sure he was the right person to tell. After burying the map at the edge of his yard, Fiona watched him for a few weeks. Almost every afternoon she rode her bike around their neighborhood, passing his house three or four times. She had a small cassette recorder taped to her handlebars and she played music dubbed from her uncle's collection, a bunch of loud songs that told the world to stay far away.

She would see Alistair in his yard, sometimes in his garage. She would see him through windows, eating meals and watching television. She would see him on his walk home, arguing and roughhousing with his sister. Whenever Alistair looked at her, Fiona looked up at the trees. She knew this must have appeared strange, but she figured being strange was better than being a spy. Because that's what she was, a spy.

She wasn't sure what she was hoping to uncover, though. Something to prove Alistair was clever? Or villainous? Maybe something to prove he was brave?

She didn't see anything other than a kid being a kid.

The next time she was called to Aquavania, she invited Toby to join her on a swing made of vines, where they munched on star fruit and let the breeze tussle their hair.

"I don't know if I picked the right person," she told him.

With his mouth full, Toby responded, "How . . . ya know he's . . . right person . . . mm-less you . . . give 'im a chance?"

"I want to be sure he has secrets," Fiona said. "That he keeps secrets."

Toby swallowed and replied, "Everyone keeps some secrets. Nobody tells everything."

"Apart from you," Fiona said.

"Exception to the rule."

Fiona had followed Jenny's advice. She had shut herself off from the other worlds in Aquavania. She kept her wishes to material items, sent no signals, went nowhere near the folds. But the isolation was getting to her. She wasn't enjoying being in Aquavania anymore. To know the Riverman was still out there, draining the souls of others while she hid, caused her too much guilt to carry.

She decided to take a chance on Alistair. Her spying had at least taught her that he was still the quiet guy she remembered, and that he didn't have many friends. To hook him, she appealed to his storytelling instincts. She recorded an invitation to write her biography and delivered it as a present.

Alistair bit.

Within a few days, Fiona was in his room, sitting on his bed, starting from the beginning, dictating her earliest memories. He seemed genuinely interested, but when she reached the part with the talking radiators, he got spooked. He asked her to leave.

It could have, and maybe should have, ended there. But a few days later, Alistair dug up the map and Fiona knew there was no turning back.

Fiona was called to Aquavania, and she invited Toby to join her on the swing again. "I've been careless," she said. "Alistair's sister saw me bury the ammo can. What if the Riverman is in the Solid World too? If some girl knows what I'm doing, then surely the Riverman could figure it out. So I burned the map. I won't let him get his grubby paws on it."

Toby kicked his legs, giving the swing some juice. "Here's a thought," he said. "Why do you have to stop the Riverman?"

It was a question she had never once considered. "Because he's hurting people."

"He's not hurting you."

"Should that matter?"

"Maybe that's all that should matter," Toby said, kicking again and piling on the momentum. "Don't go back to the Solid World. Stay here and don't invite anyone in, and you'll be fine. Is this world not good enough for you?"

Even if she didn't always like what he said, Fiona had always loved Toby. But she didn't love him now. Why was he talking like this?

"Of course this world is good enough for me," she said. "But what about the other worlds? You told me that Aquavania is the place where stories are born. The Riverman is stealing all of those other stories."

"Maybe your story is the only one worth saving," Toby said.

The vines that held the swing were so long that they carried Fiona and Toby high enough to look down on the animals and the waterfalls and so many of the things Fiona had brought to life. All at once, she was ashamed of it. This world was a cliché, a little girl's fantasy, a silly tropical paradise that wasn't worth squat.

"Who are you?" Fiona asked Toby.

"I'm Toby."

"No," she said. "Who are you really?"

"I think you know."

"Maybe, but tell me anyway. Say it out loud."

"I'm you," Toby said. "Everything in your world is you."

Fiona did know this, but not in a conscious way. She knew it in the way that she knew the hair and the fingernails that grew and she cut off were her, and the tears that fell from her eyes and soaked into her clothes were her, and the words that she set loose on the world were her.

"And if I were to wish you away?" Fiona asked.

Toby clasped his hands together and said, "You'll wish me back eventually, in one form or another."

Fiona nodded. "Goodbye, Toby. Be safe," she said. And she jumped off the swing and landed in a pile of dandelion fluff, where she made her most revolutionary wish.

It seemed at first as if Fiona were growing, but she knew that wasn't possible. Toby and the animals and the island and the ocean were getting smaller, contracting around her until it all looked like the insides of a snow globe. An ammo can appeared in Fiona's arms, and she was able to pick up the shrunken world and place it inside.

Fiona was now standing on a flat black plane. The only horizon was the haze of the folds. There was nothing in every direction. She wished a shovel into her hands and she used it to dig a hole. She dropped the ammo can in the hole and buried it. She smoothed out the ground until there was no evidence that it had ever been disturbed.

For the next few weeks she walked, in no particular

direction. And she thought about what she might do next. When she wished something into existence— like food, or a bed—she shrank it down and buried whatever she was finished with, whatever she didn't use or need. It was lonely at first, but she viewed her loneliness as punishment. For losing Chua, and Boaz, and Rodrigo.

When she finally decided to stop walking, she wished for a comfortable chair and desk and a note-book and pen. She sat and wrote her story down, start-ing from the moment that she arrived in Aquavania, up until the moment she was sitting in that chair. And when she finished writing it, she buried that story too.

Then she wrote Chua's story. She wrote every de-tail about Chua's world she could remember. And she wrote about the things that Chua said. And she wrote about Werner. And Boaz. And Rodrigo. And Jenny. And all the kids she'd ever heard about who had come to Aquavania.

It took her a year to write all their stories. Whenever she finished one, she buried it and moved on to the next.

Finally, she decided to write the story of the River-man. She knew nothing about him other than the destruction he had wrought. She figured that after writing about all the kids, she'd have some insight into what drew the Riverman to them.

But it was no use. She started and stopped countless

times. She had no idea what made the Riverman who he was. She had no idea what she would have to do to stop him. She had done everything she could. What else was there?

She decided to go back to the Solid World.

The next day, Alistair approached her in the school cafeteria with an apology. Only a week had gone by in the Solid World since she had first given Alistair that cassette tape, but she had spent over a year in Aquavania during that time. She was fourteen now, and he was still twelve.

"Why don't I come over to your house and we can talk about Aquaville?" he asked. Fiona thought it was cute how he called it Aquaville, and she was charmed that he seemed genuinely sorry and that he wanted to help. Fiona's grandmother, who she called Nana, had taken ill, so she decided it was best if they spoke somewhere other than her house. She suggested the place where they had made their pact, the rock shaped like a frog.

Over the course of a few days, she told Alistair her story. She told him about the missing children. She offered evidence to convince him she wasn't crazy. She asked him to help stop the Riverman.

Alistair was a good listener, and that was perhaps all she wanted at first. Yet the more she spoke to him, the more she realized he cared. He was as invested in this as she was. And by sharing her story, she was discovering things she wasn't able to discover on her own.

For instance, the Riverman's ability to find the children had puzzled Fiona. Somehow he always knew exactly what each kid needed. With Alistair's help, she came to realize that perhaps the Riverman's pen held not only the souls of the children, but also their thoughts. And in that collection of thoughts were the needs and wants and friends and memories of every child he'd ever stolen. Which meant he knew about Fiona. Fiona assumed the only reason he hadn't come for her yet was because there was one thing he didn't know, one thing she hoped that no one knew.

What she needed.

Nana died on the night of Thursday, October 26. She died in her sleep, and that was a relief for everyone. She had lived a long and full life, and it was time. Fiona's dad arranged a wake for Sunday, and her mom rented a cabin in the mountains for two nights. The family was supposed to gather there and reflect on Nana's life.

But like always, the Loomises kept to themselves. Fiona's dad and uncle went deer hunting. Fiona's mom bought produce from a market and passed time by jarring pickles and jam while listening to old records. Derek and Maria drove to a nearby town both mornings, to shop and eat and call friends from a broken pay phone they had discovered that made free long-distance calls.

Fiona spent the days alone on the screened-in

porch, where she made a list of what was good about her life in the Solid World and what was good about her life in Aquavania. She also made a list of her regrets, of things she would do over if she ever had the chance. At the top of that list of regrets was: *I wish I never knew about the Riverman.*

She suspected that many kids in Aquavania shared the same regret. If she was to believe the legends, then she knew the Riverman had been around for ages. So why hadn't someone stopped him yet? Surely kids more powerful and smarter than Fiona had tried. Chua and Rodrigo—even Boaz—were perfect examples.

It became clear to Fiona. Maybe the Riverman couldn't be stopped. Nana's death was inevitable. So maybe the loss of all these kids was inevitable too, and the Riverman was some sort of a balancing force, some kind of necessary evil. Maybe Aquavania couldn't exist without him.

When she returned home, she invited Alistair to the wake. They took a walk in the graveyard that was to be Nana's final resting place. They sat on the steps of a mausoleum and Fiona laid bare her guilt, about how she was to blame for Boaz and Rodrigo's disappearance, about how she had no idea how to find the Riverman, about how she was grasping at straws.

And Alistair asked, "What if I told you I know who the Riverman is?"

And Fiona thought about this. And she decided that it didn't matter. For the first time . . . she didn't care.

She was called to Aquavania that night.

She stayed in Aquavania for twelve years.

"How is that possible?" I asked. "What could you do for twelve years?"

"I can't tell you that," Fiona said. "It's too private. But I grew up. I became a better person. A smarter person. I learned there are things you can control and things you can't."

Fiona climbed onto her bike. It still had the ragged ribbons on the handgrips and slivers of duct tape on the handlebars.

"You matter," I said. "I need you to know that you matter."

"I know that," she said. "And you matter too. I'm going to handle this, on my own, in my own way."

"What are you saying?"

"I'm saying thank you. For being you. But that's all you need to be. I don't need your help anymore. Good night, Alistair."

She kissed the tips of her fingers and pressed them to my forehead. And that was that. She started pedaling, and by the time I had gotten on my bike and caught up, she was turning into her driveway and heading for the darkness of her garage.

Thursday, November 2

———◦—◦———

SCHOOL WAS SLIPPING AWAY FROM ME. MY GRADES WERE proving that. The next morning in math class, I received my latest pop quiz back. I got a 43 percent. A solid F. I had never scored so low.

Mr. Baker left a note at the top of the paper: *See me after the bell.*

I did, and he asked, "What's going on?"

I told him, "Nothing. Maybe I'm not trying hard enough."

"There are tutors."

"I know."

"You look tired, Alistair."

"I know."

"What are we supposed to do here?"

"Try harder, I guess."

Between classes, I scampered through the halls, constantly on the lookout for Trevor, and Mike, and Charlie, and Fiona. I made eye contact with no one. Instead of going to lunch, I smuggled my brown bag into the room near the gym lockers where they kept the wrestling mats. I built a little fort out of some of the smaller mats and ate my PB&J in the dark and soft silence.

I understood the appeal of being alone. I liked it most when I was lying in my bed, door closed, lights off. Sometimes with music playing, sometimes not. Sometimes the wind was enough. But a year alone? In the middle of nowhere? Doing nothing but writing? That didn't seem possible. No one, not even the greatest of hermits, could live like that.

And what about the twelve years? And what about those twelve . . . freaking . . . years!

Back when Fiona was telling me about monsters and missing kids, I could apply it to her uncle, but the latest installment of her tale was indecipherable, and her indifferent attitude toward everything was beyond confusing. Was she truly losing touch with reality? Had she really given up completely? Did that mean I should give up too? I was beginning to feel like I was on Fiona's blank slate. No view of the future. No one to count on but myself. And why even count on myself when Fiona didn't count on me anymore?

We had a test in Social Studies on Reconstruction in the South. I answered maybe nineteen out of the forty questions. Mostly I watched my classmates. I wasn't copying off their papers. It was more about observing them in deep thought. Some of them chewed their pencils or closed their eyes and bit their lips. Kelly Dubois was downing cough drops at what seemed like an alarming rate until I realized she was using the wrappers as crib sheets. The insides were covered in tiny boxy words—an innovative, if strange, cheating technique. I considered snitching on her in order to complete my transformation into the school's pariah, but I didn't have the energy.

I handed my test in unfinished, grabbed a hall pass, and headed to the bathroom. My favorite stall was unoccupied, and I went in without even thinking about the message I'd posted:

In the story of Aquavania there is a Riverman and a girl. Who is the Riverman? Is the girl in danger?

There was a new response, written with the sloppy penmanship of a kid who must have given teachers fits. The identity of the Riverman wasn't revealed, but that didn't matter. A more important question was answered.

The place where stories are born? Who claims to have been there? She is in danger.

I analyzed every word.

The place where stories are born: that was what Fiona called Aquavania.

Who claims to have been there: *claims* was the important word. Liars claim.

She is in danger: she is in danger.

I pulled out my Sharpie and wrote: *Fiona Loomis. What did she tell you? Please let me know ASAP: 798-5291.*

I didn't consider that I might be inundated with prank calls. I needed to hear from someone immediately.

I made it through the rest of the day without saying a word to another person. Even on the walk home with Keri, I kept a few paces ahead as she yammered on about some tiff she was having with Mandy. At home, I took the cordless phone to my room and I got in bed and set it on my chest and waited.

It rang. Not right away, but a few minutes before dinner, sending vibrations through my ribs and into my blood.

"Hello."

"Is this Alistair?"

"It is."

"I got it."

"Kyle?"

"The thing. It's here."

Friday, November 3

Kyle's van was waiting at the end of our driveway when Keri and I left for school the next morning. The engine was purring, and the passenger side door was open. Kyle's hair was wet and combed back. He didn't have to say a word. I climbed in.

"You and Dally have fun at the rumble," Keri teased. "Say hi to Ponyboy for me."

A couple of weeks earlier, I might have responded to such a comment, but what did Keri know? I sneered, and the kid walked west toward school. We men drove east.

"Are we on our way to get it?" I asked.

"No," Kyle said. "I got it already. We're on our way to take care of your problem."

A frost had settled in, dusting the weedy fields and the patches of woods on the outskirts of the neighborhood. We weren't going into town. We were heading the other way, into the infinite hilly stretches of pig and dairy farms, of state forests and Indian reservations.

Kyle wasn't talking, so I assumed it meant he had nothing to say. The radio was tuned to a morning show, and they were playing a parody song about East Germans climbing the Berlin Wall. I didn't really get it, but I laughed anyway, trying to lighten the mood. Kyle's face was stone serious.

"You know what's funny?" he asked.

"No, what?"

"I think I knew from the beginning who you were talking about. From day one. When you were asking questions about how you can tell if a girl is lying or not. It's the Loomis kid, right? I've seen her riding her bike by your house before."

We were going close to eighty down a road with no center stripe. Anything in the van that could rattle did rattle.

"Yeah," I said. "Fiona. But it's not that I wanted to keep her name from you."

"No sweat," Kyle replied. "It's cool. True studs don't kiss and tell. Her older sister, Maria? She's a fox. And your girl is too. Or will be someday. You can see that already."

"Thank you."

This coaxed a grin out of him. "You're welcome."

"Where are we going?" I asked.

He pointed through the buggy windshield. "About five miles down there's a dirt road. Leads to a field where someone cut a runway. Guess you could land a Cessna on it if you had to, but that ain't what the runway is used for. It's for these guys. Grown men, like our parents' age. They go out there with these radio-controlled airplanes and launch 'em and fly 'em all around, up over the fields and the trees and all that. Ain't something normal guys do, but it's Disneyland for these creeps, and I'm guessing they just love to bring little boys and little girls out here too. Show them the loopty-loops and whatnot. Makes me sick."

"And we're going there?"

"Yes sirree, Bob."

The frost was melting and leaving dew on the dying cornstalks that lined the dirt road. At the end of the road was a muddy patch that served as the parking lot. There was only one other vehicle there: Dorian Loomis's truck. We pulled up behind it.

From the lot you could see the runway. It was probably fifty yards long and twenty yards wide, with manicured grass like you'd find on any suburban lawn. Dorian stood in the middle of it, holding a large remote control with multiple levers. A tiny red biplane flew overhead.

"Freakin' Charlie in twenty-five years." Kyle sighed.

"How'd you know he'd be here?"

"After our chat at Gina's, I put two and two together and figured you were talking about this chump. So I followed him yesterday. Plus there's that sticker." Kyle raised his chin to Dorian's truck, and I saw an emblem on the rear window that featured a propeller plane, a golden crest, and the words *The Mini Airmen of Thessaly.*

"What are we doing?" I asked.

"No *we*. Me. *I'm* handling this."

I looked into the back of the van, where it was a land-scape of clothes and burger wrappers. And I checked Kyle's coat, a ratty brown canvas thing with red flannel lining at the collar. I was searching for a gleam or a lump. "You're not gonna . . . ?"

"I'm gonna have a chat with the man. I can be persuasive."

"He was in the Army. He was—"

"He's fat and he's old and plays with toys," Kyle said as he opened his door and jumped out over a puddle. Before shutting it, he pointed at me. "Stay, boy."

I did, and Kyle moved down the path toward the runway, his swagger exaggerated, one arm in front and one in back, swaying to some unheard beat. It was half street corner hustler, half cowboy. Yet it went unnoticed, at least to Dorian, who kept his face to the sky. The sky was a weak blue, a watercolor sky. The acres of fallow land that surrounded the runway were watercolor too—blurred and flat. The only real punch of life was that brilliant red plane.

When Kyle reached the runway, Dorian finally paid attention. He shot Kyle a sharp wave, the exact same wave as the one he'd given me on Halloween night. The van windows were tinted, and I doubt Dorian could have recognized me, but I still didn't want him to know that someone was in there watching. I slumped down as far as I could while still maintaining a view through the driver's side window.

The two talked for a bit, but didn't look at each other. They were both watching the plane. It dipped and twirled, and I was amazed that such a thing could exist. I owned a few remote control cars, but they moved slower than a jog and could barely make it to the end of the driveway and back before their batteries ran out.

All I could hear was the high-pitched buzzing of the plane, which sounded a lot like a weed whacker. I would have given anything to know what Kyle and Dorian were saying. If their postures didn't seem friendly, they at least didn't seem hostile. They looked like two men waiting for a bus, chatting to break the boredom. On occasion, Kyle was capable of having a calm head, and I desperately needed this to be one of those times.

The violence in Kyle, the rage, I'd felt it before, lingering on his breath and beneath his twitching fingers. But I'd never seen it. Charlie had never seen it either, or at least that's what he'd said: "He's decent to me most of the time, never hit me or anything like that." But Charlie also told me that the rumors were true, that Kyle had indeed broken a bottle over a kid's head at a party, that he'd definitely pulled his butterfly knife more than once, and that he'd come home countless times with bruises and scratches that he explained away as injuries from pickup football games.

So when the rage came, it didn't come as a surprise, but it gutted me nonetheless. Kyle lifted his right arm and brought it down like a scythe and cut the remote control out of Dorian's hand. The remote control hit the ground, rolled, but didn't break. It stopped a couple of yards from Dorian, upside down in the grass. The two men faced each other, fists clenched. *Buzzzzzzz* went the plane, now spiraling out of view.

Dorian tested the tension of the air, bending his knees and leaning forward, ready to pounce. Kyle peeled the left half of his jacket from his body, showed me the outside and Dorian the inside. I saw nothing and I couldn't say for sure what Dorian saw, but I could easily guess. Dorian stopped, raised his hands, and drew back.

Buzzzzzzz . . .

Crack!

It sounded like a tree trunk broken in a storm. Glass splintered, veins formed. Red! In my face and then falling away. I flinched, not knowing at first whether it was a bird, a bullet, or what. It was the model plane. It had crashed into the windshield and was rolling down to the hood. The buzzing was gone. The plane was broken, dead.

And I could hear voices now.

"Two in the skull! That's all it will take!" Kyle yelled. Hands up, Dorian trembled.

Kyle zipped his jacket, turned back to me, and started walking. It was no longer a swagger. It was a march, methodical and tight. Over Kyle's shoulder, I could still see Dorian, bloated and scared and not doing a thing, and through the windshield, on the hood, I could see the wing of the plane.

It was clear now. This was the wing I spied poking out from beneath the towel in the front of Dorian's truck that night. It wasn't some kid's toy. It was *his* toy.

When Kyle reached the van, he grabbed the broken plane and flung it sideways like so much trash. The key was poised in the ignition, and I reached over and gave it a twist.

Ca . . . ca . . . caaaaa . . .

Nothing. Kyle opened the door, slid into the driver's seat, stomped the clutch, and employed his expert touch.

Pu . . . pu . . . pu . . . purooooom.

"Pathetic coward," he growled, and he fed the truck gas and jammed it into gear. The wheels spun for a second in the mud, gripped and dug, and then we flew backward. Kyle spun the wheel, slapped the shift, and we were off.

At the Skylark, Kyle bought me a piece of apple pie and a coffee, which I loaded with sugar until it tasted more like hot chocolate. School was out of the question by now, but we hadn't yet concocted a suitable lie to explain my truancy. We needed some time to right our heads.

"Why won't you tell me what you said to him?" I asked.

"Didn't say much," Kyle replied as he forked the yolks of his sunny-side-ups. They bled yellow across the plate until a wall of sausage dammed them up. "Actions speak louder. A picture paints a ton of words."

"You didn't leave it in the van, did you? You still have it on you right now, don't you?"

He dipped a corner of toast in the yolk and pointed it at me. "Not another peep about it." He chomped the toast like he was killing it.

The Skylark was full of old people and a few workmen who sat at the counter and ate efficiently. No one seemed to be listening in on our conversation, but I understood Kyle's hesitation.

"Thank you," I said. "For everything."

Kyle chewed and nodded. He lifted his mug and clinked it against mine. Then he dug into his pocket and laid its contents on the table. Keys, coins, a napkin, and a paper clip. At the end of our booth was a miniature jukebox. Kyle continued to gorge himself as he turned the knob and flipped through the little pages of songs. When he found one he liked, he fed the machine a nickel.

A guitar riff, playful and quick, shuffled out and across our table. This was the type of music my parents listened to, and even though Kyle had only six years on me, choosing a song like this made him seem so much older.

"That thing I told you a little while ago," he said between bites. "It might be happening sooner rather than later."

"Oh." I had wanted to forget about "that thing," but I couldn't. Every move Kyle had made in the last two weeks I had associated with his desire to escape Thessaly in one way or another.

"Not because of this morning," Kyle went on. "It's just time."

"You spent your money, though," I said.

"Some of it. An investment. Will make me more cash in the long run."

I didn't ask him to elaborate. I didn't want to know. "I took Fiona here the other night," I told him instead. "It was a date, I guess."

"You pay?"

"I did. Well, with a gift certificate."

"Good enough."

"She appreciated it," I said. "She appreciated just being here and knowing what was going on with me and hearing stories about Thessaly."

Kyle eyed me suspiciously. "Your point?"

I took a bite of pie as the singer sang about his one true love. "It's not such a bad place."

With a contemptuous sniff, Kyle said, "Someday you'll be telling that to the mirror. And the mirror ain't gonna buy it either."

We drove forty minutes to the nearest multiplex, bought two tickets for a matinee, and spent the rest of the day hopping from screen to screen, checking out the latest movies. There were talking babies and a movie about a bear and one about a guy made of electricity. They were okay, but after the third one I was getting pretty bored and I pitied Kyle if this was his typical day.

Driving home, we didn't say much, mostly kept our comments focused on the one-liners and the explosions. Kyle dropped me on the edge of the neighborhood where no one would see us.

"If Uncle acts up, you know my number," he said as I stepped down from the van.

"I'm sure you scared him straight," I said. But I wasn't sure. If I was wrong about the plane, then what else was I wrong about? And as Kyle drove away, I began to go over every little incident in my head. Our rides in the van. My talks with Fiona. Dorian in the backyard, Dorian the deviant. The sleepover and the box in the road. The wake. Halloween. Today.

At the library, there was a shelf of Choose Your Own Adventure novels. Charlie liked to read those books backward, searching for the happy endings first and figuring out the path of least resistance. I always read them the correct way, and I'd invariably find myself lost in a cave or bitten by a scorpion. I rarely made it through without a misstep.

If only I could read my life backward, I thought.

When I got home, the sun was still up but low. Keri was in the driveway with a can of silver spray paint, coating a group of Cabbage Patch Kids that were laid out on a sheet of newspaper.

"What in the heck happened to you?" she asked.

"Nothing."

"Mom and Dad are crazy worried." She held her nose and deployed another layer of paint. "Don't worry, though. I'm not a snitch. I didn't say a word about your ride with the Fonz."

"Thanks."

My parents were in the kitchen, speaking to each other in hushed tones. As soon as the door shut behind me, they clammed up. They looked at me like I was a stranger.

"So?" my dad said after a short silence.

"I know, I know, I know."

"You know?" my mom said with a gasp. "I'm told you never showed up for school. I call home. No answer. I drive home and you're not here. And you're telling me you know? *You know?*"

"I'm sorry," I said. "I've had some tough things going on."

"Skipping school is your solution?" my dad asked. "Where'd you go?"

"I don't know. Nowhere. Walking."

"Walking? All day?" my dad asked.

"And what's this Mrs. Carmine is telling us about a fight on Halloween?" my mom added.

"Oh come on, like you've never made mistakes!" I snapped.

"Of course we have," my mom said. "But this is not you. *This? So not you.*"

"Who is it, then? Who am I?"

When they didn't answer right away, I stormed out of the room. "There will be consequences," my dad yelled to me, but I kept moving.

The cordless phone was sitting on the dining room table. It rang as I passed, and I snatched it up and barked, "Hello."

"I'm sorry. I need you to know I'm sorry."

I didn't respond. The timing of the call couldn't have been worse.

"Alistair? Are you still there? You don't have to say anything if you don't want to. But we're best friends, and best friends are honest with each other. I don't know why I do the things I do sometimes. I never mean to hurt anyone. I don't mean to hurt you."

I couldn't listen to this anymore. I pulled the phone away from my head and held it at arm's length.

"Screw you, Charlie!"

I hung it up.

My room was the only place I felt safe, and I stayed there all night. I skipped dinner, and every time my mom or dad came to my door saying "We need to talk to you" and "Everything is going to be okay" and "We're not angry as much as we're concerned," I responded with "Please leave me alone!" over and over again.

Not long after dark, I turned off my light and crawled into bed. I punched my mattress to burn away my anxiety and I flopped onto my back, closed my eyes, and tried to listen to my pulse as my blood pumped through my neck, across my temples, and into my scalp. I have no idea what time it was when I finally fell asleep.

SATURDAY, NOVEMBER 4

———⸱◆⸱———

THERE'S ANOTHER STORY MY DAD OFTEN TELLS.

It's about his college friend Peggy. After graduation, Peggy got her doctorate in botany with a concentration in desert plants. Botanists do a lot of fieldwork, and the young scientist spent a good chunk of her time in the American Southwest. She preferred to work alone and without the hassle of permits, so she often parked her car along dirt roads and set out on foot with a pack of supplies that could sustain her for a few days.

On one such solo expedition, she was eight miles south of the U.S. border when she came upon an interesting collection of cacti. She didn't have the time to study and collect samples and make it back to the car before dark, so she laid out a sleeping bag for the night. No tent was needed. Rain and bugs were rarely a problem, and she preferred a roof of stars to a roof of nylon. Sure, it could get cold, but she had a wool hat and, as every boyfriend had told her, her body always ran as hot as a furnace.

When Peggy woke the next morning, her body was running hotter than ever, particularly in the abdomen. She unzipped the bag to let the cool morning breeze waft away the heat, and there, to her surprise and horror, was a rattlesnake on her belly.

Peggy had heard about snakes sneaking under the hoods of cars and soldiering through cold nights by sleeping on warm engines. This predicament, however, was something she had never contemplated. The snake was probably six feet long and as thick as Peggy's dainty wrists. Curled up—its head tucked down in the center and its rattle draped over the top of the coil—it was about the size of a dinner plate.

She was lucky that the snake was a sound sleeper. Opening the bag had done little to rouse it. Peggy didn't want to take any other chances, so she held her breath and clenched her muscles. Unfortunately, this had the opposite effect. Her breathing—the up and down motion of her stomach—had been like rocking a cradle. Once it halted, the snake stirred.

The rattle rose first, a periscope seeking out a disturbance in the water. Peggy could feel the body expanding and spreading, and she could see the scales moving to accommodate the new shape. It would be only a matter of seconds before the head popped up to say *good morning*. Thinking fast and acting faster was of the essence.

Three. Two. One.

Peggy grabbed the rattle and tore the beast from her body. The snake snapped like a whip, and Peggy released it at the ideal moment. It somersaulted, its body undulating in the air, and it landed on the bend of a giant saguaro cactus, where the needles impaled the reptile's soft underbelly.

Gasping, Peggy jumped to her feet and ran her hands all over her body. Everything was intact. Tears and laughter burst forth, and she pointed at the creature that was now writhing away its last moments of life, pinned to the cactus.

"I win! I win, you slithering piece of—"

And another snake bit Peggy on the ankle.

It was a little bugger and its bite felt no worse than a bee sting. Peggy shook her foot in annoyance, but when she saw the other snake stealing away into the brush and she noticed the two red marks near her heel, she knew that fate was having a grand laugh.

She rifled through her pack to find her first aid supplies. Tearing them open, she remembered a note held by magnets to her refrigerator door: *Buy snakebite kit.*

The note was still there. Like so many errands, it was one Peggy neglected. With no towns nearby, her only hope was to walk the eight miles to the border, then the other three to her car. Peggy might have been a procrastinator, but she was no quitter. Once her tears had dried and she had gulped down a full quart of water, she set off.

By mile seven the venom had caused her foot to swell so much that she had to remove her boot. One-legged is no way to walk the desert, so she took off her shirt and ripped it into pieces, which she wrapped around her hands and knees. She continued on all fours. The sun beat down on her back. Fatigue and nausea colonized her body. It was becoming obvious. She probably wasn't going to make it.

She had crawled just over the border and into the U.S. when a patrolman approached her. Big hat, mirrored shades, Stars and Stripes on his lapel—he was an imposing but distinctly American man. Dark-haired and sunburned, Peggy, on the other hand, was of ambiguous ethnicity. The patrolman had no reason to believe he wasn't coming upon an illegal alien.

"So where are we scooting off to?" he asked.

Peggy's throat was so parched that she couldn't speak, so she reached into her jeans for her passport. She chose the wrong pocket, and a small vial of white powder fell on the ground. The patrolman picked the vial up and held it to the sun. "What do we have here?" He twisted the cap off, dipped a pinkie in the powder, and took a taste.

If she had the strength and the voice, Peggy would have said, *It's not what you think it is!* and *I'm a scientist and I use that to measure the pH of soil!*

If she knew sign language, Peggy would have done the sign for *poison!*

The patrolman collapsed.

That was it. Peggy threw in the towel. As the patrolman sputtered and coughed on the ground, she set her head on his chest. She looked up, expecting to see vultures. She saw only the brilliant and cloudless desert sky. She faded off to sleep.

When she woke, her body was running hotter than ever. She could feel something coiled up on her stomach. *No,* she thought. *Not again.* She couldn't bear to look.

It was a breathing tube. And as the ambulance barreled down the dusty road, carrying Peggy and the patrolman to the nearest hospital, a paramedic used a towel to pat the sweat off the unlucky woman's brow and made a quip that has become something of a catchphrase for Peggy and her family.

"Bet you weren't expecting this when you woke up today."

Saturday, November 4

Part II

I WOKE UP TO FIND FIONA IN MY ROOM. COLD AIR ROLLED through the open window. The clock read 2:06. Her whisper sought out the warmth of my body.

"Alistair . . . It happened . . . Alistair."

Whenever my dad told the story about Peggy, he said that it had two morals.

Moral number one: It's always the second snake that gets you.

Moral number two: Don't ever assume you know what's in the vial.

In the story of that early November morning when Fiona snuck into my room, I was like Peggy, but I was also like the patrolman. And Fiona's whisper was like the first snake, but it was also like the vial. The morals, however, didn't come into play until a little later.

Fiona sat in my beanbag chair. Her hair wasn't out of

place. Her clothes—that neon jacket, those faded jeans—weren't ruffled or dirty or wet. Her skin was the same pale it always was. Yet she looked defeated.

"What are you doing here?" I asked as I sat up.

"It happened," she said again.

I pushed the covers away and kicked my legs over the edge of the bed. The floorboards creaked as I stood. "You can't be here," I whispered. "I'm already in enough trouble with my parents."

"Then come outside with me," she said as she struggled to rise. *Beanbag chairs.*

I reached out and pulled her up. The cold air bounced off her and into me. My fleece pajamas were cheap and did little to stop the chill, and I didn't like that standing so close to Fiona could feel so cold. "Give me a minute to get dressed," I said.

My room was on the ground floor, and the window was big enough that sneaking in wasn't much harder than climbing a tree. She nodded and eased herself through the window.

"You scared the crap out of me," I whispered a few minutes later when I joined her outside, now sufficiently clothed for the weather. Tiny snowflakes fought to stay afloat in the air, dipping and rising and swirling around us.

"I knocked on the window. I opened it and called for you. I made lots of noise. You were dead to the world, my friend."

That may have been true, but I needed her to keep quiet

now. I put a finger to my lips and ushered her away from the house and my parents, two notoriously light sleepers. As we reached the edge of the yard and I turned left, Fiona told me to go the other way.

We walked amid the flurries, side by side in the middle of the road. The snow wasn't piling up yet, but the streetlights showcased the gloss it left on everything. To me it looked like the neighborhood was being encased in a thin, clear candy shell.

"It looks so real out here," Fiona said. She held her hand out so that flakes would land on her skin. She examined them with the eye of a scientist.

"What happened?" I asked her. "You said something happened."

"They're not all unique in Aquavania," she explained, still looking at her hand. "The snowflakes. There are only so many designs there. Ten. Maybe twenty. But here in the Solid World, the possibilities are infinite. It's funny. There was a time when I thought it would be the other way around."

"What happened?" I repeated.

Fiona shook the snow off herself—steeled herself—and said it. "I saw the Riverman."

"You saw the Riverman?"

"Yes."

"You *saw* the Riverman?"

"*Yes.*"

"Of course you did," I snapped. There was plenty of anger behind my words, but frustration was pushing them harder. I had held this in for far too long.

"What's that supposed to mean?" Fiona asked.

"You live with him! You see him every day!"

"Huh?"

"Your uncle? Dorian? He's the Riverman. That's what you've been trying to say, right? He murdered all those kids . . . and maybe your grandma . . . and I don't know what he's done to you, but . . . but Aquavania . . . it's like your . . . I don't know . . . the place you make up to deal with it all. We both know that. We've both known that since the beginning."

I'm not sure I could have said anything worse. She exhaled as she kept walking. Clouds of breath rose and spread in the air, and there was so much of it that I was surprised she had enough left in her lungs to speak. Her voice was both wistful and worried. "Alistair. Kid. Don't you dare treat me like this."

"Like what?" I asked.

"Like a stupid little schoolgirl." Was she disgusted or was she ashamed? Was she livid? Whatever the case, she didn't look at me.

"I'm not," I said. "I'm not."

"You are," she replied. "And I'm not naïve. Haven't been in forever. I didn't expect you to believe me. Not about everything. What I expected you to do was listen. Obviously you weren't even doing that. Because here you are talking about Dorian like he's some . . . well, I don't know what you're talking about."

I thought about Kyle hitting that remote control to the ground and the plane crashing into the windshield. I thought about the rage and the red and Dorian's unreadable face.

"Did he get to you?" I asked. "Was Dorian angry because of Kyle? I was worried he might take it out on you." I placed my hand on her shoulder. She brushed it away with a flick of her fingertips.

"Uncle Dorian is a nice man. He's a sweet man. He has nothing to do with any of this. I don't know why you would think he does."

"Because," I explained.

"Because what? Because I have a portal in my basement that leads to a magical world full of candy and teddy bears and unicorns?"

She had never mentioned any unicorns, but I wasn't about to point out that inconsistency. I kept my mouth shut and kept walking.

"That's fine," she went on. "Go ahead and see this as pure craziness. What do I care? But please also see that this is something I believe in. I believe in it more than anything else."

I took a step in front of her and turned to face her. She stopped. The spot where her nose had been broken all those years ago—that knobby bit of cartilage right below her eyes—made me imagine that a tiny asteroid had crashed into her face and had determined the orbit of her life. She probably hated that asteroid, but to me it was essential. She wouldn't be Fiona without it. Her hair fluttered a bit, and the snow tried so hard, but failed, to make her hair less black. Fiona was right. Everything looked so real out here. She looked so real.

"Why?" I asked. "Why do you believe?"

Fiona drew three breaths, full and thick, and then she said, "In the beginning, when I was really little, I was only called to Aquavania once every year or so. Then it was every few months. Then sometimes weeks or days. But there was never any pattern to it. The radiators spoke, and I followed, and I was happy to go. I figured it was random.

"I was called an hour ago, and I went in thinking I might stay forever. Or as long as I could. I mean, it's what I've been doing for most of my life. I know it so much better than *this*."

She put her hands out as wide as possible. *The Solid World.*

"On that first night back in Aquavania, I had a thought when I was fading off to sleep," she continued on. "I let my guard down and made a wish that Aquavania couldn't deliver, and that wish . . . that need . . . well, it invited something across the folds. Because I woke up and there was a figure standing across from my bed, watching me sleep. 'Fancy meeting you here,' it whispered.

"At first I thought it was Toby and I told him to buzz off. When it didn't move, I turned on a lamp. The room didn't brighten much. Most of the light came out of the lamp in wisps and threads and swirled through the air until the body of the creature absorbed it.

"The creature was my size. A bit heavier, a bit stouter, but no taller. And he was shaped like a human, but he didn't have the color of a human. He was the color of nothing and everything, of everywhere and nowhere, of the spaces between the stars in the night sky.

"He held a glass pen full of sparkling ink. 'Do you know why I've spared your soul?' he asked me. His voice was not deep or draped in evil. It was young. Precocious.

"I had been waiting years for this moment. I had been *fearing* it, but I had practiced countless times. Before he could say another word, I had an icicle in my hand and I was plunging it into his chest. The nothingness of his body swallowed it whole. 'Riverman, Riverman, blood to ice,' I chanted.

"I was so close to him. Our cheeks were practically touching. His mouth was next to my ear, and I waited for him to wail or cry or whimper. Instead, he wrapped an arm around me, holding me tight, and he spoke.

"'Such a cute little phrase, but it doesn't work, darlin'. People will believe anything they read. They rarely ask who wrote it.' I felt the tip of the pen brushing along the tiny hairs on my earlobe. 'This is when I win,' the creature said.

"I winced. I assumed it was all over. But he pushed me away and I fell back onto my bed. Frantic, I assaulted him with questions. 'Who are you? How did you find me? Why are you doing this?'

"He laughed a little, fanned out a hand, and said, 'Let's start with the first question. Who am I? I have many names. Some, like you, call me the Riverman. I call myself the Whisper. For my voice is the voice in the water that calls out and asks you to come play.'

"Now that I've thought about it, the voice from the radiators did sound a bit like his, but I couldn't actually believe they were the same.

"'Question two: How did I find you? A stroke of luck and a stroke of intuition. Fiona Loomis, there are many people in Aquavania, including many Fionas, in fact, and you shouldn't be counted as more special than any of them. And yet you are. But not because of the person you may be. It's because of the person you know.'

"I thought this might be a reference to Chua, Boaz, or Rodrigo. But the fact that the Riverman used my last name puzzled me. I had never told my last name to anyone in Aquavania.

"'And your final question. Why am I doing this? Simple. For fun.'

"The whole time he was talking, he was gesturing wildly, and while I couldn't make out a face, I could see the shape of his hands from the little bit of light that was still swirling in the air unabsorbed."

Fiona crouched down. There was a thin layer of snow on

the road now, enough for her to dip her finger in and draw. She outlined what looked like two hands, misshapen and incomplete. Three fingers on one hand, two on the other.

She looked up at me and continued with her story.

"'What if I wished myself back to the Solid World right now?' I asked the Riverman.

"He chuckled. 'So you can come and get me?'

"'Maybe.'

"'How will you accomplish that?' he asked. 'I'll know you're coming. And what will the Solid World think of Fiona Loomis the vigilante? How will that work out for you, and your family . . . and the ones you love? No. We deal with this right here. Right now. I have spared you and I will leave you in peace, so long as you give me one thing.'

"'And what's that?'

"'Him.'

"'Who?'

"'Alistair.'"

Fiona stood up and looked me in the eyes as she ran her foot over the drawing in the snow, whiting it out. There was a reason she had led us this way. We were standing on the road next to Charlie's house.

The second snake in the story. The contents of the vial.

"No," I said.

"Charlie is the Riverman," Fiona said. "I know it. I feel it. It seems impossible, but it's the truth."

The Dwyer house was dark, every window. Kyle's van

and the family cars were in the driveway, collecting the snow. I had known these people my entire life.

"I was ready to do anything for you!" I cried. "I was going to give everything for you! This is not the story! This is not how it goes!"

Fiona tilted her head. Her eyes were sympathetic, but not sympathetic enough. "You're so much better here," she said.

"I don't know what that means!"

"I'm going back," she went on, "as soon as I'm called. And I'm finishing this. But I needed to tell you. If things turn out differently, at least now you know. Charlie is not the kid you think he is. He's something else."

"No. No. No. No. No."

"I wish I could have done everything better," she said. "But you can't change your mistakes. You can only try to make up for them."

And she turned away. As she walked back in the direction of her house, she left footprints in the snow. Fiona left footprints everywhere. That was her problem. She was always walking away, inserting herself and then going, needing me and then not needing me. She left reminders of herself, but she didn't leave herself, and I was sick of it. I hurried after her.

"You don't do this to me," I said. "You don't bring me this far and tell me these things and then leave."

She paused for a moment. "I'm sorry. I've been selfish. But I'm trying to be better. Tell you what. When it's all over, meet me out by the rock."

"When what's all over?" I asked.

She didn't answer. Instead, she smiled and kissed the tips of her fingers again, like she had a few nights before when we were on the side of the road with our bikes, and as she raised her hand to touch it to my forehead, I caught her by the wrist.

"No," I said. "Please. A real kiss."

She stared at me for a moment. I lowered her hand and placed it on my chest so she could feel what she was putting me through. She did, and she sighed. And she wet her lips with her tongue. Finally, she closed her eyes, leaned in, and pressed her lips to mine.

It only lasted a second, and as soon as it was over, she walked away. I hardly remember what it felt like, but I'll always remember that look—that *finally* look—on her face as she pulled away. Yes, it was a *finally* look. Trust me. It couldn't be anything else.

SATURDAY, NOVEMBER 4

PART III

THE MORNING CAME, AND I'M NOT SURE HOW TO DESCRIBE this exactly, but I felt an absence, a dreadful sensation that something was missing from my body. In bed, looking up at the ceiling, it was like all the cracks that had been spreading over my world had finally opened up and things were slipping into them.

The snow held until the sun came out, and then it escaped as vapor into the air or it seeped as water into the ground. In slippers, I walked through our soggy yard and pulled the thin Saturday morning newspaper from the mailbox and held it under my arm as I looked up the street toward Fiona's house and down the street toward Charlie's house and across the street through the cluster of houses that made up the only place I had ever called home.

This place was the same place it had always been. The street was the same street I had walked and biked along so many times. Yet everything felt different, slanted, peeled of its skin. And it felt like that for the rest of the morning.

When the afternoon arrived, it brought news of what was gone.

The phone rang, and my dad answered.

"Hey, buddy, it's been ages," he said into the receiver. "Really . . . that's . . . oh, buddy, I'm so sorry to hear that. Of course I'll ask him. And if there's anything else . . . we'll, well, I'll ask him. And I'll get right back to you. Good-bye."

He set the phone down and ran a hand across his face and into his hair, as if wiping an awful image from his mind.

"What is it?" I asked.

"Fiona." He sighed. "Her parents haven't seen her since last night. You haven't seen her, have you?"

I shook my head and I got up from the couch, and I grabbed on to my dad and hugged him like I hadn't hugged him in forever, and I wanted nothing more than for him to pick me up and carry me away.

Sunday, November 5

——— and ———

Monday, November 6

There was still no word from Fiona on Sunday. The police went door-to-door. Families from the neighborhood collected in their yards or in their driveways. Watching, waiting, trying to figure out what they could do to help. My mom cooked a big Sunday dinner, as she always did, but this time she made an extra pan of lasagna, which she wrapped in foil. Because she didn't want to "be a bother," she set the pan on the Loomises' front step with a note that read: *We're here for you. Anything you need, simply ask. Love, The Clearys.*

By Monday, Fiona's picture began appearing on the television news and in the newspaper. At school Principal Braugher held another assembly, and the same officer who had warned us about the dangers of fireworks now warned us about the dangers of keeping information from the police.

"We all want to see Fiona home," he said. "If you know something, anything, you need to tell us. There's a girl out there who depends on it."

I was called to the police station that evening, and my dad joined me there. We sat at a round table in the middle of the station with two detectives—one man and one woman—both eating fried chicken and coleslaw as they asked me about my relationship with Fiona.

"She was my girlfriend, I guess," I told them.

"And how long had you been dating?"

"A few weeks."

"Did she ever talk about running away?"

"No."

"Was there anyone who might have reason to hurt her?"

"Have you talked to her uncle?" I replied. "Have you investigated the death of her grandmother?"

They didn't record this. They didn't take notes. They nodded at my answers and they ate. I couldn't be coy anymore. I had to lay it all out there.

"Fiona knew about these other missing kids," I went on. "Chua Ling was one of them. And there's a kid from Germany named Werner. Then there's Boaz and Rodrigo, and probably lots more, all over the world. I don't know all the details, but there must be databases of missing kids. I think her uncle Dorian kidnapped them."

The woman was Detective Driscoll, and she was like a ventriloquist without a dummy. When she spoke, her lips hardly moved. "And did Miss Loomis tell you that her uncle was responsible for the disappearances of these children?"

"Not in those words exactly. But she made up these crazy stories and she implied it."

The man was Detective Jackson, and he spoke with the cadence of a man who knew more than he was ever willing to tell you. "Here's the thing. We've spoken to Dorian Loomis already. And there is no reason to believe this guy wants anything other than his niece home safe and sound."

"But the other kids," I said. "You have to look into them. It would have happened over the last couple of years, and—"

Driscoll chuckled under her breath, still not moving her lips. "That would be quite a feat, because Dorian Loomis hasn't been much of a traveler. For the last couple of years he's been a ward of the state on account of his persistent recreational activities."

Jackson pinched his thumb and forefinger together and raised it to his mouth like he was smoking something. He squinted and nodded to my dad.

"A what of the state?" I asked.

"Incarcerated," Driscoll said. "In prison."

I stuttered. "But he . . . he . . . Then what about Fiona's grandma? Her death might not have been . . . natural."

"Eighty-two years old with a weak heart and dementia is as natural as it gets," Jackson remarked.

Driscoll sipped her coffee and watched me over the rim of her mug. "Tell us a bit more about Kyle Dwyer," she said.

I told them that Kyle was my friend and that I had

confided my suspicions about Dorian to him. But I didn't tell them about the gun. I didn't tell them about his plan to leave. I assured them that Kyle had nothing to do with Fiona's disappearance. And they let me go.

On the drive home, my dad didn't scold me or ask me to explain myself. All he said was, "When I was young, there was a widow named Mrs. Maynard who lived down the street. We'd knock on her door and she'd invite us kids in and sit us on the couch and give us ribbon candy and pop. She didn't expect anything but a chat. Then we'd be on our way. We didn't tell our parents about it because we worried they'd think we were taking advantage of her. She was quite senile, you see. Starting to lose touch with reality. Some things she said were so off-the-wall that we decided she must have been receiving transmissions from outer space. You know, beamed down through the atmosphere and into the silver fillings in her teeth? We believed it too. It's amazing the stories you can make yourself believe."

We drove the rest of the way in silence.

Tuesday, November 7

———— ◆◆ ————

THREE DAYS AFTER FIONA DISAPPEARED, ON A WINDY evening when the air smelled like bark and gravel, I rode my bike to her house. News vans and police cars were already regular visitors there, but for a short window that evening the only vehicle in the driveway was Dorian's truck. The only lights on were the ones in the garage.

Mrs. Carmine sat on her front steps, watching me. "What are you doing, Alistair?" she asked.

"Never mind," I replied.

"I told you to keep your distance from that man," she said.

"You didn't tell me what he did. You didn't tell me the truth."

She shook her head. "You're confused. Go home."

"Not until I talk to him."

"He's been talked to already."

"Not by me."

She sighed and didn't say anything else. A few minutes later she went inside, and I rolled my bike down the driveway, walked to the garage door, and knocked on it. The knock was answered by the grind of a chain and the door drawing up and open. Dorian stood at the threshold, his black T-shirt covered in little flecks of wood. I squeezed the handgrips of my bike and pushed all my confidence into my shoulders.

"I carved this for her," Dorian said before I could get a word out. He presented his hand. Resting in the palm was a small wooden figurine with big ears and a tail. "She has this stuffed animal from when she was real young. Calls it a bush baby. I based it on that. She loves monkeys and stuff."

Loves. Present tense. Not *loved.* I noticed that immediately.

Dorian pushed the wood at me, urging me to take it. I did, and I was struck by how smooth it felt. "It's almost like glass," I told him.

"Been whittling and sanding it for near two hours." In his face I saw a mixture of pride and sadness—a smile that wasn't a smile, a downward brow, eyes squinting to slits. Behind him, on a workbench, I saw the stuffed animal from his truck. I saw that long thin blade resting in a pile of sawdust and wood shavings.

"The police asked me about her, but I don't know where she is," I told him. It was not what I had planned to say, but they seemed like the words he needed to hear.

"I know you don't," he said. "I've spoken to the cops too. Sorry, but I had to tell them about your pal with the van."

I didn't respond. I kept running my hand over the wood, entranced by the grace of the thing.

"Not sure who you two think I am," he went on, "but it ain't accur . . . it ain't the truth." He noticed how much sawdust was still on his shirt, so he gave it a shake, unleashing a swarm of wood particles.

"I made some mistakes," I admitted. I was there to tell him that I was sorry, but this was the best I could manage. Dorian's innocence was devastating. It meant I was a fool. It meant I knew nothing.

He nodded, but he wasn't nodding a yes. "No one's blaming you," he said.

A nice man, a sweet man. That's what Fiona called him. Did that mean he was also an honest man? A wise man? "What do you think happened to her?" I asked.

He shrugged limply. "Fi wasn't happy here. I could see that. It wasn't like she was sulking about or anything. She was smart. Clever. Quick with a joke. But she was making phone calls to other parts of the world. Dreaming of escape, I guess. She was never really part of this place, if you catch my drift."

I did.

"And sometimes a kid has to get up and go," he went on.

"I know. Someone so young? It don't make much sense. But that's what the police think, anyhow. I mean, there's no evidence of anyone messing about the house. And they've dealt with younger runaways. Kids who hop a bus and end up in a new city and . . . Well, you can imagine how this sorta thing goes."

The idea of Fiona wandering alone through a landscape of skyscrapers and graffiti made me sad in a way I hadn't felt yet. In the past she had asked me for help, but before that moment, I had never thought of her as completely helpless.

"You think she'll be okay?" I asked.

He shrugged again. "You care for her, don't you?"

"Yessir."

"And she cares for you. When Ma passed, Fi asked if it was okay to invite you along to the memorial. We asked why, and Fi said that it was because 'Alistair is a kid you can trust, a kid you can count on.'"

"She said that?"

"She did. And Fi is a damn good judge of character. That's why I'm asking you . . . if there's anything . . . anything you haven't told the cops, even if it's a secret between you and her, you're gonna have to tell them. You're gonna have to be that kid, the one Fi says you are."

Our conversation ended there. Dorian insisted that I keep the figurine, and so I brought it home and set it on my nightstand.

Wednesday, November 8
— TO —
Friday, November 10

THREE MORE DAYS. I WENT TO SCHOOL, I CAME HOME, I SAT
with my family at dinner, I did homework. The phone seemed
to ring incessantly. One of the calls was from Charlie.

"Tell him I don't want to talk right now," I told my mom.

"He says that's fine. He's says whenever you're ready."

Charlie is the Riverman. Charlie is the Riverman. Charlie is the Riverman.

I said it over and over to myself, as if saying it over and
over could make it seem possible. But it wasn't possible.
Aquavania wasn't possible. Charlie was Charlie. That's all
he could ever be—the kid who had shared a sandbox with
me and who had been there for the birthday parties and the
games of flashlight tag and for everything. For everything.

So what was Fiona telling me? Was she jealous of my
friendship with Charlie? Was she trying to pull us apart?
Why bring Charlie into this?

By the end of the week, school was hardly school anymore. Almost every class was dedicated to talking about our feelings. On Friday afternoon, Keri and I were walking home when she began to cry. I'd seen her cry plenty of times, but never out of the blue like this. She sat down while still wearing her backpack and buried her face in her knees.

I looked around to see if anyone was watching, but we were alone. So I sat down beside her with my back against a tree. "Are you all right?" I asked.

"No," she said. "Of course not. No one's all right anymore. It's so unfair. It's so stupid and so unfair."

A news van rumbled past.

On Friday night I waited until I was sure my parents were asleep and I went outside for a stroll. It wasn't quite midnight, but it was late. In the past, the neighborhood was usually pretty dark at this hour, but the fear had become contagious. Most of the houses had at least a few lights lit. TVs were on even if people weren't watching them. *Don't try anything because we're awake* was the message to the peepers and the prowlers and the restless souls like me.

It had been a week since I'd seen Fiona, since we'd walked through the snow and stood outside of Charlie's house. I followed the same path, replaying our conversation in my head.

You're so much better here.

I still didn't understand what she meant by that. Except

for the occasional vacation, I had never been anywhere but Thessaly. Maybe it was Fiona's way of saying that while *I* fit in here, *she* didn't. Maybe it was her way of telling me not to follow her. As if I had any idea where she went. Or even *if* she went. Maybe someone did get to her. But if not Dorian, then who?

I stopped in front of the Dwyer house. Kyle was leaning against the side of his van and smoking a cigarette. He motioned for me to join him.

"Hey," I said.

"Hey."

"You okay?" I asked.

Kyle opened his mouth but didn't breathe. The smoke drifted out slowly, hugging his face and climbing into the air. When it had all escaped, he said, "What'd you get me into, kid?"

"I didn't—"

"They searched my van, my room, took my fingerprints."

"They didn't find . . . ?"

"They didn't find anything," he assured me. "Because I didn't do anything. What happened, kid? They're saying Uncle's not a suspect?"

"That's what they told me."

"And did they also tell you that I am?"

"Sort of."

"Chriiiist." He took another drag.

"I know you didn't do anything. And I didn't tell them anything. I'm a kid who can keep secrets."

Kyle sent a blast of smoke out his nose and looked up at the moon. "So if I hit the road like I've been needing to, what are people gonna think? They're gonna think I'm some perv running from justice."

"No they won't."

"How old are you again, Alistair?"

"I'm almost thirteen." *Almost* was relative. I still had a few months to go.

"Yeah, and someday you'll be eighteen."

I didn't know what to say to that, so I didn't say anything. And we stood there for a few minutes, looking at the moon. As soon as Kyle burned it down to the end, he flicked his cigarette at a puddle near the edge of the driveway and walked to his house.

Back in my room, I pulled out the box Fiona had given me and I put on her grandfather's tweed jacket and I sat in the corner in the beanbag chair and I listened to the tape of that first interview we did. It was only about a month old, but it felt ancient, an artifact from another era, an age when Fiona was solid and real.

Play. Stop. Rewind. Play. Stop. Rewind. I listened to it so much that it came to a point where I didn't even need to hit *Play* anymore. I could summon the words whenever I wanted. Fiona's voice was in my head.

Because we're weirdos, Alistair. We're the aliens.

VETERANS DAY

———◆———

THERE WAS A PARADE FOR VETERANS DAY, AND A FEW DOZEN uniformed men marched through the center of Thessaly, followed by the football team and the cheerleaders and bagpipers and anyone, it seemed, who liked to parade. Dorian wasn't there. I wasn't sure if he even owned a uniform anymore.

Actually, no one in Fiona's family attended, but there were missing posters stapled or taped to every utility pole that lined the street. The Elks Club made their way through the crowd with clipboards and asked people to sign up for search parties. Our family was camped out in lawn chairs near the memorial tree. When the clipboards reached us, my mom only put down two names: hers and my dad's.

"Why didn't you put me and Alistair on the list?" Keri asked.

"We don't want you coming upon something that your mind will never shake," my dad said.

He had a good point. I didn't want that either. Not all memories rot away. Some sprout fungus. "What happened with you and Fiona's parents?" I asked. "You used to be good friends."

My dad looked at me like he did whenever he had to report that it was time to turn off the TV or to go to bed. "We didn't like them," he stated. "I know that sounds harsh, but it's that simple."

"They're individuals," my mom added. "Let's leave it at that."

"No," my dad snapped. "For once, let's not leave it at that. The kids should know. The Loomises didn't love that girl. They didn't want that girl. They told us as much."

"They told you what?" I asked.

I had never seen my dad so riled up about something. My mom gave him a disapproving look and whispered, "They didn't say that, Rich."

"They might as well have," my dad replied. "They're our neighbors, so we gave them a shot, but sometimes what's worse than people lying to you is people being too honest."

"Did they really not love her? Not want her?" I asked.

My mom shook her head. "That was years ago. All parents get annoyed and say things they don't mean. She's their daughter. Of course they love her. And they miss her dearly. They're in a terrible place right now. I've been speaking to her mother on the phone almost every night. They can barely function. They need our support. Everybody's. The whole town's."

At the tail end of the parade, a group of veterans carried spools of wire and bulbs. Firemen propped ladders against the memorial tree, and the veterans climbed and strung up the blue lights, wrapping them around the tree in a spiral, passing the spools from ladder to ladder. As always, they were going to wait until Christmas Eve to turn them on.

"Why don't they do this on Memorial Day?" Keri asked. "Isn't today when you're supposed to remember the ones who lived?"

"It's tradition," my mom said. "A tribute to start the holiday season."

"Do you have to die in war to get a light?" Keri asked.

"That's why they call it a tribute," my dad said. "These people made the ultimate sacrifice for you and me and the entire country."

"They should have lights for anyone who died who shouldn't be dead," Keri added. "You know, anyone who died too early."

I knew what she was getting at, and I started to say, "You mean like—"

But my mom cut me off. "Oh, Keri," she said with a sigh. "Don't talk like that. Don't even think like that. We don't know anything yet."

SUNDAY, NOVEMBER 12

—— TO ——

FRIDAY, NOVEMBER 17

THE NEXT WEEK WENT MUCH LIKE THE ONE BEFORE IT. MY head buzzed. My bones ached. I flew through the days on autopilot, hardly knowing which one was which. Teachers tried to return our classes to the normal and the comfortable, but school was plagued with rumors about men in rusty cars and old farmhouses in the woods with secret cellars where someone could be squirreled away.

"They worship the devil," Sanjay whispered to me in gym class. "Out there in the boonies. Sacrifice cats and stuff. I saw it once, drove out with my brother, and he showed me some bones and spray-painted pentagrams."

Police officers came and went from the main office, and a security guard was hired to make sure no one was sneaking out at lunch or during study hall. Kids who lived within walking distance of the school had to bring home release forms for parents to sign. My parents signed, but made Keri and me promise not to walk alone.

It was impossible to avoid Charlie. Even though I knew his schedule and planned my routes through the halls around it, he was always there at lunch and on the front steps in the morning, joking with new friends like Ken Wagner and Kelly Dubois, who were either impressed by Charlie's deformed hands or by his omnipresent laptop and his satchel full of floppy disks. Those hands were no longer wrapped in gauze, but Charlie wore thin leather gloves. Stuffing filled the empty glove fingers, so it was hard to tell which ones were flesh and blood and which ones were fluff.

Whenever Charlie saw me, he gave me a respectful nod and mouthed the same thing.

Sorry.

Word spread that Fiona was my girlfriend, and I got a lot of sorrys like that, including ones from Trevor and Mike. Even Kendra and Fay-Renee sat next to me at lunch one afternoon and pulled out a Ziploc of Oreos. Kendra passed me a few, and they each took a handful. We ate in silence, until Fay-Renee closed her eyes and rested her head on the table. Kendra rubbed Fay-Renee's back and then stood, pulled Fay-Renee from her chair, and led her out of the cafeteria, but not before telling me, "We're sorry for being jealous. Fiona really liked you."

It was meant to comfort, but it didn't. Instead it made me feel like this was all the result of my mistakes. That if

I had tried harder, or listened better, or done just about anything other than what I had done, then this wouldn't have happened. And maybe that was the truth of it.

Each evening there was an update on the news about the search for Fiona. My parents accompanied every group that combed the woods and the fields. Divers descended to the bottom of lakes and experts came from somewhere in the Midwest to help dredge the Oriskanny. A yearbook picture appeared on milk cartons. There were no suspects and there was no evidence, at least not any the media was aware of, so numerous sources still listed Fiona as a possible runaway.

I heard that Derek and Maria had been driving from city to city, as far as New York and Boston and even Montreal. They brought along the missing posters and handed them out at homeless shelters and to groups of wayward teens who hung out in parks and under bridges.

Back in the neighborhood, I would see Dorian's truck sometimes, and Kyle's van sometimes, quietly gliding through the streets like they were trying to evade detection. Or maybe that was just how I perceived it. Maybe that's how they always drove. Maybe, suddenly, I was the one who wanted to stay hidden.

Charlie is the Riverman. Charlie is the Riverman. Charlie is the Riverman.

I kept telling myself this, because it was the last thing that Fiona told me. She wanted me to know it, to believe it.

In my basement we had our own boiler, tucked in the

corner where the floor was concrete. I spent Friday night sitting on a plastic tub of driveway sealant with a flashlight in my lap, and I watched that boiler. It didn't disappear. It didn't speak to me. It hardly made a sound.

Before going back upstairs, I peeled the top off the tub of driveway sealant and pointed a beam of light into it. It was a colorless liquid, but it shimmered. I wondered what Charlie would look like if he were coated in the stuff. I tried to imagine a tiny version of him, rising out of the tub like a creature made of the night sky. But all I could see was a specter of my face reflected in the shimmer.

I put the sole of my slipper on the top rim of the tub and I tipped it back and held it at an angle. It started to tip over, so I let it. The tub hit the concrete floor, and the liquid spilled out and spread. The slope of the floor pulled the liquid away from me, and soon there was a black river running across the basement. I spent the rest of the night mopping it up.

Saturday, November 18

The weekend started when the doorbell rang and I was like the salivating dog in that famous experiment. The bell was more than a bell to me. It meant Fiona.

I launched myself from bed and was at the door before I realized I wasn't dressed for company. Not that I cared. The only thing that mattered was finding her on that doorstep and making a pact to start over. Pledging to do whatever she needed this time around, so long as it kept her home.

That hair. That skin. Those eyes. They were nearly the same, but the person at the door wasn't Fiona. It was her mom.

"I'm so sorry to wake you," she said.

"It's okay. I was up."

She held out a key. "Your mom is expecting this. We're

leaving for a few days. The police know where, but we're ridding ourselves of reporters for a bit."

I took the key. "Yes, ma'am."

Her empty hands suddenly perplexed her. She stroked and tapped the fingers of one hand with the fingers of the other. "How are we doing?" she asked.

"Um . . . okay. And you?"

"Getting by." She giggled the words out, but it wasn't really like she was laughing. Her shaking fingertips then touched her lips, but instead of bringing them to my forehead like Fiona might have done, she held them in the air for a second. "Thank you, Alistair. You've always been a good boy."

The Loomises' station wagon was in our driveway, engine running. She turned and hurried back to it, skipping from our steps to our brick walkway like someone half her age. Dorian sat in the backseat next to Maria and Derek. From behind the wheel, Fiona's dad was watching me. I closed the door so I wouldn't have to look him in the eye.

When my mom got out of bed a few minutes later, I gave her the key.

"I'm watering the plants, feeding the fish, getting the mail. Neighbor stuff," she explained as she hung the key on a hook in the kitchen. "It's good for them to get away for a bit. And Dad and I think it might be good for us to get away too, at least for today."

* * *

We drove south on hilly back roads full of apple orchards. The trees were picked clean and looked like talons reaching out from birds buried upside down in the cold earth. Our stereo played a book on tape my mom had borrowed from the library. It was something the entire family was supposed to enjoy, a tale of giants and dwarfs and elves. I couldn't concentrate on it. All I could think about were Fiona's tales of Aquavania. *Aquavania is where stories are born.* That's what she had said. But what did it mean?

For lunch we stopped at a diner, a shiny-shelled converted railcar with mirrored walls on the inside that made it seem infinitely big when there were really only a handful of booths and counter seats. I ordered a turkey club and an iced tea, and as Keri chattered on about the latest drama dictating the terms of her friendship with Mandy, I watched our fellow customers. I started making up stories about them in my head.

An obese man sat at the counter, pouring salt from a shaker into his glass of cola. I imagined that he was skinny once, back when he was a teenager, but on prom night he was driving his date home and the car spun out of control, hit a drainage ditch, and flipped. His date died, and in a way, he died too. His soul was reincarnated as a vessel for guilt, and he began feeding the guilt with junk food. Although a promising student, he never showed up for college and had been living at home ever since, occasionally making money by selling ephemera at flea markets. After years of sucking down sweets, his taste buds had changed until nothing but salt could deliver flavor. So he put it on everything he ate and drank. Even his cola.

A woman in a flannel shirt and jeans ate at a booth with a man in a basketball jersey and sweatpants. I imagined she was a disciplined and courteous trainer of sheepdogs and he was her irresponsible younger brother, still recovering from a night of partying. She was pregnant, but hadn't told their parents yet on account of the fact that she wasn't married to the father. For the first time in their lives, roles were reversed. She was the one with the secret, the mistake, and she was asking him how he handled difficult things. How did he deal with constantly disappointing their parents?

A little girl sipped a milk shake as her dad got up to go to the restroom. The girl stared at the mirrors, marveling at how the layers of reflections went on forever. Like the mirrors, this girl would go on forever. Even though she didn't know it yet, she was the first immortal ever born. Her blood contained DNA that could repair any part of her body that was failing. If she lost an arm, a new one would simply grow back. Scientists would study her. The world would celebrate her, and that world would die all around her. As she lived on.

So Aquavania was where the stories were born, but was it an actual place? I was making up stories right then, in my head. That's where stories were born, which meant Aquavania was really just another word for Fiona's imagination. There was only one question left, the question I kept asking myself, the question I kept getting wrong. Where did she get the details, the inspiration?

I got my inspiration from the things in life that I feared to be true and the things in life that I hoped to be true. I didn't know anything about the people in the diner, but my hopes and fears flavored my stories about them. I couldn't see why Fiona's hopes and fears didn't flavor her stories as well.

"You know what I think happened to Fiona?" I said to my family after I took the last bite of my sandwich. "I think she ran away. I think the reason she read newspaper articles about missing kids is that she wanted to be a missing kid. Her parents didn't love her. Her brother and sister, her uncle, her grandma . . . Fiona didn't want to end up like them. She must not have liked how her future looked here. So she decided to start over somewhere else. Maybe somewhere warm. Palm trees. Colorful birds. Near the ocean. She's there right now with all the other kids who got away."

My mom took a deep breath and folded her hands together like she was saying a prayer. "Is that what you talked about when the two of you were together?"

"Not about running away, but we talked about creating new worlds, about saving people, about starting over from scratch," I said. "We talked about how your thoughts and imagination are your soul, and how you gotta make sure no one ever steals your soul."

"She's twelve years old, Alistair." My dad sighed. "I don't doubt she has an amazing imagination, but if she ran away, then they would have found her by now. She's too young to know how to disappear."

"Just because she's twelve doesn't mean she's not as smart and capable as anyone else," I said. "*This* is what happened to her. *This* is Fiona's story."

Keri slurped at the end of her milk shake and flashed me a thumbs-up. "I like that story, little bro," she said. "It's better than anyone else's."

As we drove home, my mind was occupied by that nagging refrain: *Charlie is the Riverman. Charlie is the Riverman. Charlie is the Riverman.*

Charlie stole my story. The Riverman stole stories. Fiona's dislike of Charlie was no secret, so maybe her tales of the Riverman were also elaborate warnings. We were weirdos, Fiona and I. Creative minds like ours were the minds of aliens. And the soul-suckers, the plagiarists, the malicious people like Charlie? They were sapping us. It was our mission to get away from them. So that's what Fiona did. And she was inviting me to do the same thing.

Yet the thing was, I wasn't ready to get away, not from Thessaly, not even from Charlie. I had been angry with him, but what he had done was so minor in the grand scheme of things. I didn't see him as malicious. I saw him as weak, and weakness was something I could forgive. With Fiona gone, I was essentially alone. Forgiveness was the only option I had.

So when we returned home that evening, after I had thought for a while about why we tell the stories we tell, I picked up the phone and dialed a number my fingers had memorized years ago.

"Hey, Charlie," I said. "Let's hang out together tomorrow."

SUNDAY, NOVEMBER 19

THE RAIN STARTED EARLY, PUMMELING MY WINDOW AND reminding me I had somewhere to be. Even with an umbrella, I was soaked by the time I reached Charlie's house. He answered the door with a towel draped over his shoulder. Handing it to me, he said, "Good morning, sunshine."

The video game was cued up to the point where we had last left off. One final level to defeat, an absurdly difficult maze through a dungeon to the big boss, an armored ogre who was both brutish and magical.

"It's been a few weeks," I told Charlie. "I'll be rusty. I'm not sure I'm up to it."

"You're up to it," he assured me. "If it takes all day, it takes all day."

That it did. I played through the morning and into the afternoon, only grabbing a quick break for lunch. Charlie was patient, never chiding me for my mistakes or resorting to *I told you so* when I failed to follow his advice. He had said *sorry* so many times over the previous two weeks that the word didn't really mean it anymore. So now he was making an effort to show it by tolerating my deficiencies. For Charlie, this was a big step, and I wondered if he had actually grown up a bit.

By evening, I had mastered the dungeon, but I still couldn't defeat the big boss. Even using the sharpest sword and all the potions and enchanted objects, I could only get his energy levels down halfway. It was Sunday, and Sunday dinner at my house was the most important one of the week. My mom always spent hours cooking something special. I knew she would want me home, but I felt like I had to stay and finish what I had started. At least something in my life had to be solved.

I called my mom and told her I'd be home in a few hours. "If that's what you need," she told me.

Charlie's dad fetched some Chinese takeout, and he and Charlie's mom ate their dinner in front of a TV in the basement while Charlie and I ate ours on the couch in the back room with the video game on pause. Chopsticks weren't an option for Charlie, but he was already adept at holding a spoon pressed to his palm with his pinky and thumb and shoveling the food into his mouth.

"Shouldn't we save some for Kyle?" I asked.

"Nah," Charlie responded as he lifted another pile of sweet-and-sour chicken. "Don't even know if he's coming home or not."

Outside, the rain continued its onslaught and the clouds were so thick that nighttime didn't wait for sunset. Darkness swallowed everything beyond the glow of the game. I finished my dinner and dove back in.

It was shortly after nine o'clock, and I had gotten no further at defeating the big boss. It was time to go, as much as it pained me to admit it.

"Let's take a breather," Charlie suggested. "Try a few more times. All you need is one perfect round."

"Okay. But only one more. Then I have to leave."

Charlie nodded in agreement. "I'm going outside to feed the cats. Should be a few minutes. Mom got an electric can opener, so I'm all set on that front. You take a moment, walk around the house, do whatever you gotta do to clear your head." He patted me on the shoulder with his gloved hand and headed for the kitchen to find some tuna.

I made a quick trip to the bathroom and then lingered in the hallway to look at photos on the wall. There were framed shots of Charlie and Kyle from when they were babies and toddlers. They both looked so happy and young, but true to Fiona's theory, there were twice as many pictures of Kyle.

My gaze eventually wandered from the pictures, down the hall, and through the open door to Charlie's bedroom. I hardly ever spent any time in there. It was always too messy, so we usually hung out near the TV or in the basement. In fact, it had been years since I'd even entered his room, and yet something caught my eye and compelled me to step inside. Sitting on Charlie's dresser, underneath his mirror, was an object I recognized.

A fishbowl. Full of water, but no fish inside.

The image of Thessaly's first missing child, of the boy named Luke Drake—splotchy and purple and staring back at me through the microfiche screen—was the only thing that compared, the only other thing in my life that tore my eyes out and put them back in upside down. Something familiar was suddenly something completely new.

A distinctive chip in its rim told me that this was Humbert's fishbowl, the fishbowl that haunted my dream when I was six years old, the one that disappeared from my dresser and left a floating orb of water in its place. But it was also something else. It was a gateway. An object beneath it confirmed the fact.

The fishbowl sat upon a thick notebook, which I pulled out to examine its cover.

GODS OF NOWHERE

The title didn't mean much to me, so I opened it to the first page.

The Whisper
Once upon a time at Alistair's house I heard a
whisper in a fishbowl. I went inside the bowl and

*met the whisper. We fought in the land of icicles
and I won. I am the Whisper now.*

The handwriting was barely more than a scribble. Next to the words was a crayon drawing of two boys, one lying on the ground, the other standing and holding a pen in the air. In the background was something that looked like a rainbow-colored snake.

I turned to the next page.

*The Tale of Trina Cook
Trina Cook lived in a world made of zebra fur and
I found her by mistake. She laughed at me and I
defeated her like I defeated the Whisper. Zebra
fur only looks black and white. Deep down it has
all the colors.*

The handwriting was better, but there was no picture with this story. I flipped to the next page: "The Song of Simon Abrams."

Then the next: "The Adventure of Purvi Patel."

Then the next: "The Chronicle of Gaby Noonan."

It went on like that, page after page, story after story, kid after kid. I didn't read most of them, but as I skimmed, I noticed that the handwriting got better and the stories became more sophisticated.

Near the end of the notebook, I had to stop.

The Tragedy of Werner Schroeder
Werner Schroeder was a silly boy with a silly
heart that was forever bound to a chick named
Chua Ling . . .

I closed my eyes and the notebook. That was enough. In fact, that was too much. I pounded the dresser with my fist, and the water in the fishbowl splashed over the rim and onto my knuckles. Opening my eyes, I snatched the bowl and poised it on my shoulder like a shot put. To hurl it into the mirror, to smash all the glass to bits—that was what I really wanted to do. My reflection wouldn't let me, though. It urged me to turn away.

In the middle of his bed, Charlie's silk comforter was a tussled mess, its folds forming a series of valleys. With no reflection to scold me, I gave in to my next temptation. I poured the water all over the silk, where it found the crags and crevices and followed the paths it was given.

For myself, I saw only one path. With the empty fishbowl in hand and the notebook tucked under my arm, I bolted through the house to the back door.

The rain was still heavy when I stepped out to the backyard. A light mounted above the door cut through only so much of it, and I couldn't see Charlie until I was halfway to the clubhouse. He was crouching next to the entrance, a polka-dotted umbrella shielding him from the worst of the downpour. Under his chin he held a flashlight that pointed at the ground and illuminated the seven or eight cats that circled him and ate from the cans of tuna distributed in the grass.

Peering up at me, he smiled and said, "Well, looky here . . ."

I was already soaked to the guts. Wind was pulling the rain sideways, and the cold air was crisping it up. When the water hit my skin, it stung and incited blood to my cheeks. My face ran hot and cold. In the distance, thunder rumbled.

"What are you holding, buddy?" Charlie asked, rising up and straightening his back. He took the flashlight from his chin, balanced it in his gloved hand, and aimed its beam at the fishbowl.

The bowl had started to fill with rainwater, maybe as much as half an inch. "I don't get it," I said. "It makes no sense."

"What's to get? Back when we were kids, you threw out Humbert's fishbowl. I picked it out of the trash and took it home. It's called recycling. Saving the Earth."

"Did you mean for me to find it?"

Charlie gave his umbrella a twirl, kicking a pinwheel of droplets into the air. "Nothing in life is meant. Things go the way the wind blows."

"Where are they?" I asked.

"Who?"

"Where is she?" I yelled.

"Who?"

In a single motion, I pulled the notebook out from under my arm and flung it at Charlie. My hope was that it would sail like a giant ninja star and strike him in the face, but it hardly made it six feet before the wind opened it up and swatted it to the ground.

Charlie pointed the beam at the notebook until we could both see the open page. The handwriting was sloppy. The broken curves and squiggly lines matched the ones I'd seen in the bathroom stall, the ones that spelled out the response to my questions about Aquavania.

The author was missing fingers. That was the reason the writing was nearly illegible. The key word is *nearly*. Because even in the dark, at a distance, I could make out the title of the story.

The Legend of Fiona Loomis

Ink bled as the paper sucked up the rain and the words began to die. Charlie moved the beam to my face.

"'Aliens of the Sixth Grade' or whatever title you used," he said. "That was actually my story, you know?"

"What?"

"Back when I first thought it up, it was called 'Aliens of Fourth Grade,'" he explained. "But now we're talking minor details. We were younger then. We were having a sleepover, and I told you the whole idea. Kids who weren't kids. Kids who were older. Kids of another world. Sure, you might have written it down first, but you stole that stuff from me."

"I don't remember that."

"No surprise there. You zone me out. Always have. Doesn't mean my ideas don't get lodged in your noggin."

The notebook was fattening with water, and the words were almost entirely gone. Regretting my decision to throw it, I stepped forward, and Charlie closed his umbrella. As I bent to grab the notebook, Charlie skewered it with the umbrella tip and pulled it away from me. A flick of his wrist sent the notebook sliding across the wet grass and into the darkness. Some of the more timid cats scattered.

"How could you?" I cried.

"What?" he howled. "They're stories!"

"You took them! You took her! Where are they?"

Charlie raised the umbrella like a sword and pointed the tip at my face. Stepping closer to me, he said, "You chose her. You hardly knew her. While you've known me your entire stupid life. But you chose *her*."

"I didn't choose anyone."

He touched the tip of the umbrella to my forehead. "You said I was your best friend. *Best!* And where were you when I blew my fingers off? Where were you all those times I called? Where have you been for the last month?"

"I've been here. But people change, Charlie. You have to understand that."

Before he could respond, the glow of headlights and the distinctive rattle from Kyle's van pulling into the driveway grabbed Charlie's attention. I seized the opportunity, swinging the fishbowl and using it to knock the umbrella from his hand.

"Careful now," Charlie whispered, stepping back.

"What? Are you afraid that I'll break this?" I shook the bowl in the air.

"I'm afraid you'll get hurt."

"It's your way into Aquavania, isn't it? That wasn't a dream I had, was it? And when I didn't answer the call, you took my place, right? If I fill this bowl with water, it will disappear, and if I touch the water—"

"Fill that bowl with water and you can put sea monkeys in it."

"Screw you."

"Would you believe me if I told you I have no idea where Fiona is?"

"No," I said. "Would you believe me if I told you I was going to hit you over the head with this fishbowl?"

"No."

Thwack.

The glass was so thick that it didn't shatter, and the blow reverberated through my arm and into my clenched teeth. Charlie doubled over, dropped the flashlight, and raised his gloved hands to his head. He stumbled backward, groaning, "What is wrong with you?"

"Tell me you're the Riverman. Say you're the Riverman."

"This is how you treat a best friend?" he asked as he struggled his way toward the clubhouse. I kept after him, the bowl raised and cocked for another strike. As Charlie threw open the clubhouse door, one of the hinges popped off and the door tilted and smacked me in the nose. Blood let loose. I pulled my arm to my face. It gave Charlie a precious few seconds to get inside.

With my bleeding nose tucked in the pit of my elbow, I stepped into the black and dank of the clubhouse. Even with that bleeding nose, the odor was overpowering. Wet fur. Cat urine. My lungs burned with the stink. I hacked and coughed, which was met with a chorus of hisses. All around me, red eyes. I could see nothing other than those eyes.

"Get outta here!" I shrieked, swinging the bowl wildly in the air. The cats began to scatter. Up and down and past me. The awful smell was now joined by the awful sound of claws on wood. One cat even nipped at my calf as it slunk out into the rain. I flinched and floundered until my shoulder hit the wall. An exposed nail tore open my wet shirt and the skin underneath.

Someone had boarded up the windows long ago, and while the place was a calamity of holes, dark clouds were keeping all of the moonlight out. I was essentially blind, and thanks to the rain drumming on the roof, I was close to deaf too. Getting my bearings was nearly impossible. Not that it was a very big clubhouse. It was perhaps the size of a small bedroom. But it had a lofted space on top and a crawl space below. I didn't know whether Charlie was above me, beneath me, or standing right in front of me, ready to dig his thumbs into my neck.

"Where are you?" I groaned.

"*Prrrrack!*" Charlie's voice volleyed off the walls.

"What's that?"

"That's the sound of me shooting you with the gun I'm holding."

He was above me. I was pretty sure of it. I started drawing the fishbowl back so I could hurl it upward, and I said, "You don't own a gun."

"No, I don't. But Kyle does. And the fool hides it in here."

I stopped. As much as I wanted to believe Charlie was lying, I knew he wasn't. No one ever dared enter that nasty clubhouse. It was the only sensible place for Kyle to hide the gun. "Okay," I said. "You have a gun. But why would you shoot me?"

"Um . . . nothing to do with the fact that you thumped my skull with an aquarium."

It was the brand of sarcasm I expected from Charlie, but I didn't find it the least bit amusing. He was pointing a gun at me, and it was as if he was pretending this entire thing was a game. Only he wasn't pretending. This *was* a game to him. Everything was a game. And I realized if I was going to stop him, I needed to play.

Weaknesses. Spot them, exploit them, and you win. That was the key to every video game. Only what were Charlie's weaknesses?

"So how's this gonna go, Alistair?" he asked. "You seem very upset with me. But all I want is to talk this out, address our differences."

Talking was Charlie's strength. I wasn't about to fall for that. I had to defeat him physically, and while I was stronger than he was, the gun in his hand negated my advantage. The gun in his hand negated almost *every* advantage, and there in the dark, shivering and bleeding and desperate, I couldn't see a way around that fact.

Until, suddenly, I could.

The answer came in the form of a memory, a vision. Fiona standing in the snow, drawing two shapes. Hands. The left one with a thumb, a pinky, and a ring finger. The right one with only a pinky and a thumb. Charlie was a righty.

"You'd really shoot me?" I asked.

"Only to defend myself," he said. "Wouldn't anyone?"

"Defend yourself? I have a fishbowl."

"And you have a broken heart. I don't know what you're capable of."

I tried my best to pinpoint exactly where his voice was coming from, and I drew the fishbowl back again. "You sure don't," I said.

"I can see you, you know? I have the eyes of a bat. You throw that at me and I might have to pull this trigger."

"How?" I asked.

"How what?"

"Are you going to pull it without any fingers?"

The fishbowl was in the air as soon as I posed the question. I can't be sure what it hit, but I heard a thump, and I heard Charlie cough, and I heard the metallic percussion of the gun falling and tumbling across the floor. I dropped to all fours and scoured. I had no plan other than getting my hands on it.

"You think you know everything," Charlie said, coughing. "You think you've got it all figured out. You don't have a single clue."

I felt the muzzle first and pawed until I found the handle. I pulled it to my chest, sat down, and braced it against my sternum so the barrel was pointing out. I held it with both hands. Gingerly, I tapped the trigger, making sure I knew where it was.

"Fiona Loomis?" Charlie went on. "That's what you care about? That girl is pathetic. You know how I got to her? The same way I get to anyone. I figure out that itch they can't scratch, that thing they need but can't have."

I scooted on my butt across the floor until my back was against the wall. It didn't seem possible, but the rain was coming down harder than ever, determined to pound the clubhouse to bits. Breathing was a battle.

"Sometimes people will surprise you with what they need. But not Fiona. She was predictable. Like so many stupid and pathetic girls, all she needed was a boy. All she needed was *you*, Alistair. And she will never . . . ever . . . have you," the Riverman said.

As the words stabbed me in the heart, a beam of light struck me in the face. It was a reflex more than anything—I pulled the trigger. And the blast echoed like thunder.

Sunday, November 19

---◆---

Part II

For a second or two, a man stood in the doorway of the clubhouse. Then he wobbled, let out a low groan, staggered, and leaned back as if someone were there to catch him. But there was no one else, and as the man fell into the yard, the flashlight in his hand tipped upward and cast its glow onto his face. His features were twisted, wincing from the shock. Still, I could see who he was.

"What did you shoot? Who did you shoot?" Charlie shrieked.

My body toppled, slid against the wall until I was lying on my side. It was like I was back in that cardboard box in the middle of the road, or back in my shower, letting the world pour over me. I stayed curled up for a few moments, and I might have stayed like that forever, if not for the sound of a wheezing voice calling from outside.

"It's okay, kid. It's fine."

Fine? Fine was impossible, but sometimes you believe the things you need to believe, and I needed to believe in *fine*. So I willed myself back to my feet and lumbered to the doorway. With the gun pinned to my chest, I stepped out into the rain.

Prack!

A blast of nearby lightning illuminated the backyard for a second, and I saw Kyle lying on his back. On the ground next to him, the flashlight was highlighting the bleeding hole in his stomach. The notebook, spread open in the grass, was destroyed by the rain. Scattered on the edges of the yard, cats.

"Come here," Kyle groaned.

I obeyed, and soon I was hovering over him, waiting for his next command.

"You shot me," he said with a gurgle in his voice, liquid in his throat. "Right in the . . ."

"I'm sorry, I'm so sorry."

"Here." He reached his hand up and I gave him mine.

"On three," I whimpered, assuming he wanted me to lift him.

"No." He coughed. "Give it to me."

Rain ran down my arm and poured off the barrel of the gun like it was a teakettle. I peeled my hand from Kyle's and swapped the gun in its place. It didn't seem at all strange to give a gun to the person I'd shot. At that point, I trusted him more than I trusted myself.

"I didn't mean it," I said. "It was dark and—"

"Saw the . . . flashlight," he mumbled as he drew the gun to his body. "I was like . . . great, cops found the . . ." He pressed it against his chest like a keepsake.

Prack!

Lightning again, and thunder even louder than the gunshot. My body jolted and I bumped into Charlie, who was now standing next to me, shoulder to shoulder. The fishbowl rested in the crook of his elbow.

"What's it feel like?" Charlie asked, crouching down. If there was concern in his voice, it was buried deep in curiosity.

"Not . . . good." Maybe the shock of being shot had numbed Kyle at first, but it was obvious that the pain was now digging its heels into his face. He squeezed his eyes shut.

"I'll call 911," I said.

Charlie set the fishbowl in the grass where it collected more rain.

"This . . . is really . . . bad," Kyle whispered. "I'm not sure . . . this is what . . . I really . . ." He gulped twice, searching for the rest of his voice. He couldn't find it.

Charlie didn't say anything either. He pulled the glove off of his left hand, and for the first time I saw the damage. It doesn't bother me to tell you that it looked like a claw, because that's exactly how it looked. And as Charlie—as the Riverman—waved that claw over the wound in his brother's stomach, like some shaman or some faith healer, I saw every side of him. I saw the boy, the man, and the monster.

"I'll make the call," I told them, turning away.

I could have called from the Dwyers' house, but I wanted nothing to do with that place. Yes, minutes were precious. Even seconds were. Perhaps it makes me a bad person, but I ran all the way home.

I entered through the garage and opened the door to our kitchen. The cordless phone was in its charger by the door, mounted above the hooks where the keys hung. Grabbing it, I stepped back into the garage.

I dialed 911, and as soon as the operator answered, I said in as clear a voice as I could muster, "There's been a shooting. Send an ambulance. 132 Seven Pines Road. Backyard."

I hung up and stepped inside. I replaced the phone in its charger and my eye caught the shine of the key to Fiona's house. I headed toward my room.

"There you are," my mom said as she turned from the TV and spotted me creeping by the dining room table in the dark.

"I forgot my umbrella," I told her as I passed, hoping she wouldn't spot the streaks of blood. "Gimme a second to change."

"We're glad you're home. Hope you had fun with Charlie."

I stepped into the hallway, and Keri poked her head out of her room. "You been swimming?" she joked.

Filthy sanguine water dripped off my body and onto the floor. "It's not how it looks," I told her. "Don't ask me what happened. Just make sure they know it's not how it looks."

She paused for closer inspection, and a mask of worry slipped over her face. "You bet," she assured me.

I escaped into my room.

Fresh underwear, dry pajama bottoms, and a new T-shirt, but I could still feel the dirt and the blood. I sat down on the edge of my bed. I figured the police could be at the door within a few minutes, and if they arrested me and searched my room, I might never again get the chance to hear Fiona's voice. Reaching down between my legs, I pulled out the tape recorder and her grandfather's jacket. I slipped the jacket on. It was still too big for me, but I liked the feel of the silk lining on my bare arms.

With the tape recorder in my lap, I ran my fingers over the buttons, but stopped before pressing *Play*. I needed more time with her voice.

A minute later I was pulling the key off the hook in the kitchen and sneaking into the garage.

A minute after that I was outside, under an umbrella, rushing to Fiona's house.

Another minute and an ambulance screamed by.

One more minute and I was at the door, inserting the key.

It had been years since I had been in the Loomis home. Back when I was younger, I probably noticed the furniture and knickknacks that made it a distinct place, but I'm quite sure I didn't notice what made it so eerily familiar to me now. It had an identical layout to my house, a matching skeleton. Under other circumstances, I might have explored a bit and puzzled out the variations, taken note of where they set their TVs and how they dealt with the awkwardly shaped kitchen. Under these circumstances, there was only one room I wanted to visit.

I climbed the stairs and opened the door to what, in my house, was my dad's study. Here it was a bedroom, painted light blue, with two walls lined with white dressers and short white bookshelves that were overflowing with haphazardly arranged paperbacks. The ceiling slanted above the two walls to accommodate the angle of the roof. A bed with a looping iron frame was set against the back wall, and a window with gauzy drapes was above the bed. No posters. No pictures. A clean and simple room to read and dress and sleep. I stared for a bit, thinking about all the time Fiona had spent in here.

I climbed onto the bed and stretched out over the covers. My blood couldn't maintain its fury for much longer. My body rejoiced at the surrender. I placed the tape recorder on my chest and closed my eyes as I pressed *Play*.

"Kilgore here will keep the record straight . . ."

I woke a couple of hours later. The tape had stopped. So had the rain. I expected to hear the sirens from police cars, but I didn't hear a thing. It was dead quiet in the house, and lying there, looking up at the ceiling, I decided it was time to put an end to this.

I was going to turn myself in. There was really no other option. I would reveal every detail: my fears, my suspicions, Fiona's tales of Aquavania. I would tell them about Kyle and the gun and Charlie and *Gods of Nowhere* and the Riverman. All of it and everything. And while I couldn't be sure they'd count me as sane, I wasn't sure if I should be counted as sane anymore.

I sat up, and as I did, my sanity was given one final test. The radiators began to click.

Fiona said the radiators spoke to her when they clicked. I don't know everything they said to her, but I can tell you what they said to me.

"We've waited so long for you."

And yes, they did sound a bit like Charlie, but they sounded like other people too. I had no choice but to follow.

Everything can change in an instant, and everything did change in an instant. The boiler was there and then it was not. The cylinder of water hung in the air, next to the dangling lightbulb, in the room full of boxes in Fiona's basement. It was both the loveliest and the scariest thing I had ever seen.

I reached out my hand.

Monday, November 20

———◆———

Ten years ago today was when they declared Luke Drake missing. Ten years since he fell into the Oriskanny and was snatched away from his brother, swept away from his future. Ten years since he became Thessaly's lost child, and almost ten years since I saw him. That's ten years in the Solid World, obviously. For those of us who've spent time in Aquavania, it's been significantly longer.

That's right. When I touched that cylinder of water, I went to Aquavania. And I stayed for a very long time. To get home, back to the Solid World, has taken me ages. Now that I'm finally here, sitting on Fiona's bed again with Kilgore in my lap, it helps to revisit how it all started. My memories of the events that took place over those six autumn weeks in 1989 feel like they're only minutes and days old. Because they are only minutes and days old. But they're also much older and much more important than people might realize.

I think about Luke Drake a lot. He is a constant reminder that the meaning of a memory can change, even when the details remain the same. A boy waving hello is not always a boy waving hello. A girl who needs a guy might not need him for the reasons people suspect. Goodbye kisses are not always goodbye kisses . . . because gone for now is not necessarily gone for good.

There are many more memories I could share on this recording, but I'm not sure I want to do that. I'm not entirely proud of some of the things that I've done. Instead, I'd rather share one last story and then bury this tape out by Frog Rock, where someone can find it when the time is right.

Don't worry. The story is a short one. Don't ask me where I heard it. Just trust me when I say that it's true.

THE LEGEND OF FIONA LOOMIS, PART VI

At the beginning of those twelve mysterious years in Aquavania, Fiona had a perfect day. Her world was still a blank slate, but the time had come to build her most ambitious project yet. She made a wish.

The ground shook, and a bed rose out of it. The bed frame struck Fiona on the legs, knocking her onto a firm mattress. Covers emerged and cocooned her, tucked her in tightly. Beneath the bed, a floor materialized, wooden slats shooting across in a wave. Walls sprouted next, topped by a ceiling. Then it all climbed upward as an entire house grew around her.

Fiona was in a bedroom identical to the one she had in the Solid World. She stripped the covers off, leapt from the bed, and skittered to the hall and down the stairs. She ate a breakfast of cereal in her family's kitchen. Then she put on her neon green jacket and went to the garage to fetch her bike. Wheeling her bike outside, she was confronted with a gorgeous autumn day—an invigorating chill in the air, a bright but forgiving sun.

The neighborhood was also a replica of the one from the Solid World. Next door was the Andersons' house. Across the street was the Carmines'. The telephone lines sagged and swayed in the breeze exactly as they did back home. Fiona pedaled down the street, playing music from the recorder duct-taped to her handlebars, and she looked up at the splatter of red and yellow and green and brown leaves.

Animals roamed about—squirrels and cats and birds—but there were no people, and Fiona pedaled alone. She continued past the school, past the memorial tree and the Skylark, by the graveyard where her grandma was buried, along the banks of the Oriskanny, until she reached a road on which she had never biked or walked. As soon as she turned onto the road, she was beyond the limits of her memories of

Thessaly, beyond the limits of what she had built. She began biking on her blank slate. It was a flat stretch of nothing, with only the haze of the folds on the horizon. Such emptiness held no appeal for her anymore, so she turned around and headed back the way she'd come, into the realm of the familiar.

When she reached her street, she closed her eyes. She made another wish.

When she opened her eyes, the same houses and lawns and cars were there. Only now the street was lined with friends from the Solid World, such as Kendra and Fay-Renee. Alongside them were all of the kids Fiona had met and heard of from Aquavania, all of the kids she had written stories about. Chua and Werner, Boaz and Rodrigo. Plus many, many more. They waved to Fiona and said hello and seemed extremely happy to see her.

Fiona hopped off her bike when she reached the replica of Alistair's house, bounded up the brick walkway, and rang the doorbell. As if on cue, a version of Alistair answered within seconds.

"Come out and meet everybody," she said.

Peering cautiously over her shoulder, this version of Alistair said, "You know I'm not the real Alistair, right? You know that all of this is your memories and your impressions of me and of them and of everything? We're like the real thing, but we're not the real thing. You created us. You know that this could never really happen?"

"Of course I know that," Fiona said. "But for today, let's pretend. For today, let's believe that anything is possible."

ACKNOWLEDGMENTS

The story of how this book came to be is one with a large
cast of characters. If I could, I'd single out every author who
has inspired me, and every friend or stranger who has enchanted me with a tall tale. I don't have the memory to do
that, but there are a handful of people whose contributions
to this book I will never forget:

Joy Peskin. An editor with vision and courage and an uncanny ability to see the beauty in odd birds.

Michael Bourret. A tireless advocate, a good-humored
geek, a spinner of gold.

Nova Ren Suma. A great friend to writers and an even
greater writer herself.

Kate Hurley and Karla Reganold. Talented word wran-
glers who might object to this sentence fragment.

**Angie Chen and the secret squad at Farrar Straus
Giroux Books for Young Readers.** Unassuming magi-
cians who make books appear in your hands.

Elizabeth Clark and Yelena Bryksenkova. A designer
and an artist who took my words and gave them a lovely and
indelible face.

Jim and Gwenn Wells. Your support and encouragement
keep me afloat.

Mom and Dad. They love a good tale, and me.

Tim and Toril. Not to mention all the muddy kids who grew up and ran wild on Cleveland Boulevard and in Brookside. This is a novel about us.

Cate. Our story is my favorite story.

AARON STARMER

What did you want to be when you grew up?
A movie director or a soccer player. Preferably both. Maybe I'd make a soccer movie.

When did you realize you wanted to be a writer?
Very early on, probably in first grade when my teacher let the class write and perform our own play. I proposed that we write a play called *The Magic Leopard,* and everyone agreed. Coincidentally (wink, wink), I just happened to have a leopard costume left over from Halloween that fit me perfectly. So I got to play the lead!

What's your most embarrassing childhood memory?
An "accident" in first grade. We'll just leave it at that.

What's your favorite childhood memory?
Exploring the forests near my home, building forts, and making movies on camcorders with my friends.

As a young person, who did you look up to most?
My parents. They've always been kind, clever, and encouraging, which I hope I can be with my daughter.

What was your favorite thing about school?
Class discussions. I loved to talk about books and if they had any deeper or hidden meanings. I still love that.

What were your hobbies as a kid? What are your hobbies now?
As a kid, I liked making up songs and stories (big surprise). These days, I like to take a break from stories by cooking, jogging, and doing outdoorsy things like kayaking and skiing.

Did you play sports as a kid?
I was a big soccer player when I was young and then picked up lacrosse when I was older. I played lacrosse all the way through college.

What was your first job, and what was your "worst" job?
My first job was as a soccer referee but it only lasted a few games. My worst job was as a liquor store clerk, a combination of boring and depressing.

What book is on your nightstand now?
Code Name Verity by Elizabeth Wein. Lovely novel.

How did you celebrate publishing your first book?
By writing another!

Where do you write your books?
I write them at home, at the library, or in a café, depending on where and when I can find a quiet spot for a few hours.

What sparked your imagination for *The Riverman*?
I wanted to write a story about what would happen if a girl like Alice (from *Alice in Wonderland*) came home. What would her friends think of her story? Would they believe her or would they think she was going crazy?

Did you have any girls next door growing up?
No, and I'm glad I didn't! There were plenty of girls I had crushes on, but they all lived in other neighborhoods. If they had lived nearby, it would have been torture because I was so shy, and even though I'd see them constantly, I probably never would have had the guts to talk to them.

What got you interested in fantasy/magical realism?
I'm not sure. I've always liked stories that are very realistic but then the reality twists or bends in a way that challenges the characters.

How did you pick the names Alistair and Fiona?
I'm not entirely sure where the names come from, but I know the idea of "staring" is important for Alistair. When you stare at something, you look at it intensely, but you don't necessarily understand it. The name Fiona might have originated from an e-mail newsletter I often receive from the Scottish tourism board. It always says it comes from someone named Fiona. Scotland reminds me of a medieval fantasyland, and I think the name Fiona will now always have a fantasy connotation to me.

What was your favorite scene to write?
The scene near the end where Alistair and Fiona walk together in the snow. It's full of emotions and revelations, which are always exciting to write.

What can readers expect from the next book in the Riverman Trilogy, *The Whisper*? No spoilers, please!
They can expect answers to some lingering questions, some outer space adventures, and a strange, but polite, hummingbird.

What challenges do you face in the writing process, and how do you overcome them?
The hardest part is making the story emotionally believable, logically believable, and entertaining all at the same time. I'm not sure I accomplished that, but I hope I came close.

Which of your characters is most like you?
I guess Alistair is most like me, though I'm sure there are bits of Charlie in my personality. I'd like to say I'm like Fiona, but I'm not sure I'm that brave.

What makes you laugh out loud?
My daughter laughing.

What do you do on a rainy day?
Read a book, go to the movies, and cook. Ideally all three.

What's your idea of fun?
Exploring a foreign landscape or city, then sitting down for a great meal with family and friends.

What is your favorite word?
Orangutan. I just like saying it. And they seem like a nice bunch of primates.

If you could live in any fictional world, what would it be?
Anyplace without talking animals. Talking animals kind of freak me out.

What's your favorite song?
It changes all the time, but while writing *The Riverman*, I'd say "Thirteen" by Big Star was the most influential.

Who is your favorite fictional character?
Cool Hand Luke!

What was your favorite book when you were a kid? Do you have a favorite book now?
As a kid, it was probably *George's Marvelous Medicine*, one of the more obscure (and pitch-dark) Roald Dahl books. These days, it's Truman Capote's *In Cold Blood*, which is a master class in writing. Precise, poetic, and powerful.

What's your favorite TV show or movie?
It's hard to beat *Breaking Bad* for TV: a perfect TV show. And though I don't think it's my favorite, the one movie that always makes me smile is Richard Linklater's *Dazed and Confused*. It came out my senior year of high school so it probably hit me at just the right time.

If you were stranded on a desert island, who would you want for company?
My wife and daughter, of course. Don't be cruel. Don't make me choose! The island is big enough for all three of us, isn't it?

If you could travel anywhere in the world, where would you go and what would you do?
I've always wanted to hike the Inca Trail to Machu Picchu.

If you could travel in time, where would you go and what would you do?
I'd go see the dinosaurs. And I'd probably do a lot of running and screaming.

What's the best advice you have ever received about writing?
Don't ever be satisfied with something that's "good enough." If it's only "good enough," then it's not good enough.

What advice do you wish someone had given you when you were younger?
Slow down. Be patient. Everyone has a different timeline for writing. It's not a race.

Do you ever get writer's block? What do you do to get back on track?
All the time. Only cure is to keep writing. I sit down and force myself to do it.

What do you want readers to remember about your books?
That, as readers, they were surprised and they were emotionally involved in my stories.

What would you do if you ever stopped writing?
I doubt I'll stop, but if I do, I hope I find a new creative outlet. Maybe renovating an old house. Maybe gardening. Maybe painting.

If you were a superhero, what would your superpower be?
I'd have to agree with Fiona in *The Whisper*: stopping time.

Do you have any strange or funny habits? Did you when you were a kid?

Whenever I'm anxious about something, for example, if someone is late to meet me somewhere, I become obsessed with counting things. Birds, cars, etc. Alistair does the same thing in *The Riverman*.

What do you consider to be your greatest accomplishment?

Each time I finish a book, it's a bigger accomplishment than I ever thought I could manage when I was younger. I started and gave up on writing at least half a dozen books before I ever finished my first one.

What do you wish you could do better?

Sing. And play an instrument. Any instrument. At all.

What would your readers be most surprised to learn about you?

That my best subject in school was always math. I only got average grades in English because I've always been a slow reader. But I was never that interested in math. Maybe because there are right and wrong answers and I like answers (and characters) that fall somewhere in between.

ALISTAIR IS DETERMINED

to find his own way to Aquavania to search
for Fiona. But if it is anything as strange and
unexpected as Fiona's tales of it are,
will Alistair ever be able to find her?

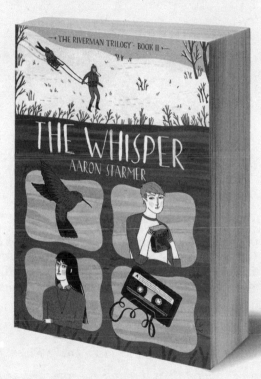

Read on for an excerpt of

THE WHISPER

November 19, 1989

———— ◆ ————

A whisper is a monster with many mouths. It invites, it infests, it assures: I am not for all ears, I am just for you. There are whispers in the water, as strange as that may seem. But it's only strange to the ones who don't hear them. The ones who do hear them have a choice. They can ignore or they can follow.

On a rainy November night, Alistair Cleary chose to follow. The whispers came out of radiators. "We've waited so long for you," they said.

He followed them down to the basement of Fiona Loomis's house, where a boiler, tall and round, disappeared, revealing a cylinder of water. The water was unbroken, immune to gravity, suspended in the air.

Alistair reached out and touched it. His body tingled and then crossed over. What was once a basement became an entire world, a place smudged sick and gray. His eyes burned. Tornadoes of ash swirled around him, while in front of him a colorful river raged. With an arm over his face, he rushed toward the sound of the current.

This is how Alistair's tale began.

CHAPTER 1

————◆————

WATER, LUMINOUS AND GAUDY, SLAPPED AGAINST LAND, AND the boy named Alistair Cleary lay on the edge of the liquid and the dirt where a river had coughed him out. He ached—head and body. An oaky film of ash coated the roof of his mouth. The sun pummeled his bare skin.

Alistair was twelve years old, a slight, bony kid with a round nose and a birthmark on his chin and a curiosity that sometimes lapsed into foolishness. Groaning, he stood, and water licked his calves. He rolled his head, and his neck crackled like a campfire. Behind him, a river churned with color—it was sherbet and gumballs, sunlight on an oil slick, and it cut across a lifeless landscape of black and gray. Yet in front of him it met an abrupt end. Weird.

There was no lake or ocean for the water to empty into, but the river was disappearing, merging into the land like wet paint becoming dry paint. It was transforming into a wide field where waves of yellow grass billowed and flattened in conversation with the wind. Someone had even flipped a switch on the sky. Behind him, it was putrid and smoky. In front of him, it was bright, tinged with a healthy green. Water becoming earth, a sharp border between death and life—Alistair had never seen anything like it.

What is this place?

It was part of Aquavania, he knew at least that much. In fact, he knew more than he cared to know. He knew that he had touched some kind of liquid portal in his friend's basement and he had ended up in a windstorm of ash. He knew that to escape the storm, he had jumped into a brightly colored river and the river had carried him to this place. He knew there was no clear path home from here.

Send me home. Bring me home. There's no place like . . .

He wished over and over again to be transported back to his friend's basement. That's how it worked in Aquavania. At least that's how he *thought* it worked. You wished and your wish was granted. But it wasn't working, and the more he wished, the more he began to wonder if that was a blessing, if home was actually the best place for him to be at the moment. Because he also knew that back home they might call him something terrible.

Killer.

He started to cry. He took two steps into the field, but that was all his body could manage. He collapsed to his knees and surrendered to the tears. The guilt, the terror—they were invading his body, pirates looting his blood and oxygen. His hands were sore, bruised by the recoil of a gun, and he brought them to his face, drove their heels into the bony upper rims of his eye sockets.

This isn't real. I didn't do those things. I didn't shoot Kyle. Fiona isn't gone. Aquavania doesn't exist. I've been dreaming since that snowy night on the road two weeks ago, when I last saw Fiona. Two weeks of dreaming. Two weeks of fiction.

He slapped himself in the face. Hard. That's what people do in dreams to rouse reality. But he didn't wake up, because this was his reality now.

In the distance, movement. A band of men cut through the waves of grass. As they got closer, Alistair could make out their numbers. Six, walking shoulder to shoulder, spears held tight to the chests of the inner four, leather slings dangling from the hands of the outer two. Straggly-looking guys. They appeared to wear animal fur, but it was darker than any fur Alistair was aware of and it was flecked with sparkling white dots. Their hair was tied in long ponytails, and their skin was covered in streaks of mud and clay. War paint? They stopped about twenty yards from where the river ended, but they didn't poise their weapons. Water dripped off of Alistair's body. He was smart enough to stay quiet and still.

They're here to punish me for what I've done.

The tallest of the men took one step forward and leaned on his spear as if it were a staff. His bright blue eyes were ambiguous beacons. They were alive with curiosity. Or was it rage?

"Stand," the tall man said.

Alistair was in no position to object. He did as ordered.

"You swim?" the tall man asked.

Alistair was astounded that such an odd-looking person would speak English, or what seemed like English. Alistair could understand it, in any case.

"I . . . can swim," Alistair replied cautiously.

The tall man nodded. The other five remained stoic.

"This is your quest?" he asked. "Or you come to take our land?"

"I . . . I . . . am . . . not taking anything," Alistair stuttered. "I'm lost. I'm looking for someone. A girl."

The tall man nodded again and said, "She is here." Then he pounded his spear on the ground twice.

One of the others, a wrinkly and oafish character with scars on his cheeks, stepped forward and took a deep breath. His throat ballooned, all supple and bullfrogish. It was beyond strange. It was impossible.

"I don't know what—" Alistair started to say, but he shut his mouth as soon as the frog-throated man opened his. Because what filled that throat wasn't air. It was dragonflies.

Elegant insects, with wings veined in neon, streamed out from the man's gullet and toward Alistair's face. He struggled with two conflicting instincts. Swat? Or swoon? He couldn't choose either, though. Because once the dragonflies had swarmed around his head, his free will was gone.

Alistair was their captive.

*   *   *

To lose control of your body seems a horrible fate, but to Alistair it felt like a relief. His anxiety wafted away, and whatever fear he had of the men was replaced by a deep reverence. He stepped forward, marched, in fact—one, two, three—right into the band of strangers. They clustered around him, their weapons held casually but confidently. They showed no signs of fear, but they kept their distance as they ushered him in the direction of the high-hanging sun.

All logic told Alistair he should try to escape, but his brain was not beholden to logic. He walked with the men. He didn't question them. He didn't fight. The dragonflies, which orbited his head, had rendered him a lamb.

"We will not harm you, swimmer," the tall man said with a grave but respectful tone.

Perhaps it was the influence of the dragonflies, but Alistair believed this. Or perhaps it was something else that inspired his trust. Alistair wanted—or more accurately, he *needed*—to believe the other thing the man had said.

She is here.

They hiked at a steady pace, the sun wicking the moisture from Alistair's damp clothes. The field went on for at least a mile. No change. The yellow grass sashayed back and forth and tickled Alistair's bare arms. He was wearing jeans and a T-shirt and white socks with red stripes, his standard uniform from home. He wore no shoes, because he came here with no shoes. He was beginning to regret the fact. Luckily the earth was soft and free of stabby things.

Finally, a patch of trees appeared in the distance, the first sign that this world was not all pastures and tribesmen, and right before the trees, a perfectly round rock came into view. The rock was about twice Alistair's height and it rested in the field like a marble dropped from the heavens. The men approached the rock cautiously, keeping a buffer around it as they circled, but the dragonflies led Alistair straight to it.

There were images on the rock's surface. Bears, bulls, lions, and horses. Cave paintings—Alistair had seen similar ones in books. Only these didn't seem ancient. They looked fresh.

"We honor you and bid that you release the night," the tall man said. "Then we will feast."

A feast where I will see her? Alistair wanted to ask, but it was as if the dragonflies were speaking for him. "Yes, sir," he whispered instead.

The tall man pointed with his spear at the rock. The others followed suit, pointing if not with their spears, then with their fingers. Alistair waited for more instructions, but none arrived. So the dragonflies took the reins, guided him ever closer to the rock. The men let out deep, satisfied grunts. Alistair leaned in and examined the animal paintings.

They were shimmering. They were trembling. It was more than a symptom of the sunlight; it was as if tiny creatures lived in the pigment and were wiggling their way to the surface. Alistair looked back at his companions and saw that their weapons were poised. A bad omen. And yet it was irresistible. The paintings begged to be touched, like feathery scarves hanging in a costume store, like a freshly shaved head. Alistair reached out and placed his fingers on the rock and, as if startled from their sleep, the images jumped to attention and scampered from his hand.

Running, leaping, galloping, the silhouetted creatures circled the surface of the stone. They were more than paintings. These things were suddenly alive, and Alistair stood there transfixed. A lion tackled a horse and tore into its throat as the other horses scattered, only to be confronted by the bears. The bears stood on their hind legs, defending their corner of the stone with drawn claws and teeth. The bulls, swept up in the commotion, scuffed their hooves and prepared to charge, and when their charge began, there was no stopping it.

Alistair felt them before he saw them and tumbled to his back as the bulls leapt off the stone and emerged in the field, three-dimensional and fully grown. They weren't made of flesh, though. Their bodies had a solid black sheen, and their joints, horns, and eyes consisted of twinkling stars. It was as if they were carved from chunks of the cosmos. As the bulls plowed through the field, the dragonflies scattered. Finally in control of his movements, Alistair bolted, worried about what might leap out next.

The horses leapt next, followed by the lions, and finally the bears. Their bodies were also black and speckled with stars. None of the animals seemed particularly interested in Alistair as they fled the rock. Alistair's touch had lit a fire in them, and they seemed determined to burn, burn away.

The men were far more prepared than Alistair. They had spread their ranks and were now running among the bulls at speeds that didn't seem humanly possible. The two men with slings were twirling them so fast that blurry halos appeared over their heads, and when they snapped their wrists to deploy their weapons, disc-shaped stones rocketed out and struck a bull on the head with a one-two punch. *Thwack! Thwack!* The bull collapsed to the ground.

Before the lions or bears could reach the wounded prey, the four men with spears had it surrounded. The tall man lanced the bull's neck, and its body jerked for a second, then deflated. Blood, red and true, spilled out. It was a stunningly fast kill.

Ahead of them, the other bulls lifted their hooves. The confines of the rock couldn't hold them and neither could the confines of the ground. They dug those hooves into the air and took to the sky, where they charged right at the sun. The other animals streamed past the band of men and took to the sky as well, their dark and sparkling bodies amassing above like a murder of hulking crows. They roared and growled their way upward, speeding and then spreading, blacking out the green tinge until the sky was their bodies and their bodies were the sky. The sun faded and dimpled and transformed into a moon.

It was no longer daytime. Alistair had set free the night.